To G. with love

*It soared, a bird, it held its flight, a swift pure cry,
soar silver orb it leaped serene, speeding, sustained . . .*

James Joyce, *Ulysses*

The South of Ireland
1984

Part I
SPRING

One

The place brought to mind a sinking ship. Wood creaked on the floor, across the pews, up in the gallery. Around the walls, a fierce March wind chased itself.

The congregation launched into the *Our Father* as if every last soul was going down. *Heaven. Bread. Trespass. Temptation.* The words whisked past Shell's ears like rabbits vanishing into their holes. She tried wriggling her nose to make it slimmer. *Evil.* Mrs McGrath's hat lurched in front of her, its feather looking drunk: three-to-one odds it would fall off. Declan Ronan, today's altar boy, was examining the tabernacle, licking his lips with half-shut eyes. Whatever he was thinking, it wasn't holy.

Trix and Jimmy sat on either side of her, swinging their legs in their falling-down socks. They were in a competition to see who could go higher and faster.

'Whisht,' Shell hissed, poking Jimmy in the ribs.

'Whisht yourself,' said Jimmy aloud.

Thankfully, Dad didn't hear. By now he was up at the microphone, reading the lesson like a demented prophet. His sideburns gleamed grey. The lines on his massive forehead rose and fell. This past year, he'd gone religion-mad. He'd become worshipper extraordinaire, handing out the hymn books, going round with the collection boxes every offertory. Most days he went into nearby Castlerock and walked the streets, collecting for the Church's causes. On Sunday mornings, she'd often glimpse him practising the reading in his bedroom. He'd sit upright in front of the three panelled mirrors of Mam's old dressing table, spitting out the words like bad grapes.

Shell, on the other hand, had no time for church: not since Mam's death, over a year back. She remembered how, when she was small, Mam had made her, Jimmy and Trix dress up clean and bright and coaxed them through Mass with colouring pencils and paper. '*Draw me an angel, Shell, playing hurling in the rain*'; '*Do me a cat, Jimmy, parachuting off a plane.*' Mam had liked the priests, the candles and the rosaries. Most of all, she'd loved the Virgin Mary. She'd said '*Sweet Mary* this and that' all day long. *Sweet Mary* if the potatoes boiled over, if the dog caught a crow. *Sweet Mary* if the scones came out good and soft.

Then she died.

Shell remembered standing by Mam's bed as she floated off. Dr Fallon, Mrs Duggan and Mrs McGrath had been there, with Father Carroll leading a round of the rosary. Her dad had stood off to the side, like a minor character in a film, mouthing the words rather than saying them. *Now and at the hour of our* . . . On the word 'death' Shell had frozen. *Death.* The word was a bad breath. The closer you got the more you

4

wanted it to go away. She'd realized then she didn't believe in heaven any more. Mam wasn't going anywhere. She was going to nowhere, to nothing. Her face had fallen in, puckered and ash-white. Her thin fingers kneaded the sheets, working over them methodically. In Shell's mind, Jesus got off the cross and walked off to the nearest bar. Mam's face scrunched up, like a baby's that's about to cry. Then she died. Jesus drained off his glass of beer and went clean out of Shell's life. Mrs McGrath put the mirror Mam had used for plucking her eyebrows up to her mouth and said, 'She's gone.' It was quiet. Dad didn't move. He just kept on mouthing the prayers, a fish out of water.

They'd waked her in the house over three days. Mam's face turned waxen. Her fingers went blue and stiff, then yellow and loose again. They threaded them with her milk-white rosary beads. Then they buried her. It was a drama, the whole village bowing, the men doffing their hats. There were processions and candles, solemn stares, prayers, and callers night and day. *I'm sorry for your trouble,* they'd say. A feed of drink was drunk. Shell didn't cry. Not at first. Not until a whole year passed. Then she'd cried long and hard as she planted the grave up with daffodils on a November day, the first anniversary.

The less religious Shell got, the more Dad became. Before Mam died, he'd only ever gone through the motions, standing in the church's back porch, muttering with the other men about the latest cattlemart or hurling match. Mam hadn't minded. She'd joked that men fell into two categories: they were either ardent about God and indifferent to women, or ardent about women and indifferent to God. If she'd been alive now, she wouldn't have known him. He was piety personified. He'd sold the television, saying it was a vehicle of the devil. He'd taken over Mam's old role and led Shell, Jimmy and Trix in a decade of the rosary every night, except Wednesdays and Saturdays, when he went straight down to Stack's pub after his day of collecting. He'd given up his job on Duggans' farm. He said he was devoting his life to the Lord.

Today, he was almost yelling. Avenging angels, crashing temples and false gods resounded in the small church, hurting the ear. Mrs McGrath's hat slid off when the shock of the word *thunder* set the microphone off in a high-pitched whine. Dad's eyes flickered. He was momentarily distracted. He looked up at the congregation, staring into the middle distance, seeing nobody. He clenched the lectern's sides. Shell held her breath. Had he lost his place? No. He continued, but the steam had gone out of it. Jimmy punched the bench, making it boom, just as Dad faltered to the end.

'This – is – the – word – of – the – Lord,' he trailed.

'Thanks be to God,' the congregation chorused. Shell for one meant it. He'd done. Jimmy smirked. He made the hymn sheet into a spyglass and twisted to inspect the people in the gallery. Trix curled up on the floor, with her head on the kneeler. Dad came down from the altar. Everybody stood up. Shell averted her eyes from Dad as he shuffled up beside her. Bridie

Quinn, her friend from school, caught her eye. She had two fingers up to her temple and was twizzling them round as if to say, *Your dad is mad.* Shell shrugged as if to reply, *It's nothing to do with me.* Everybody was waiting for Father Carroll to do the Gospel. He was stooped and old, with a soft, sing-song voice. You could go off into a sweet, peaceful dream as he pattered out the words.

There was a long pause.

The wind outside died down. Crows cawed.

It wasn't Father Carroll who approached the microphone but the new curate, Father Rose. He was fresh from the seminary, people said, up in the Midlands. He'd never spoken in public before. Shell had only seen him perform the rites in silence, at Father Carroll's side. There was a quickening interest all around.

He stood at the lectern, eyes down, and turned the pages of the book with a slight frown of concentration. He was young, with a full head of hair that sprang upwards like bracken. He held his head to one side, as if considering a finer point of theology. When he found the place, he straightened up and smiled. It was the kind of smile that radiated out to everyone, everywhere at once. Shell felt he'd smiled at her alone. She heard him draw his breath.

"'The next day, as they were leaving Bethany . . .'" he began.

His voice was even, expressive. The words had a new tune in them, an accent from another place, a richer county. He read the words as if he'd written them himself, telling the story about Jesus throwing over the tables of the moneylenders outside the temple. Jesus raged with righteous anger and Father Rose's mouth moved in solemn tandem. The air around him vibrated with shining picture bubbles. Shell could hear the caged birds under the arches, the clink of Roman coins. She could see the gorgeous colours of the Israelites' robes, the light shafting through the temple columns. The images and sounds cascaded out from the pulpit, hanging in the air, turning over like angels in the spring light.

'Please be seated,' Father Rose said at the end of the reading. The congregation sat. Only Shell remained standing, her mouth open. The tables of the moneymen turned into hissing snakes. The multitudes fell silent. Jesus became a man, sad and real, smiling upon Shell as she stood in a daze.

'Be seated,' Father Rose repeated gently.

There was a rustle around her and Shell remembered where she was. *God. Everyone's staring.* She plumped down. Trix tittered. Jimmy dug his spyglass in her side.

Father Rose came down the altar steps and stood before the congregation, arms folded, grinning, as if welcoming guests over for dinner. There was a mutter at this departure from practice. Father Carroll always went to the pulpit for his sermon. Father Rose began to speak.

'Well. We've had some real gloom and doom today,' he said. 'Blasted temples, God being angry. But' – he put his two palms upwards and looked piercingly into the congregation's heart – 'has it ever occurred to you that where there is no anger, there is also no love?' The sentences fitted and sparkled like precious gems in a necklace. His raiment glittered as he gestured. His thick hair spangled with blonds and browns. He spoke of choices and temptations. He spoke of new beginnings. He described how he'd just given up the fags. He'd jumped on the packet, he said, and ground it into the earth to expel the nicotine curse from his marrow. Maybe that was like the tables going over in the gospel story. He spoke of angels and rebirth. Shell leaned forward, her hands clasped tight. A miracle happened. Jesus came out of the bar and got right back up on the high cross. Mam danced in heaven, waltzing with the spirits.

When Father Rose finished, everyone got to their feet and sang, 'Praise, My Soul, the King of Heaven'. Between the notes was a hum of gossip. Nora Canterville nudged Mrs Fallon, the doctor's wife, with a grimace. Mrs McGrath fanned her face with her hat, as if the devil had passed by. Dad's eyebrows pulled together, dark as beetles.

'*Ransomed, healed, restored, forgiven . . .*' Shell sang at the top of her voice. She hadn't the voice of her mother but she could carry a tune. She caught Declan Ronan imitating her, shutting and opening his mouth like an anguished fish. '*Praise the everlasting King*'. She scrunched her nose up at him and looked away. Even when she remembered she'd to cook the mutton dinner, with Trix and Jimmy plaguing the kitchen like flies, and recalled the schoolwork that she wouldn't do, and the dark, heavy future of her life, nothing mattered. Jesus Christ had come back to earth in the shape of Father Rose. He was walking among them, the congregation of the church, in the village of Coolbar, County Cork.

Two

She floated on a cloud of Father Rose the rest of the day. His face – or was it Jesus's? – floated in the potato peelings in the washing bowl. It shimmered in the mirror as the light failed and floated in the dark as she drifted off to sleep.

The next day, they were up early to pick up the stones in the back field. Dad had been making them do it since the winter. He never gave a reason. If he was planning to plough it over, he gave no sign. By now, she, Jimmy and Trix had a great cairn growing in the north-east corner. Most mornings, they'd be three silent sentinels going up the hill in the half-light, stooped over with their loads.

Today, Shell picked up the old holdall they used to carry the stones. She was cold and hungry. It was spitting rain.

'Dad,' she said. He was sitting in his usual chair by the fire, with the poker resting loosely in his hand. He was staring into the flames as if they contained the answer to life's riddle. '*Why* do we have to pick up the stones?'

He glanced up. 'What's that?'

'Why do we have to pick up the stones, Dad?'

He frowned. 'Because I say so. Isn't that enough?'

'It's raining today, Dad. We'll be wet through all day at school.'

'Beat it, Shell. Go on. Double-quick.'

'Only—'

He dropped the poker and came towards her, his hand up, making as if to strike. 'Scram.'

'I'm off,' she said, scooting through the door.

Trix and Jimmy were already huddled over the soil. Shell joined them as they trudged up the hill. The stones always seemed to reappear overnight. However many they picked up, there were always more. Halfway up, Shell doubled right over and stared at the world upside down through the triangle of her white, thin legs. If anger and love went together, like Father Rose had said, it must mean that she loved her dad. She knew she had done once, long ago, when he'd swung her in his arms and let her climb up him like a tree. She could dimly recall it. She imagined all the hate pouring out of her brain, trickling out through her ears. Perhaps it worked, because when she stood up, she felt lighter. She looked over the field to the rusty gate, across the road, up the slope and into the yellow soup of sky.

'Thank you, Jesus, for the stones,' she said.

Jimmy threw one at her. 'Hate the stones,' he said. 'Hate Jesus. Hate you.'

The stone hit her right in the belly. Shell rubbed where it hit, and then looked Jimmy in the eye. His face was twisted up. The whiteness around the freckles stood out. She'd been sharp with him of late, she knew. Just the other day, she'd slapped him when she'd caught him stealing one of her new-baked scones from the cooling rack. Then when he'd asked to go to the funfair last Saturday she'd snapped a no. She'd have liked to go herself but there'd been no money. No mon, no fun, she said, and he'd stopped talking to her ever since.

She stretched out her arms. 'Throw another,' she said.

Jimmy looked at Trix, Trix looked at Jimmy. 'Go on,' she said. 'Both of you. For the love of God.'

They picked up two stones and threw them. One missed, the other grazed Shell's cheek.

'Go on. Don't be afraid.' *Scones,* she thought, smiling. *Not stones. Imagine them as soft, light scones.*

They threw again. On the road, Shell heard a car trawling up the hill. On the third throw, she yelped despite herself.

'Go on,' she squeaked.

'No,' said Trix. ''S boring.' She ran off down the field, singing something. But Jimmy picked up a big stone, the size of three scones in one. He squinted, as if the devil was sneaking a peek out of his eye.

'This'll hurt,' he said.

'That's right, Jimmy. Fine man. Throw it.'

He heaved it up to his shoulder with both hands, a miniature Superman. He grunted.

'Ready,' said Shell. 'Do it.'

'Stop.' A voice, dark and deep, like an underground earthquake, called over to them.

Shell closed her eyes. 'Do it,' she whispered. A

breeze fanned her fringe. Inside her eyelids, yellow rockets burst.

'Drop it, boy.' It was a command, urgent but not harsh.

She opened her eyes. The devil catapulted out of Jimmy in two shakes. She turned round. Father Rose had pulled up by the gate. She could hardly see him or the car in the strong early light that broke through the heavy clouds. He'd wound down the window.

'We were only messing,' Jimmy hollered, dropping the stone. He ran off down the hill.

Father Rose looked towards Shell. 'What was that about?' he asked.

Shell shrugged.

'You're the Talent girl, aren't you?'

She nodded.

'What's your first name?'

'Michelle. But everyone calls me Shell.'

He nodded back and started up his car. 'So long, Shell.' She thought he was going to add something, but he sighed instead. He let down the handbrake and took off up the hill. She blinked. The car flashed purple as he rounded the bend.

Shell sat down on the damp earth and breathed out hard. She stroked the lumpen stones of the Pharisees that had glanced off her mortal body. '*He who has not sinned,*' she murmured, '*let him cast the first stone.*' She took up the last stone, the one Jimmy hadn't dared to throw, and cooled her cheek with it. She lay back on the ground and was still. The cold spring morning went deep into her bones.

Three

She saw Father Rose again soon afterwards.

Dad had been collecting for the starving nations of Africa. One week it was flood victims of a sub-continent, the next it was refugees from a minor theatre of war, but when each week ended, he'd seal the money in an envelope and tell Shell to take it to the priests' house. It was the one job she liked: first, because she'd steal a few pence for herself and buy some gums at McGraths', and second, because if Nora Canterville, the priests' housekeeper, answered, she'd get a wedge of coffee and walnut cake.

Before she left, Dad grabbed her arm. 'If you steal it, even a penny of it, I'll know. Father Carroll'll tell me and all hell will be let loose.'

'Yes, Dad. I know.'

And she *did* know. The money he collected was always more than the money he sent in. She might be a thief, but he was a worse one. She'd seen him filching the larger coins, even notes, and dropping them into his pockets. The man was as mean as a blood-sucking midge. When he gave her the money for the shopping each week, he'd grab her wrist and tell her to bring him back the change down to the last penny and every last receipt. There was no such thing as pocket money in their house. And since Mam died, he'd made herself, Jimmy and Trix wear the same school uniforms three sizes too big, so as to save on having to buy new ones when they'd grown out of the old. They were the scarecrow pupils, the laughs of the townland. Shell's school had a song for her, courtesy of Declan Ronan, Coolbar's unholiest altar boy, and the cleverest boy in the Leaving Certificate year:

> *Shell looks worse than brambles*
> *Or empty tins of Campbell's.*
> *She smells of eggy-scrambles,*
> *Her greasy hair's a shambles.*

Whatever about his charity collecting, her dad had a black shrivelled walnut for a heart.

The meanest thing she'd ever seen him do was steal Mam's ring off her corpse. Mam had only the one, the gold band on her left hand that meant she was his wife. When married women die, Shell knew, they get buried with their wedding rings on, so that they can take their loving and faithfulness to the grave. There the rings stay until time ends, surviving the flesh and even the bone.

But her dad couldn't bear to see a good bit of yellow gold go to waste. The ring had loosened up in her final wasting. Before they put the coffin lid on, he'd said, 'Please: one last prayer, one last goodbye, on my own.' Everyone had left him to it. Everyone but Shell. She'd stopped outside the room behind the door that had been left ajar and peeked in through the crack. She saw him unravelling a portion of the milky white rosary from her mam's hand. She glimpsed a yellow flash dropping into his top waistcoat pocket. Then he fiddled with the rosary again.

'You can cover her over now,' he'd called to the undertaker. 'I'm ready.'

What he'd done with the ring, Shell didn't know. It wasn't in with his socks – she'd checked. He'd probably sold it when he was next in town.

Dad and his demented readings. Dad and the stones in the back field. Dad and the rattle of the collection tins. She trudged up the back field with the envelope of small change tucked underarm. The sun was out, strong and pale. The lambs had arrived. One skipped up to her and baa-ed, then darted off again, its legs like airy springs. *This is the Lamb of God, which taketh away the sin of the world.* The thought of Dad faded. She reached the top of the hill. The clouds might have been lamb-cousins in their fluffiness. The trees brimmed with white blossom. She felt like a bride as she passed below them. Two fields on and Coolbar appeared before her in a fold of slope. She sat on a bank of grass and peeled the envelope flap open with a steady hand, watching the strands of gum stretch and shrivel as she tugged. She took out five pieces of silver and hurled them into the air for the poor of the parish to find in their hour of need.

'So there, Dad,' she shouted.

The coins sparkled, scattering to earth. She laughed and resealed the envelope, then walked down through the last pasture to human habitation.

She meandered along the village pavement. At McGraths' shop the sweet aroma of newspapers and cigarettes made her linger. They sold postcards and beach balls all year round, liquorice, ice-cream cones, plastic buckets and spades. She felt the money calling to her from inside the envelope and wished she'd kept the pieces of silver for herself. She didn't dare take any more. A ball of longing itched her belly. She'd only had an egg all day.

Mr McGrath saw her from within the shop. He beckoned, his bright red cheeks and big forehead wagging like a toy dog. Shell shrugged her shoulders, as if to say, *If only*. He came out with a handful of bubblegums. He gave them to her, putting a finger to his mouth.

'Our secret, Shell. Don't be going telling, or I'll have all Coolbar on to me.'

'No, Mr McGrath. I won't. Promise.' She blushed as pink as the bubblegum wrappers and went on down the street rejoicing. Jesus had surely rewarded her for the money she'd sprinkled earlier for the parish poor.

The priests' house was a little way up the street, beyond the church. Father Carroll had lived there ever since Shell could remember with his housekeeper, Nora Canterville. The curates came and went, but they two stayed. Nora, it was proclaimed, was the best cook in the whole of County Cork, famed for a consommé soup as clear as a newborn baby's soul. Dad always said that if you were invited for a meal, you'd leave half a stone heavier than you'd come.

Shell wasn't expecting to encounter Father Rose. She thought he'd be out on the parish rounds, up at the community hospital or out on Goat Island, the nearby peninsula, saying the mid-week Mass. She rang the bell, thinking of coffee cake, not him.

There was a long wait before anybody answered. She was about to go, when she heard steps on the stairs, then an approaching tread, sure and measured: too firm for Nora; too swift for Father Carroll. She held her breath. Her stomach fluttered.

The door opened. Father Rose looked upon Shell, an eyebrow raised, but said nothing.

'My dad,' she said, holding the envelope forward, 'said to give this to you.'

He took the envelope by its top, so that the money slid to the bottom. Her cheeks burned at the vulgar clink of change. Money and the Word of the Lord were far from fast friends, as he'd said last Sunday. He was surely thinking of the tables of the moneylenders.

'It's charity money,' she said. 'For the starving of Africa.'

'That campaign ended last month,' he said. 'Maybe it's for St Vincent de Paul? That's who we're collecting for now.'

Shell shook her head as if to say she didn't know.

'Your dad. He collects it in his spare time, doesn't he?' The money kept jingling. In devastation, Shell stared down at Father Rose's feet. With a shock, she saw they were bare. His dark priest's pants stopped short just above his white, long toes.

'His whole time is spare, Father,' she stammered. 'He's no job.'

'No job?'

'Not since Mam died. He left off the farm work over at Duggans' on account of his bad back.' That was what Dad gave out anyway.

'He's the job of keeping house and being mother and father to you and your brother and your sister, hasn't he?'

'S'pose.' She could have said it was herself did most of that.

'He's a religious man, your father. So Father Carroll tells me.'

Shell shrugged. 'S'pose.'

'Do you want to come in for a glass of something? Nora's shopping in town, but I can rustle up something for you.'

Shell nodded. He didn't move to one side. Instead he made a tall bridge of his arm, so that she could walk under him, through the open door. As she passed beneath, she took care not to tread on his bare feet by accident. The smell of the woven wool carpet and the heavy velvet tick of the big wall clock made her feel the size of an infant.

'This way, Shell,' he said.

The way he said her name was like a blessing.

He opened a door to the best room, at the front, where Shell had never been before. He waved her onto a huge chair of dimpled leather. Then he got a cut glass from a cabinet, and took a small bottle of bitter lemon from a drinks trolley.

Shell had never liked bitter lemon until then. But as she sipped it now, it fizzed like sherbet on her nose and lip and slipped over her tongue, sweet and sour at the same time. He leaned against the arm of the matching leather sofa as she drank. He folded his arms and watched. He smiled. A slow warmth filled the room.

'I'm glad you called when you did,' he said.

'Why's that, Father?'

'I'd been having a struggle.'

'A struggle?'

'With myself. A terrible craving for the fags.'

Shell chortled, remembering his sermon. 'You're still off them?'

'For all Lent, I hope. Please God I last till Easter.'

'Will you go back on them then?'

'Maybe. Maybe not.' He shook his head. 'Desperate things, the fags. The hold they have on you. Don't *you* ever go on them, will you?'

She didn't like to say she'd already had a few. Declan Ronan shared one around at school some-times, swapping it between herself and Bridie Quinn: a token of honour, he'd quip, for the founding members of his harem.

'I hope you don't mind me asking,' Father Rose said, as if he'd read her thoughts, 'but shouldn't you be at school?'

Shell held up the glass to her face. She peered through the diamond ridges. 'School?' she said. ''S nearly over. We break up soon.'

'I see.' He got up and walked the length of the room. He stopped at the casement window and stood for a long moment.

'The other morning,' he said with his back to her. 'In the field. Why were you letting your brother and sister throw stones at you like that?'

Shell almost drank the fizzing lemon the wrong way.

'As I came up the hill,' he continued, 'I saw you, standing with your arms outstretched.' He turned to face her.

Her eyes slanted over to the vase of silk flowers inside the fireplace. She finished the drink.

'For a moment I thought I was seeing things,' he said. 'A vision from the gospel.'

'We were only messing.'

'It seemed an odd game, Shell.'

There was something in the way he said the words that drew her eyes to his. A soft bowl of light sat in his look, so she told him the truth. 'I was praying, Father. I was making them hurt me so that I could feel the praying. Really feel it. Strong and hard.'

He got up and took the glass from her. 'Would you like another?'

'No, Father.'

'Well, on you go, so.'

'Yes, Father.'

He showed her to the door, but as she stepped back out onto the front path, he stopped her with a hand on her shoulder. She felt it there, a firm, kind touch.

'Shell,' he said. 'Prayer doesn't have to be painful. Trust me.'

She looked up. The wisdom of ages was in his eyes. 'I do, Father,' she said.

He let her go. She hurried down the path, through the gate and up the road. She knew he was watching her as she departed, for she did not hear the sound of the front door closing after her.

Four

After tea that day, Dad led the usual decade of the
rosary. They were on the first Sorrowful Mystery,
the agony in the garden. Jesus was waiting in anguish
of mind to be arrested. Jimmy had his tongue poked
off to the side so that his left cheek was like a tent.
He stared at the old piano longingly, and wiggled his
fingers as if he was playing it. Trix sat back on her
heels and stared up at the flypaper Dad had hung
up earlier from the lampshade. The first trapped fly
was stirring on it, dying. Shell closed her eyes. Dad's
voice drifted away. Instead Jesus joined her in his
trouble of mind. She walked with him along the
gravel path of the priests' house garden. They
approached the tall pampas grass, waiting for the
soldiers to arrive, and sighed together to think of the
coming cross and nails. *Jesus*, Shell said, *I wish I could
have the nails instead.* He turned to her and took her
arm. He had the face of Father Rose, but instead
of priestly vestments he wore a long linen tunic of
dazzling white. Beneath it, his feet were bare. His
face was unshaven, his hair longer. *Shell*, he said in

his dulcet Midlands tone, *your sweet love is all the comfort I need on this dark day.*

'Shell!' Dad's voice, stern. 'You've stopped praying.'

'No, I haven't,' Shell said. 'I was talking to Jesus in my head.'

'That's blasphemy,' he snapped. He thrust the rosary at her. 'You do the next five beads. And you, Jimmy, stop your wriggling, or I'll put an axe to that piano.'

In bed that night, after the light was out, she returned to her visions. She found herself in a boat. Jesus was on the far side of the lake, walking on the water. When she climbed over the side, the surface was elastic, like a trampoline. She crossed over, bounding like a spaceman on the moon. He took her hand and they traversed the lake as the sun went down and the stars came out. As she drifted into sleep, he turned and said something to her. She leaned towards him to catch the words and suddenly the surface of the lake shifted. She was falling into the grey-green depths below. Silence, thick and heavy, was everywhere. Then from afar came the steady tick-tocking of a clock.

Five

On Wednesday morning, after they'd done the stones, Dad said there'd be no more mitching off from school. They were to go in, quick march.

'I thought you said we could have the last week off,' Jimmy moaned.

'I don't *wanna* go to school, Dadda,' Trix said. She always called him 'Dadda' when she wanted her way but today it didn't work.

'You'll be at school in two shakes or I'll have the washing line down to the three of you,' he said. 'I'll not have any more interfering phone calls.'

Shell's ears pricked up. Somebody from school had been on to him again.

She helped Trix get ready and kept them both quiet with a bubblegum each she'd saved from yesterday. She hurried them over the field to the village and left them off at the national school. Then she caught the bus to Castlerock town for secondary school.

She arrived just on time. Bridie Quinn sauntered over to her before the bell went. She and Bridie were the only girls from Coolbar in their class. They were the two bad apples of the fourth year and fast friends, whenever they weren't mitching. Bridie's dad had vanished years back. She, her younger brothers and sisters and her mam lived in a mouldering three-room bungalow the other side of Coolbar, on the road to Goat Island. They'd a TV and calor gas, but no bathroom, and they washed in an outhouse. Nobody knew how they all squeezed in. Bridie had to share a bed with her mam, a fate worse than death. She'd a thistle for a tongue but was Shell's only friend.

'Shell Talent, you're a sight,' she announced.

Shell looked down at her grubby dress and around the playground. She was the only one in summer uniform, a maggot-green shapeless shift with a narrow belt, sleeves to the elbow and stripes of navy on the flat, wide collar. The weather was fine. She'd thought the whole school would have switched over from winter to summer by now.

'I guessed wrong,' she moaned.

''S not the *dress*,' Bridie said, waving a hand. The dangers of the morning guessing game at the change of the season were well understood. 'It's the cut of you under it. You've no bra on.'

Shell wriggled. 'So?'

'In that dress, I can see them drooping.'

'No!'

'I can. They're like two jellyfish.'

'Shut it.'

''S true.'

Shell sighed. 'I don't *have* a bra.'

'You should get one.'

27

'Dad'd never give me the money for one.'

'Will we pinch something from Meehans' stores? They'd never notice. I could pick you out a nice one. Lacy blue. Underwired. Whatever you fancy.'

Shell giggled. 'Would you?'

'I would. You'd have to tell me your size, first.'

'Dunno my size. I've never been measured.'

'Not even the size of your cup?'

'My cup?'

'*You* know.' Bridie clumped her two hands in front of her chest.

'I've no notion,' Shell admitted.

'Looking at you, I'd say you're a C for sure.'

'A C?'

'A C, Shell.'

A seashell. She liked the sound of it. She thought of the round creamy shells on Goat Island strand. 'A seashell,' she murmured like an incantation. 'Is that big or small?'

Bridie fluttered her eyelids as if Shell was Miss Ireland for Ignorance.

'Big enough that you need a bra,' she said. Her voice softened. She slipped her arm through Shell's, a thing she rarely did. 'I didn't like it when mine grew,' she confided. 'But now I'm used to them. A bra makes them stick out. People notice. I'm a thirty-four D, but don't be telling anyone.'

'I won't,' Shell promised.

'Come with me after school,' Bridie said. 'We'll pop into Meehans'. I'll slip it out of the box – into my school bag – and away we go.'

'You *sure* we won't get caught?'

'Sure. I've done it before. Often.'

The bell rang.

At break time, Shell resumed the conversation.

'Bridie. Did they have bras in the olden days?' she asked.

Bridie pondered the question. 'They must have,' she concluded. 'Otherwise, women would have wobbled all over the place. Like yourself.'

'D'you think,' Shell whispered, 'that the Virgin Mary wore a bra?'

Bridie hooted. 'You wait till I tell Declan that one. Maybe he'll think up a joke about it.'

'I'm serious.'

'Under all those loose blue robes and cloaks? She must have, mustn't she? When you've had a baby, you quadruple in size. I know. My mam told me. You've to carry around all the milk.'

Shell thought of the cows she'd seen with machines on their udders in the milking parlour over on Duggans' farm. 'How much milk, d'you think?'

'A good few pints, I'd say. There's Declan. I'm off.' She ran after Declan's distant figure. He was making for the games hut for a fag. Shell shrugged and turned away, pondering the mystery of the milk of various nursing mammals.

At lunch, Declan Ronan came up to Shell and invited her behind the hut for a drag on his fag. Bridie had to stay indoors and do a detention.

'I've a great one. What kind of bra did the Virgin Mary Mother wear when she was lactating?' Declan said.

Shell pondered. The word lactating puzzled her, but she wouldn't admit it. 'Dunno,' she said. 'Give up.'

'A thirty-three J Wonderbra,' he said. 'Get it?'

'Not sure,' she admitted.

'A three for the Holy Father, a three for the Holy Spirit, and a J-cup for your man, Jesus, so's he could drink his fill of the eternal life.'

'And grow up wonderful?' Shell suggested.

'You've got it,' he said, passing her the fag.

She took a long drag and passed it back. They sat together in the sun. Theresa Sheehy poked her head round the corner as if to join them but Declan shooed her away.

'Why don't you let her join us?' Shell said after she'd vanished.

'Her legs are too fat.'

Shell clouted him. He gave her another go on the fag, then clamped his hand on her calf. 'Not like yours.' He ran his hand up to behind her knee and tickled.

'Gerroff.'

'Good and skinny.' He took his hand away and smirked. 'Miss Shambles.'

'You, Bridie and me, Declan,' Shell smiled, blowing out the smoke. 'We're the Coolbar Club, aren't we?' She remembered Declan as a familiar torment down the years. In national school he was forever chasing the girls around the playground, yanking up their skirts. In secondary school he'd sometimes ride the bus home with her and Bridie, taking it in turns who he'd sit next to.

He took the fag from her and snorted. 'Coolbar,' he said, 'is an excrescence on the face of the earth.'

'Too right.' She nodded sagely, though she didn't know what an excrescence was.

Six

Stealing the bra from Meehans' didn't feel like a sin, even though it was. Bridie did it on Shell's behalf. She picked a bra out of its box when nobody was looking. It was white, with a criss-cross back. She slipped it between her homework books, and then investigated the nightgowns. She nearly stole a skimpy robe of pink, but Shell stopped her. They made their getaway. They nearly died laughing all the way up the street to the town clock. Over the way, near the garda station, was Dad, standing on his own, shaking the can. Shell saw a shopper crossing the road to avoid walking past him.

'Not that way,' she gasped, falling back before he could spot her.

'Rather no dad than a dad like that,' Bridie said, raising her eyes to heaven.

'Too right,' Shell said. They slipped down a side street to the quays and headed the back way to the bus stop.

Bridie passed her the bra. 'I'm not going home yet,' she said.

'Why not?'

'I've a date. In town.' She sounded just like a character from one of the American soaps she was always going on about.

'A date? Who with?'

Bridie jerked her chin out and tossed back her hair. ''S secret.' She waved goodbye and walked back towards the pier.

Shell couldn't wait to try the bra on. There was no sign of the bus. She dived into the nearby public toilets. By the time she'd figured out how to do the hooks and clasps, she was hot and bothered. When she emerged, the bus was sailing off from the stop without her. She'd a long wait for the next.

When it came, she climbed aboard with a straight back and her chin tilted up. The driver took her fare in slow motion, staring straight at her front. She took her seat with a regal smile. It was a coming of age. Her baggy old shift-shape had been annihilated.

She was nearly an hour late picking up Trix and Jimmy from primary school. The head teacher, Miss Donoghue, had them sitting in her room on hard, grown-up chairs. Miss Donoghue was a Coolbar fixture, having taught Shell and many a Coolbar child before her. She looked like she'd been nearing retirement for ever but it never arrived. Trix's grey socks swung between the long iron legs. Jimmy pulled a face at Shell as she came in.

'Shell's h-e-r-e,' Jimmy said. He looked over her head and mimed a bored whistle.

'Shell!' Trix said, leaping down. She ran up for a hug. 'I thought you'd forgotten us, Shell. Like that other time.'

'No, I didn't. I'd messages to do in town.' A great love descended upon her heart. She stooped and gave Trix a kiss.

Miss Donoghue opened her mouth as if about to say something, then shut it. She sighed. 'You young Talents,' she said. 'You'll be the death of me.' She smiled, then got up from behind her desk and gave Jimmy a nudge.

'Off you go,' she said. She held the door open, but not like Father Rose had done. Instead of going under her arm like a bridge, they had to walk past her. Shell still felt about seven years old as she sloped by.

'Good evening, Miss Donoghue,' she murmured.

'Good evening, Shell,' Miss Donoghue said. Her hand suddenly landed on Shell's shoulder. 'Where *is* your father anyway?'

Shell considered. 'He's probably collecting in town still. For the Church.'

The head did a tiny *tchtch* sound with her tongue and teeth and let her go.

Dad wasn't in when they got home. Shell got the tea. Still Dad didn't appear. Then she remembered it was Wednesday, his drinking night. That meant they'd hours of freedom, space and games, Jimmy, Trix and herself. They ate the tea. Shell put a saucepan lid over Dad's share of ham and cheese triangles. Jimmy opened the lid of Mam's piano. Dad had tried to sell it after she'd died, but the man from town said it was so clapped out Dad would have to pay *him* to take it away. The tune had gone clean out of it. Mass cards for Mam still sat on top.

Jimmy stood at the piano, with one foot on the right pedal. He played strange, jarring chords that mushed together. They hung in the house like sighs from a spirit world. As he played, Shell shut her eyes. She saw colourful fish, swimming in underground caves, bubbles floating up, strange weeds rippling. Then he lifted the pedal and started over. He pattered at the top notes. It was sparrows hopping in the snow. Then snow falling on car roofs. He finished his concert with loud chords of bass notes. They rang through Shell's flesh like doom-laden giant trees stalking the earth. She and Trix laughed and clapped.

Next, they went out to play Scarecrow Chase in the back field. It was her made-up game from years back; she'd shown it to the others. There were no winners, only a loser. You started with six clothes pegs, and had to clip them onto other people and not let any be clipped on yourself. Once you got rid of all six you were out. One person ended up with the pegs dotted all over, and whoever that was was the Scarecrow Loser. But now she'd grown out of it. She let Jimmy and Trix stitch her up with pegs everywhere, then handed the lot over and went indoors to the bathroom. She stripped off the school dress in front of the cabinet mirror and examined the bra, craning over her shoulder to see the criss-cross at the back. The mirror was too high, so she crept into Dad's room and played the Eternity game. This was a game of magic mirrors at the dressing table. It was a broad, wooden chest, with three mirrors attached on top: a large fixed one in the middle, and two smaller ones on hinges on the sides. She could swivel these in and out to form angles. Then a chain of Shells going on into infinity appeared. In past games she'd always tried to chat with them, to ask them what life in the mirror was like. But although they made faces, they never gave much away. Today, she ignored them. Instead she squeezed the mirror angles up tight to see what the bra looked like from behind.

She prayed to Jesus to forgive her and Bridie for stealing the bra. She listened hard for a reply. The room was quiet: no sign of hissing snakes or thunderbolts. Perhaps she was forgiven.

Then she'd an idea. She opened the wardrobe door. Inside, a sigh of polythene escaped from Dad's best suit, back from the dry cleaner's after Mam's funeral and never worn since. His other clothes jostled as she looked through the contents: shirts he pressed himself for church; pants and braces; eleven pairs of shoes; more ties than she could count, three of them black.

Dad had thrown away Mam's things long ago. But, tucked away on a hook at the back, there was one thing of hers he'd kept – why, Shell didn't know. It was a pink, sleeveless satin dress, cut short at the knee and slim-waisted.

She reached in and took it from the hanger.

Did she dare?

She did. She tried it on.

It covered her kneecaps but only just.

It fitted just right on top.

The colour set her cheeks singing.

Shell waltzed in front of the mirror. She sat on the velvet chair her mam had perched on every morning to do her make-up and looked into the triptych of reflections. She rested her chin on her hand as Mam used to do. Shell's face was slim and freckly. She undid her ponytail and shook out her foxy hair. She batted her eyelids. She began to hum Mam's favourite hymn: 'Come Down, o Love Divine, Seek Thou This Soul of Mine'.

In the gathering gloom of the spring evening Mam's spirit returned briefly to earth. She hovered between Shell's eye and the eye of the image in the mirror.

'Mam?' Shell gasped.

It was as if a hand had reached out and touched her shoulder. One of the images furthest away in the mirror smiled – it wasn't Shell's image, because the other images didn't smile at all.

'Mam!' she called to it. 'Don't go!'

She hummed the tune harder to make her stay. She didn't notice the bedroom door opening behind her.

'Jesus!' A harsh, pained voice. A dark figure hovered in the reflected corner of her field of vision. She froze. Mam's spirit fled back deep into the mirror world. Shell turned. Dad was staring at her like a stranger. She'd no idea it had got so late.

'Sweet Jesus. Is it really *you*?'

He stepped forward into the room. He put out his right hand and it hovered palm-upward over her left cheek, fluttering. She braced herself for a slap.

It did not come.

His big hand shook, drawing closer. She could see the swirls of his finger pads in the corner of her eye. It landed on her face, quivering like a leaf in wind, stroking her cheekbone. 'Moira,' he whispered. 'My Moira.'

Shell smelled whiskey and sweat. Her stomach somersaulted. He burped.

'It's me. Shell,' she shrieked.

She darted past him and ran to the door. As she passed through it, she looked back. Dad was standing where she'd left him, arm outstretched, as if the Moira he'd seen were still standing there, letting him stroke her face. In the triptych of mirrors was the image of him standing there, again and again, into infinity, reaching out forlornly into another world, a world to which Mam had gone and the living could not follow.

Seven

She fled to her own room, the one she shared with Jimmy and Trix on the far side of the kitchen. She shut the door behind her and stood against it, panting, regaining her breath. Her father didn't follow. There was no sound of him. After a moment she tore off the pink dress and hid it under her bed. She changed into her old dungaree jeans and T-shirt.

She crept through the kitchen, into the hall. Dad's door was shut. *Please God, he's gone to bed*, she thought.

She went out into the dusk to fetch in Trix and Jimmy. It was the time when the blackbirds stop singing and the bats come out.

'Quick,' she called to Trix, who'd gone into hiding. 'Or the bats will land in your hair, and we'll have to chop it off to get them out again.'

Trix screamed and ran from behind the dilapidated log shed. Jimmy blew up the bubblegum he'd saved from the morning. It burst.

'They don't do that,' he said coolly. ''Cos they have sonic vision.'

'Never you mind,' Shell said. 'Off to bed. Dad'll

have the washing line down to you if he catches you still up.'

They did as they were told and went to bed.

The house went quiet, with no sound from Dad's room. She walked out into the back field. The bats skimmed up close. She stretched out her arms and fingers and made a high-pitched whine, hoping one might land. But the sonic vision worked too well and they wouldn't. The air was soft and smooth to the feel. The moon rose like half a silver coin from behind the mountains. She climbed the gate and crept around Duggans' new-ploughed field to the copse above. A barbed wire fence was around it, but she squeezed between the lower and upper rungs without getting caught.

In the copse, the wild things of the night had started. A scuffle, then a flap. A zzzz, a rustle, a tap. A tree moaned like a rusty hinge. 'Jesus,' she intoned aloud. 'I am no angel. But hear my prayer. Please take my mad father to your holy bosom, even as you took my own dear mam. For his life is a torment to him and to all of us.' An owl hooted. Shell listened. It hooted again, nearer, then again, further off. She frowned, trying to catch its meaning. It hooted again, a little nearer. But however hard she strained to hear, the message escaped her. The wood grew quiet. A fifth hoot came from almost overhead. She jumped. Then she knew.

Wa-ai-ai-t, the owl had said.

Jesus was telling her to wait. So wait she would.

Eight

The next day, Shell put on the winter uniform even though the sun shone.

She got to school to find the place alive with maggots. All the girls had come in their shifts of shapeless green. They'd taken a leaf from her yesterday, while she'd switched back. She stuck out again like a sore thumb.

Bridie was nowhere to be seen on the playground. Shell walked around the perimeter fence, her eyes half shut. She was with Jesus and the other Apostles, heading into Jerusalem. Crowds were gathering. Palm leaves were appearing. There was a bustle around her, a sense of growing expectation. Jesus turned to her and beckoned. 'Shell,' he said, smiling. 'Would you ever run ahead and fetch me a donkey?'

Declan grabbed her by the ankle as she walked past his smoking post behind the hut. He sat there, hunched up on the ground like a gnome. He'd a new poem for her.

'*Shell smells*
of flea balls
on the dirt floor,'

he chanted.

She smiled at him, thinking, *Here, Lord, I have found you your donkey.*

He wouldn't let her ankle go. The road to Jerusalem dissolved from her head.

'Sit down, Shell,' Declan coaxed. 'Sit here and have a drag of my fag.'

She sat down. He inched up close and handed her the fag. She inhaled, then coughed.

'These are wicked strong,' she said.

'They're my gran's. I pinched some last night when she was over. They're high-tar, non-tipped. The ones with the sailor's face on the pack.'

She took another drag. 'Jakes!' She gave it back. He took three long drags.

'Mam says they're the devil's own curse of a fag. Only sailors and whores smoke them.'

'Whores?' Shell said.

'You know. Ladies of the night.'

'Ladies of the night?'

'Ladies who sell their bodies.'

'Who what?'

'You're having a rise with me, Shell Talent. You know a whore as well as I do.'

She didn't quite, but a small inspiration made her say, 'Like Mary Magdalene, you mean?'

'A whore of the first water.' Declan blew a smoke

ring and together they watched it waft into the blue air. 'That reminds me,' he mused. 'I've just read this book my cousin over in London gave me. A big thick book. *The Holy Blood and the Holy Grail.* Not by one scholar, not by two, but by three. And d'you know what they said?'

'What?'

'They said Jesus married your woman, Mary Magdalene.'

Shell's eyes opened wide. 'Never!'

'Too right. *And* they had a child.'

'A child?'

'Yeh. A girl. Apparently after your man Jesus snuffed it, Mary M. ran away with the child and crossed the water. They say she landed in France.'

'In *France*?'

'France.'

Shell imagined a boat landing on a vast tract of empty sand. Mary Magdalene and her toddler climbed over the side and walked silently through the gentle tide towards the whistling dunes, into the new country.

'Maybe she went north to Roskoff harbour,' Declan mused. 'And took the Brittany line over to Cork.'

Shell clouted him. 'You're making it up.'

'No. Honest.' He handed her the fag. This time she declined it, calling to mind the holy abstinence of Father Rose. Declan took another short puff. 'Well, the bit about coming to Ireland I am. But the rest is in that book. They claim the Holy Catholic Apostolic Church covered it up. They're in cahoots with the freemasons.'

They sat together in companionable silence, Declan smoking and Shell thinking about the hidden life of Jesus. She saw him at the carpentry, barefoot, with his small child, a girl, pulling at his robe. Mary Magdalene was kneading the bread for the tea off to one side. His piercing blue eyes looked upon her. He picked up a plane to finish off the surface, murmuring sweet words of love.

'Would you or wouldn't you, Shell Talent?' Declan said suddenly.

'Heh?'

'That's the question I've been asking myself.'

Shell frowned. 'Would I what?'

'You know.' His hand did a few cartwheels in the air. '*That.*'

'What?'

'Was she born yesterday? Go into a field, Shell. With me. Do a Mary Magdalene. Take off your clothes.'

'And why,' Shell said, 'would I do that, Declan Ronan?'

He whistled through his teeth. 'I'd never call you smelly again, Shelly,' he teased.

'You're a right one.' She got up and gave him a kick on the thigh. He caught her ankle again. She looked down on him, lanky and brown, with a curly top and a blue flash for an eye. She pictured them both in Duggans' field with the barley up, stark naked, scooting around on all fours. 'A real, right one,' she snapped, wriggling her ankle.

''S that a yes?' Declan's hand inched up her calf.

'No!'

'You mean it's a no?'

'No.' She slapped his hand away from her leg.

'So it *is* a yes?'

'No, it's no!'

He grinned up at her. 'Only codding,' he says. 'I wouldn't go with you if you were Mary Magdalene herself.' He ground out the fag on a stone before it was spent.

'Bye, then,' Shell said.

'Bye-byes, Shellies,' he sang. He started again:

'*Shell smells like—*'

Then he stopped. He pouted and shrugged, throwing away the fag butt. 'Ah, don't go, Shell. Give us a kiss,' he pleaded. 'Go on. Kiss and make up. I didn't mean what I said.'

A kiss could do no harm, she supposed. She knelt down beside him and pushed out her lips. She closed her eyes.

His hands came round her, one on the back of her neck, the other on the small of her back. His lips came up to hers. She expected a little putter on them, like she gave Trix at night – Jimmy had grown out of them – and when it didn't happen she puttered him instead. But his two hands got tighter and his lips stayed hard on hers, until a soft sliver snaked into her mouth through the crack. She jumped. He didn't let go. He got his tongue further in and ferreted round as if he was looking for a gumboil or sore tooth. The tip of his bumped into the tip of hers. The picture of

45

God bringing life into Adam through a meeting of fingertips flashed through her brain. Lightning forked from her throat to her toes. He let her go.

She jerked back, jellified.

'Not bad,' Declan said. 'For starters.'

She clouted his head and ran.

'Never mind,' he called after her. 'There's always Bridie.

Hickory, dickory
Bridie Quinn
Ring the bell
And let yourself in,'

he sang. Shell had no idea what he was on about. As she rounded the hut, she saw Bridie herself. She was looking on from a distance with a face to turn milk, then she turned away with a jerk and strode back into the sea of maggot-green. Shell raced off in the other direction, towards the entrance to the school. She didn't stop running until she'd landed safely in her classroom.

The other pupils dribbled in after her. Of Bridie there was no sign. Lessons started. Up and down her trunk, the lightning inside her darted, coming and going all day long.

Nine

The last day of term, Friday, Father Rose came to say Mass in the school hall.

A shaft of light toppled in from the high window. Shell imagined it was Jesus in disguise, gliding down from heaven, straight into the tabernacle. '*Lord, I am not worthy to receive you, but only say the word and I shall be healed,*' the school chorused.

She went up to take the Host. Father Rose placed it upon her outstretched tongue. He loomed tall in his vestment of cream and green.

'Body of Christ,' he said.

She nearly forgot to say *Amen*.

The thin papery wafer went down softly, exploding like fifty fruit-chews in her tarnished soul. She shut her eyes to blot out the sight of Declan Ronan in the white surplice. He was altar boy again. But she kept picturing him with her, scooting around naked in Duggans' field.

When she opened her eyes, the after-Communion silence had descended. Father Rose cleaned the chalice out with a white cloth, handed to him by Declan.

Declan was as tall as him. The two's shoulders almost touched. They could have been brother apostles, had Declan an ounce of religion. His altar-boy job was a ruse. His mam and dad drafted him into it when he was seven and knew no better. Now he did it, he said, because he'd always manage a good few swigs of the communion wine in the vestry when no one was looking.

'The Mass is ended, go in peace,' Father Rose said.

'Thanks be to God,' the pupils responded.

They filed out back to class. Soon after, just before lunch, the school finished early for the Easter holidays. Shell got her things and wafted through the noisy throngs of pupils in the corridors and playground in a state of grace.

Out on the street, Bridie Quinn was waiting for her.

She sprang, arms flailing. She tugged at Shell's hair and punched her face.

'You,' she said. 'You.'

Shell put her arms up, thinking of Jesus expelling the fiends from the man possessed.

'Bridie,' she shouted. ''S me. Only me.' She caught Bridie's hand, but Bridie wrenched it back, struck her, and started to cry.

'What's the matter?' Shell said, trying to touch her.

Bridie shoved her off. '*You're* the matter. You. You cheat. You whore. You.'

Shell nearly cried too. 'I'm not.'

'You are,' Bridie said. 'I saw you. Yesterday. Saw you with him. You made him do it. Kiss you. And him going with *me.*' She lunged at Shell's shirt, tearing at it. 'After I giving you that bra. I'll have it off you.'

Bridie rained down blows and kicks. A button came off. Shell knelt on the pavement, her hands protecting her head, praying Jesus to make her stop.

He did. Father Rose appeared from nowhere.

'Whoa—' he said. 'What's this?'

Bridie stopped. She gave Shell a final kick and fled.

Shell slowly unfurled. Father Rose's eyebrows rose when he recognized her.

'Shell,' he said, in his thoughtful way. Shell stood up, sorting out her gaping shirt.

'Are you all right?'

She nodded.

'Who was that fighting you?'

She nearly said Bridie Quinn. Then she remembered the years of their friendship. 'Just a girl.'

'Does she often hit you?' he said.

Shell shook her head. 'We're friends really.'

'Sure?'

'Sure.'

They stood on the street. Shell felt a bruise on her elbow coming, where it had hit the pavement. She bit her lip, trying not to cry. Father Rose looked at her with a crinkle in his face, his hand rubbing his stubbly chin. Cars passed. Rain started spitting.

'Come on,' he said. 'I'll give you a spin home.'

'I've to pick up Jimmy and Trix from national school.'

49

'I'll give you a spin there then.'

He led Shell in silence down the kerb to where his car, an ancient wreck of purple, was parked. 'Don't laugh,' he said as Shell goggled at it.

'I thought it'd be black,' she said.

'Why so?'

'Like your clothes. Or white, maybe. Like your collar.'

'It was a bargain, going for a song. I didn't like the colour at first. But it's grown on me. It gets you noticed.'

'True for you.'

'It's not too lurid, d'you think?'

Shell wasn't sure what lurid meant. She frowned as if considering hard. 'I think it's fine, Father. Like a pop song.'

Father Rose laughed. The rain got harder. 'Come on,' he said. He opened the passenger door, took Shell's school bag from her and built that bridge of his with his spare arm over the door, so she'd to wriggle under it to get in.

'There you go.' He closed the door after her.

On the seat she'd to remove chewing-gum wrappers, a map of Ireland and his driving licence, so as to sit down. She gathered them onto her lap while he rushed round the other side and clambered in, putting her bag in the back. Shell felt as if a massive pony had got on board a wheelbarrow. His hair was brushing the top of the car, his knees were an inch from the steering wheel. 'Now,' he said, closing the door. The sound of the rain changed. It kataplunked on the roof. The warmth of their breath misted the windows.

He started up the engine. It chugged and wheezed, then died.

'Don't do this to me, Jezebel.'

Shell turned and stared. 'Jezebel?'

'It's a joke of a name, I know. But Jezebel she is, for she's a devil in her.'

He tried again. The car spurted, nearly started, died again.

'She hates the damp.'

Third try, the car started. Shell stared at the contents of her lap, wondering what to do with them. Father Rose pulled out, nearly colliding with another car. The side mirrors had water streaming off them. You could hardly see a thing. He didn't seem perturbed. He was trusting to the Lord.

'Will we go the straight road, or round the coast?' he asked.

They'd no car in Shell's house since Mam died. Mam had been the one with the driving licence. Dad owned one years ago, she had heard, but it had been taken from him for reasons Shell didn't know. There was never enough time these days to walk the three miles down to the strand on Goat Island. Mam used to run them there most days in the summer, and – also in the winter – after church on a Sunday. She'd loved to watch the waves rearing high as steeples.

'Let's go the coast road. Please.'

'The coast it is,' said Father Rose. 'If we can see it for the rain.'

They drove through the town. Mrs Fallon, the doctor's wife, waddled down the street with a plastic bag over her head, joining Mrs McGrath under the shelter of the bank doorway. Shell waved at them. They stared after her and Father Rose in open-mouthed surprise as they careered down Main Street in the purple saloon. At the grotto, Father Rose turned left and headed out the C-road. The rain hammered it as they topped the hill. A sheep with a blood-red smear of paint on its side ran out onto the road before them, as if eager to be killed. Father Rose swerved. The sheep leaped back into the open field. 'There but for the grace of God, Shell,' Father Rose said, straightening up. The car jerked into a pothole. Shell's head nearly hit the ceiling. She nearly lost the contents of her lap. She grabbed the licence just as it slipped off her knee.

She couldn't help looking at it. *Gabriel Rose*, it said.

'Gabriel?' she wondered aloud.

Father Rose looked over and saw the licence. He chuckled. 'For my sins,' he said. 'My mother called us Michael and Gabriel and prayed for us both to be priests.'

Shell pictured Father Rose as Archangel Gabriel in his shining raiments, come to tell the Virgin that she was with child. 'I've never met a Gabriel before,' she mused. 'But plenty of Michaels.'

'It's not such a common name.'

'What about your brother? Did he?'

'Did he what?'

'Did he become a priest, like you?'

Father Rose's lips went flat. He stared through the windscreen, into the washed-out view, as if he were blind. He sighed, then changed down a gear as a bedraggled dog came barking out of a bungalow's front yard.

'Well, Shell, he didn't,' he answered. 'He died of meningitis as a boy.'

'Ming-ing-ji-tus?' She'd heard the word before but couldn't place it. 'What's that?'

'It's a kind of bad flu. It gets into your brain.'

The rain came down in such sheets the windscreen wipers could not cope. 'We didn't get him to the doctor soon enough.'

They drove over the high ground in a roll of cloud.

'I'll pull in here, Shell. Until the worst of this passes.'

He stopped in a lay-by. The rain got harder still. She smelled the damp seeping into the car. It made her yawn. She looked back to the licence and saw the year of his birth. She worked out his age in comparison to hers.

Shell's age = 15 going on 16
Father Rose's age = 25
Shell's age + Jimmy's age = Father Rose's age.

'Shell,' Father Rose said. 'Would you say you're happy?'

Nobody'd ever asked her that before. She didn't know what to say. She put the licence on the dashboard and scrunched up the chewing-gum wrappers.

'Happy,' she repeated.

The rain eased a fraction. They waited longer.

'I mean in your life,' Father Rose resumed. 'At home – at school?'

'School's boring,' she said.

He considered this. 'I used get bored at school too,' he said.

'Did you?'

'Often. Specially in triple Irish.'

She slapped her knee. 'I hate Irish too.'

'So we've something in common?'

Shell nodded. She held out a chewing-gum wrapper. 'And the chewing gum, Father. I like it too. Just like you.'

'I'm addicted to it,' he said. 'Since giving up the fags. But let's keep that a secret, huh? Coolbar isn't ready for a gum-chewing priest.'

Shell giggled. The rain was only spitting now. He started up the car and pulled out onto the road. The fog thinned and the hillside emerged once more.

'Father,' Shell said, 'I'm sorry about your brother.'

He nodded. 'He was a year older than me, Shell. He'd have made a better priest than me, if he'd lived.'

As they came down the hill, the sun broke over the inlet. The watery air shimmered and blue sky truckled over from Goat Island point. Shell could hardly believe what happened next. It was a holy visitation, an answer to a prayer: a rainbow appeared, half out to sea, half dangling in land. Its colours deepened, pulsating into jostling strands.

'My God,' said Father Rose in hushed tones. He stopped the car dead, in the middle of the road. The light grew strong. White horses ran races across the bay. Father's Rose's hands floated off the steering wheel, as if doing homage.

'When the sun shines in Ireland, Shell, is there any place on earth more beautiful?'

He let her off at the national school. She fetched Trix and Jimmy and brought them home.

Jimmy was unusually quiet. He'd no interest in the tinned soup she warmed. She felt him. Cold beads of sweat were on his forehead.

'You've to go to bed,' she decreed.

'No,' he said. 'Won't.'

'You must. Now.'

'No.'

'If I say you're to go to bed, you've to go.'

He stuck out his tongue and went *pfffthrwphff.*

Her right hand itched to slap him, as she'd done before. But he looked at her with such a small, white face on him the itch evaporated.

'Go on, Jimmy,' she pleaded. 'Please. If Mam were alive, she'd tell you to go. Y'know she would.'

Jimmy's face cracked like a smashed saucer. 'You're not my mam,' he wailed. 'I want her. Not you.'

Shell had heard it before. She sighed. She dragged him by his collar out of his chair. He fisted her on the arms but not so it hurt. She marched him to the back bedroom where they all slept, army like, in a line of three thin beds, crushed in tight. His bed was at the far end. Over the headboard were his colourings of black and orange felt-tip scrawled straight on the wall. He'd done them as Mam lay dying. They weren't of anything, just busy spirals warring with each other.

When she laid him down, the fight went out of him. She put the blankets over and stroked his cheek. He pushed her hand away. Trix came up to the bedside too and gave him Nelly Quirke, the chewed-up toy dog that had once been Shell's.

'There,' Shell said. 'Fine man.'

He took Nelly Quirke from Trix but pulled away from Shell, curling in a ball with his face to the wall. 'Want Mam,' he said. But now it was more of a mutter.

Shell and Trix returned to the kitchen. Trix took to the floor with some paper dolls Shell cut out for her from an old *Examiner*. The rain returned. The long afternoon passed. Shell did the dishes. She tidied out the fridge. She dusted down the piano. Then she made tea. Jimmy made no sound. She checked in on him, but he slept the day away.

Dad was due back from the collecting. He'd be hauling Jimmy out of bed, she thought, for the next decade of the rosary. They were onto the Glorious Mysteries now, the one where flaming tongues come down on the heads of the Apostles, making them speak loads of languages.

Six came and went. Dad didn't come. Shell put a saucepan lid over his tinned fish.

'I wonder where he is,' she said, more to herself than to Trix.

Trix pushed a tomato quarter off the side of her plate onto the plastic tablecloth. 'He's here,' she said. She flicked the tomato off the edge of the table onto the floor. 'Now he's dropped down a bog. He's deaded.'

Shell chortled.

She picked up the tomato and popped it under the saucepan lid onto Dad's plate. 'He's probably delayed in town,' she said.

Trix helped Shell clear up. Then she sat at Shell's feet so that Shell could brush out her matted brown curls. The job hadn't been done in days, and the nits were back. As she combed, Shell told another story about their made-up fairy, Angie Goodie. She was the size of pea but always managed to stop the bad things happening. Tonight, Shell made her fly up onto the church steeple in an electric storm and hover over the top of the iron cross. She saved the church from being struck by raising her arm with her wand at the ready. The lightning bolt hit the wand, not the church. Because she was a fairy, she didn't die. Instead her wings shone brighter and when the rainbow came out after the storm, she went sliding back down it to her nice warm bed. Trix went off like a lamb. Jimmy slept on.

Shell went to the front door and watched the darkness settle in the yard. She walked out as far as the road. She thought of Bridie Quinn in her fury. She thought of Father Rose, the rainbow and Nelly

Quirke the dog, her ear in Jimmy's mouth. In the brown hush of the country road, she thanked Jesus for the good and bad of her day. It rained again. There being nothing else to do, she went in and made some scones.

Eleven

They were out of the oven and cool when the front door burst open. Dad stood before her, a man of the night. The rain flew in around him. His old jacket flapped, his chin bristled with growth. The collecting box was around his neck, tipped upside down, with the cord dripping. His tie was askew.

He blundered in.

'Where's tea?'

Shell put the plate before him, removing the lid.

He ripped the collecting tin from around his neck and dropped it to the floor with a curse. He ate in silence.

Shell watched in wonderment. His routine was broken. What might that mean? He'd never come in before like this on a *Friday*. Only Saturdays and Wednesdays. As he munched, she seemed to see a tear fall down his cheek and off the end of his red, wide nose, onto the plate of pilchards. She picked up the collecting tin and gave it a gentle shake. It was empty. Jesus tugged at a little string she'd never even known was in her heart. Father Rose was right: anger and love must go together.

'Are you feeling all right, Dad?' she asked.

He pushed the plate away and the cutlery fell from his hands to the table. His head dropped in his hands.

'Shell,' he said. 'You're a good girl.'

His forehead wagged. There was a moistness in his eyes.

'A good girl, praise God.'

She didn't like it. She'd almost have preferred the usual recriminations. Perhaps he'd got a touch of whatever Jimmy had.

'Ah, Shell. I'm a disappointed man.' He picked himself up and stared at her. 'Make me a cup, would you?'

She got the kettle boiling and the teapot warming.

'A disappointed man.'

She set the cup down before him. 'Why's that?' she said, passing him the sugar.

He put three spoons in and blew on the surface, then belched. The reek of Stack's was high upon him.

'You're old enough to know, I s'pose. I went courting tonight, Shell.'

Shell stared, thinking, *Courting? Him? He's out of his wits.*

'I asked a lady of my acquaintance out for a walk.'

Shell wondered who he meant.

'She'd always given me a smile and the time of day. I thought we both knew where we were going.' He shook his head and half smiled, half grimaced. 'You'd have liked a new mam, wouldn't you, Shell? You, Trix and Jimmy? Because that's why I did it. I did it for you.'

Shell shrugged. 'Dunno, Dad. We're fine as we are.' She took two scones off the cooling rack and laid them before him on Mam's favourite plate, a dainty china one with ducks and reeds painted on it. He ate the first scone, cramming it into his mouth at once. The crumbs dribbled from his lips, onto the lapels of his jacket and down his tie.

'So what happened?' Shell coaxed.

He swallowed the last bit and started on the next. His eyes went bleary and his hand shook.

'What happened, Dad? Did she go out walking with you?'

'She didn't,' he said. 'She told me no.'

'Who, Dad? Who told you no?'

He stared at Shell as if she were an idiot. 'I just told you. It was Nora. Who else?'

'Nora? Nora Canterville? The priests' *housekeeper*?'

'She's been leading me on with her fine cakes and jams for months. You see, she's the best cook in the whole of County Cork.' He shook his head. 'And now she won't have me.' His hand smashed down on the table so hard the plates jumped and the teacup rattled. 'She won't bloody have me.'

Shell stepped back.

'*Mr Talent*,' he said, mimicking Nora's cultivated accent from two counties eastward. '*It's an honour you're asking, but I'd rather stay in, if you don't mind. On these wet nights we've a grand fire going in the drawing room to keep out the chill and I'm happy out. It's where I call my home.*'

Shell thought of Nora Canterville with her tight curls permed fast to her head, her quaint suit of heather wool, her stockings of thick tan. Then she thought of Mam with her pink shiny dress and long slim legs, her hair of fresh-washed chestnut, singing her way through the morning chores. The man was crazed.

'But Dad,' she said. 'She's not even pretty. Not like Mam was.'

He shuffled from his seat and grabbed Shell's arm so fast she didn't have time to dodge. The china plate went flying and smashed to the floor. 'Shut it, Shell,' he menaced. His lips snarled back to his ears, his yellow teeth glistened, with the crumbs lodged between them. 'Don't you breathe a syllable.' He gripped her wrist, wringing it hard. 'What I just said. Don't – you – breathe – a – syllable.' Each word came out a hot, boozy hiss, and his face loomed over hers, getting closer every second.

She wrested her hand from his and picked up the broom. 'No, Dad,' she said. 'I won't.' She started up a clatter with the bristles zooming over the floor, fetching in the fragments of plate and the mess he'd made eating. 'Don't worry, Dad.' He swayed, watching her work. Then he gave her a royal salute, a little wave in the air with his right hand, and staggered out the door back into the night. She heard a sound down by the gatepost like a goat coughing. She knew what that was.

She closed the door to, but didn't lock it, and put the broom away. She put the tea towel over the rest of the scones on the cooling rack. Then she vanished into her bedroom. Jimmy and Trix were sleeping. Softly she drew the bottom bolt across the door, changed into her nightdress and got under the covers.

She cuddled up to herself, listening to the sing-song breathing in the dark. Soon her mind was full of rainbows and lightning strikes. Nora Canterville was skating down the shafts of colour instead of Angie Goodie, a steaming tureen in hand. Father Rose was driving Jezebel over the cliff roads into the sky. Declan was tugging her by the arm to the top of Duggans' field. *Would you, Shell, or wouldn't you?* She slept.

Twelve

In the heart of the night, she woke to the sound of Jimmy groaning. She turned on the light and saw his legs and arms muddled up with flannel sheets, a sweat-gloss on his skin, his face mottled red and white.

'Jimmy,' she whispered.

'It's throbbing mad,' he said.

She touched his forehead and he winced. 'Where? There?' she said.

He didn't answer but flailed his arm around as if his pyjama top were too small for him. Trix stirred in her sleep. He groaned some more.

Shell had never seen him so bad. Jimmy was often poorly. Dad said he did it to attract attention. But tonight she remembered the fate of Michael Rose, the curate's brother, dead from a flu in the brain.

'Maybe you've the meningitis,' she said.

Jimmy started bawling mad.

Shell panicked. She'd never had a sickness in the night to deal with. They had a phone, but Dad had barred them from ever touching it. It sat by his bed in his room beyond the kitchen. It was off-limits.

'Hang on, Jimmy. I'm away to Dr Fallon's,' she said. She unbolted the bedroom door and ran into the kitchen. She flung on her shoes, and ran out into the night. There was a steady drizzle still. Her nightdress was soaked in minutes. She took the short cut over the fields to the village.

The night was black and terrible. Clouds covered the moon. The hedgerows were alive with scrabbles and flaps. She stumbled in a rabbit hole and grazed herself in a thicket. In her head the words of Father Rose chased round like a dog after its tail: *We didn't get him to the doctor soon enough soon enough didn't doctor get him soon* . . . The copse shivered with strange sounds. Eyes appeared like devils in the undergrowth. 'Jesus, Lord!' she yelled, out of breath. The eyes vanished. A scurry behind her, a bird of prey flapping, then clear of the last trees, down to the field. The moon came out.

Coolbar came into sight as she ran downhill. She clutched her side, staggering with a stitch, breathing hot and fast. Dr Fallon's house was close by, at the top of the village. She rammed the knocker. 'Please, let him hear us,' she gasped, knocking again. She doubled over. Yellow streaks flared inside her eyelids.

The door opened suddenly. The doctor appeared before she could straighten up. 'It'd better be appendicitis at least,' he muttered. She could see broken sleep in his cross face. His lips were hard and flat.

''S not me, Doctor,' she panted, standing upright. 'It's Jimmy. He's wicked bad.'

'Your father sent you, did he?'

She nodded.

'Couldn't he have phoned? The cut of you!'

Shell looked down. Her nightdress was wrecked. She was soiled and damp and torn. *Shell,* she heard Mam say in her head, *you're the wreck of the* Hesperus.

'Wasn't working,' she said. She started crying. 'The phone.'

'OK, Shell. Don't panic. I'll get my bag.'

In a minute they were driving back together round the roads. 'What's wrong with Jimmy, then?' the doctor said. 'Has he a fever?'

'I think it's meningitis, Doctor. The flu you get in the head.'

'Doubt it,' the doctor said. 'No outbreaks at present, as far as I know. Where'd you get that idea?'

'Father Rose, Doctor.'

'Father Rose!' The doctor snorted. He shook his head. 'What's *he* got to do with it?'

'Nothing. Only he told me about it today, see. His brother had it.'

'Did he indeed?' Dr Fallon shook his head and accelerated. 'That young curate's full of notions.'

Shell didn't reply. She thought of Jimmy in his hot, fevered agony, and Michael Rose who'd been named for an archangel, dying young. They sped round the last sharp turn. The grey breezeblock wall that marked their bungalow loomed ahead through the darkness. She realized she'd left the front door wide open in her panic.

Dr Fallon followed her into the house, through the kitchen and down to the back room, to Jimmy's bed.

Trix woke up when they came in, whimpering in confusion. Shell went over to her. 'Whisht, Trix,' she murmured. The doctor went over to Jimmy. Shell heard him say, 'Hello, young man . . .' but she didn't stop to hear more. Mam had often told her when she lay dying that the doctor's visits were private. Shell wrapped Trix up in a blanket and carried her in her wet, muddy arms to the kitchen. She plumped her down in Dad's armchair and mimed a *shush*. Then she crept into the hall, to the door that led off to Dad's bedroom. She listened at the keyhole. She could just hear the sound of him snoring. She came back to the kitchen, got out the comb and went over Trix's hair again.

Dr Fallon soon joined them. 'Where's your father?' he said.

Shell stared at him. There was a scrape in his voice. A cold fist yanked her insides. 'Is he that bad, Doctor?' she said.

'Jimmy? No – he's only an infection.'

'It's not the meningitis?'

'Of course not. You can get that notion out of your head. He's a cut below the shoulder that's gone bad. I've given him an injection and some pills.'

'So – I *was* on time calling you?'

'You were, Shell – with time to spare. He'll be right as rain. But I'm glad we didn't leave it longer. He's been running a fever. He must have cut it days ago. Did you not notice?'

Shell shook her head. 'No, Doctor. I didn't.' Days. He'd been hurt for days and she hadn't known? She hung her head. *Dear Jesus*. She thought of all the times she'd slapped Jimmy, feeling a rage with him that she didn't understand. *Dear Jesus, forgive me for my lack of loving.*

'You weren't to know, Shell,' Dr Fallon said. His voice was different. The scrape had gone out of it. 'But I'd like a word with your father.'

'He's in bed, Doctor. He's gone asleep again. Since he sent me for you, I mean.'

The doctor walked out to the hall. Shell heard him open her dad's door. He came back with a wrinkle on his nose. 'I see,' he said. He looked sharply at Shell and at Trix, who'd a thumb in her mouth, a habit she'd gone back to in their troubles. 'I see.' He picked up his bag. 'Make sure Jimmy has a pill with his food. Three times a day. And get yourself out of those wet clothes.' He shook his head, glanced around at the kitchen as if it smelled bad. 'Good luck,' he said, and left.

Shell put Trix back to bed. Then she crept over to Jimmy. 'Are you awake, Jimmy?'

He opened his eyes.

'Is it sore?' she whispered.

He nodded. 'A small bit.'

'Can I see it?'

He eased his arm out from the pyjama top. 'It stung mad when he wiped it,' Jimmy said.

An angry gash of about an inch was halfway between his elbow and shoulder. It had gone a crusty yellow, with red skin all around. She felt the hot hard mound around it.

'How'd you do that, Jimmy?'

'It was a stone,' he said.

'A stone?'

He nodded. 'The other morning. I found this sharp small stone. Only I didn't put it on the cairn. I tried it out. To see if it was sharp enough to cut.'

Shell nodded. 'I see.'

'I've it in my treasure box still.'

'You should throw it out, Jimmy. A bad stone like that.'

'No!'

'Why not?'

'It's Stone Age. It has a point. Like an arrow.'

Shell shrugged. 'Doubt it.'

Jimmy wriggled back into his pyjamas. ''Tis. I know it.'

'OK so, it is.' She smiled. 'When you're better, Jimmy, I'll get you a present. From McGraths'.'

'Would you, Shell?'

'I will. What would you like?'

He furrowed up his face to think about it for such a long time Shell thought he'd gone asleep. Then he stared up at her with hungry eyes. 'Shell,' he whispered, 'I'd like a bucket.'

'A bucket?'

'A bucket and spade. For the strand.'

'But you have them already – out the back somewhere.'

'That old bucket's split. And the spade's gone.'

'OK, Jimmy. I'll get you the bucket and spade.' She didn't know where she'd get the money. But she knew she'd done right, because soon after he dropped off to sleep with a peaceful look on his narrow white face. She couldn't sleep herself. She sat by his bed, stroking his thick head of hair. Soon her mam was sitting beside her, an arm around her shoulder. Her soft humming filled the peaceful dark, going up and down the lazy notes of a song Shell couldn't quite remember.

Thirteen

Palm Sunday came and went, with no sign of Father Rose at church. He'd to give the Mass that week down on Goat Island. Monday passed, then Tuesday. By Spy Wednesday, Jimmy had recovered. He ate his breakfast and demanded his present.

Shell remembered the five coins she'd scattered for the poor of the parish in their hour of need. She prayed Jesus to count Jimmy as one of them and went up to the fields to retrieve them. She scrabbled around for ages but found only three of them. She'd priced the bucket and spade at McGraths' already. She hadn't enough.

She searched the house high and low. A ten pence had rolled under the fridge. In the lining of her school bag was another five. She still needed more.

Dad was out collecting. She went into his room. The dressing-table mirrors enticed her over for another game of Eternity, but she resisted them. She crept to the wardrobe and went through his pockets.

She found what she needed and stole it, making the sign of the cross.

She went to the village next, locking Trix and Jimmy into the house so they couldn't run into mischief on the roads. When she explained her errand, they solemnly swore to be good while she was out.

Mr McGrath let her spend a long time choosing. She bought a bucket of apple green and a spade of ocean blue. When she came to pay, he threw in another spade, ladybird red, with a wink. 'Our secret, Shell,' he said, like he had with the bubblegums the week before. She smiled.

Before heading home, she walked up to the church. The side door was open. She crept up into the gallery, sat down and listened hard.

Jesus was somewhere close. The wood groaned again. Light played in the aisles below. She prayed to him to forgive her the theft of money. She prayed for the repose of the souls of Michael Rose and Moira Talent, her own dead mam, and of all the departed. She prayed for the troubles of the world to end. She was still on the last, when voices started up in the vestry. Father Carroll and Father Rose came through into the main body of the church, chatting. They paused by the altar. Shell crouched down behind the balcony.

'Back again, to the time of the purple cloths,' Father Carroll sighed.

'There's always a heaviness at this time of year,' Father Rose agreed.

'Nora has the lilies organized.' Father Carroll went to the lectern and turned a page or two of the Bible. 'Joe Talent's doing the readings.'

'Joe Talent? Again?'

'He reads like a rusty nail, I know. But he'd be hurt if I passed him over.'

A shudder of mirth went through Shell in the gallery. She curled over her knees to press it back down. Her pew creaked.

'It's windy today,' Father Carroll said.

'They're a poor family, the Talents, aren't they?' Father Rose asked. The way he said it made the laughing inside Shell stop.

'The poorest. The father's on the social since his wife died. He's a lost dog without her.'

'When did she die?'

'A year ago last autumn. A lovely woman, was Moira. There was a kindness to her and a voice to charm an angel. He's like a car with no juice without her.' Father Carroll must have walked down the aisle, for his voice grew louder. 'Will I lock the church now?' he mused, more to himself than Father Rose. He was right below Shell. She froze, imagining being locked in the whole day with Jimmy and Trix alone at home.

'I've met the eldest girl,' Father Rose was saying.

'No, I won't,' Father Carroll muttered. 'There might be some poor soul needs a prayer on this holy day . . . What did you say?'

'Shell. The older Talent girl. I've had a couple of chats with her. She brought the collection over for her father one day last week. She admitted she was mitching school.'

Father Carroll sighed. 'Don't I know. Miss Donoghue over at the national school's been onto me about the younger ones. What can you or I do, but pray?'

'I rang the school.'

'You *what*?'

'I rang the school. And they rang the father.'

So that was why Dad had insisted they go back to school the last week of term. Father Carroll said nothing but Shell just heard a *tctch*. He moved away again. She risked sneaking another peak over the edge of the balcony from her hiding place in the gallery. Father Carroll's two hands were clasping the communion rails. His knuckles gleamed white.

'I wonder . . .' Father Rose added. 'I mean – the cut of them – should we not *do* something?'

Father Carroll's hands dropped to his sides. Father Rose was looking at the crucified Jesus as he spoke. Shell held her breath. There was a current going between them, back and forth, hot and tight, filling the whole church.

'Joe collects for charity most days,' Father Carroll said. 'He sends me in small, regular sums. I'd say he keeps a good bit back.'

Shell bit her thumb to stop herself from making a sound. *Dad's thieving was known?*

'And I say, let him have it,' Father Carroll continued. 'He collects for the poor and that's who he is. There's nothing wrong with begging, Gabriel. Beggars have always been close to God. Talent's just a beggar of the prouder kind. Good luck to him. That's what I do for the Talents. Before God.'

Father Rose didn't reply. He folded his arms and examined the floor.

Father Carroll continued. 'He spends the money

on drink: is that what you're thinking? How should we know or judge if he does? A drop never did any harm.'

'They're not a happy family,' said Father Rose.

'How would you know?'

'I feel it. In my bones.'

'You've only been here a few weeks. You can't know.'

'I do know. From the way Shell is. I'm sure—'

'Sure of what?'

Father Rose shrugged. 'Sure something's not right. I'd have the social services onto them.'

'Shush!' Father Carroll pounded the communion rail. 'You're from a big town. That kind of talk may go down all right where you come from, but not here. In Coolbar we look after our own.'

There was a long silence. A cloud must have passed over the sun because the light in the church dimmed. Then Father Carroll put an arm on Father Rose's shoulder. 'Interfering in such cases may be sinful, Gabriel,' he suggested. 'You were seen giving that young one a lift – I'd advise you not to in future. With the scandal the church has had, we've no cause to be driving around unaccompanied females.'

Father Rose jerked away on the word 'scandal'. He in his turn grasped the altar rail so his knuckles showed. The tables of the moneylenders were about to go over. There was a hissing in Shell's ears. Father Carroll walked slowly back towards the vestry. Father Rose did not follow. At the vestry door Father Carroll turned. 'I mean the warning kindly, Gabriel,' he relented. 'You're still young in your vocation.' He drew an arc in the air. 'Leaving well alone is often wise. Mouthing off to the authorities may be no better than what Judas Iscariot did. Reflect on that. Today of all days.'

Father Carroll left. Father Rose's grip loosened on the rails, his head and shoulders slumped. It looked as if he was doing what he'd been told. He knelt at the altar rail, his head in his hands, and did not make a sound. Shell didn't move. The wood of the church creaked again. Hot angry angels were batting their wings silently all around. The painted faces of the statues of Our Lady and St Theresa looked down in anguish. But their loving didn't help him. His shoulders shuddered. From between them came a terrible sound, like a crevice cracking open the earth, narrow and deep. A sword pierced Shell's heart. The man was crying.

'Oh Jesus,' Shell mouthed silently. She clasped her hands together hard in prayer. 'My Jesus. Shell is with you in your garden of agony.'

Minutes passed. Father Rose slowly stood up, crossed himself and followed Father Carroll through the vestry exit. Shell waited. All was quiet. She crept down the creaking balcony steps with the bucket and the two bright spades. She went her way home across the fields. The spades were tucked under her arm, the bucket banged against her knees as she walked. But her glee in their bright colours had dwindled.

When she got home, Jimmy had turned the kitchen table upside down. He was sitting in the middle of it, pretending to dodge invisible soldiers through the legs and shoot them with the gun Dad kept on top of the dresser. Trix had Mam's mass cards down from the piano. She sat cross-legged by the stove, scissoring them up into misshapen dollies, leaving shavings all over the floor.

Fourteen

Dad was home late from his Wednesday night session. Shell took care to be in bed before he came in. She bolted the bedroom door again. If he noticed the mass cards had gone, he didn't say anything.

The following morning dawned fine. Shell drew the curtains in the bedroom and peered out on the back field. Light scudded over the hill.

'Wake up, Trix,' Shell said. She shook her leg, then Jimmy's. 'It's Maundy Thursday.'

'Laundry Thursday?' yawned Trix.

Shell laughed. The sheets of the house hadn't been changed since Christmas. The clothes in the bedroom where she, Trix and Jimmy slept plastered the floor.

'Laundry Thursday so it is,' she said. She conscripted Jimmy and Trix into service and started on a big wash.

The ancient twin-tub Mam had used for years had broken soon before her death and never been replaced. When she could get the money from Dad, she went to the laundromat in town. But today, all they had were two giant bars of good green soap, the kitchen sink and the bath. Shell boiled water in the pans. Trix and Jimmy used their new spades to prod the clothes as they soaked.

Dad didn't stir from his bed, so Shell didn't do his.

They pegged the clean clothes up on the line. When they ran out of space, they spread them on the hedges. The crisp white wind rippled through them and they dried crisp and bright.

Dad appeared at four. He'd shaved and put on his next-but-one best suit.

'I don't *wanna* go to the church, Dadda,' Trix moaned. ''S not Sunday.' She had the red spade in one hand, the apple-green bucket upturned on her head.

Dad seized them. 'If you don't shake a leg, I'll throw those yokes in the dump,' he said.

Trix put her two hands up in front of her face and behind them pulled an elaborate scowl. Shell shooed her out the door, bucket and spade and all.

When they got to church, they found Father Rose was in charge of the Mass. It was Father Carroll's turn for Goat Island. When the time came for the sermon, he walked down to the communion rails and welcomed everybody to the Last Supper. He said he wanted them all to go back two thousand years in time, to a modest house in the poor quarter of Jerusalem and picture a dim room, cramped, with chatter and laughter, wine and bread. 'Are you there?' he asked. Shell shut her eyes. There were chickens pecking grain from the floor, a big range and a long refectory table, such as they had at school. The apostles were clustered on a bench. There was a smell of new-baked scones and frying fish. *I'm there,* she thought.

Father Rose asked for eleven younger members of the congregation to come forward. Dad put a sharp finger in Shell's spine.

'Wake up,' he said.

Shell started. The two Duggan boys had gone up to the front, followed by the Flavin girl from Coolbar House and the younger Ronans. Shell stood up. She grabbed Trix's hand, but Jimmy wouldn't budge. She and Trix went up on their own.

That made eight. They were three short.

'Nobody else volunteering?' Father Rose said, smiling.

Two younger Quinns were ushered forward by Mrs Quinn.

That made ten.

The church was still.

Shell stared at Jimmy. He'd his tongue in his cheek again, poking it out like a tent. She imagined herself as a magnetic pole or a black hole. He was a thin pin or a clapped-out planet. He'd no choice but to come towards her. Her eyes went large as saucers with the effort. A miracle happened. He stood up. He put on his bored look and sauntered forward.

'Grand,' said Father Rose. 'I've all the apostles now, save one, who's missing tonight. And we all know why *he* isn't coming.'

Father Rose sat them down in a semicircle of chairs he'd prepared. He asked them to take off their shoes and socks. Then he came round with a bowl of water

81

and a sponge. One by one he washed their feet. Shell was last in line. In her head, she was John, the youngest, the one that Jesus loved. Her feet were rough-soled and dimpled. She'd white broken skin on her heels and soles. Her toenails were long. She'd trodden many miles of roads in Galilee. As the cold sponge went over them, she felt its refreshment first, then the pure loving kindness of the hand that held it. She sat back and watched the crown of his head, soon to be punctured with thorns. The blond-brown swirl of hair had been cut short. It was like a field of stubble, waiting to be stroked. She'd to sit on her right hand to stop it from reaching down to him. The water dripped from her toes. He held her out a small linen towel of white with which to dry them.

The congregation of Coolbar looked on, amazed.

She put her feet into the towel so he could pat them dry.

As Shell returned with her ten companions to the pews, she saw the face of Mrs Fallon pulled long and sour. The washing of the feet had never been done before in the parish of Coolbar. Passing Mrs McGrath's pew, she heard her whisper loudly to her neighbour, 'That's a Protestant notion!' But Shell was sure that Jesus, the real Jesus, had washed her feet. He was back once more among their stunted souls in the shape of Father Rose. He'd come in loving kindness to save them from themselves.

Fifteen

Next day, the Stations of the Cross were held at three.

Father Carroll, Father Rose and Declan Ronan, altar boy again, paraded the cross around the church. After each of the fourteen Stations, the congregation sang another chorus:

'At the cross her station keeping
Stood the mournful mother weeping
Close to Jesus at the last.'

After the fifth Station, where Simon of Cyrene helped Jesus carry the cross, the whole congregation turned to face the Stations hung on the back wall. Shell realized that Bridie Quinn was sitting right behind her. Their eyes met. Bridie's nostrils flared. She showed her gums. Spite was in her eye. Shell mouthed a *Sorry,* but Bridie only glared, so Shell picked up her little bag of crocheted powder-blue, the present her mam had given her on her confirmation. She drew out a shopping list she'd scrawled on the back of an envelope and a pencil stump. *Sorry, Bridie,* she wrote. *Honest to God. Didn't know you were going with him.*

She slipped Bridie the note when no one was looking. Bridie read it, frowned and thrust it back. Then she grabbed it again and beckoned for Shell's pencil. Shell slipped it to her as they moved round to the weeping women of Jerusalem. Bridie wrote something down on the other side of the shopping list, slow and hard, and handed it back, jerking her head towards Declan. *He'd make a dog sick in those robes*, it said in big scrawl. *You can have him Shell plus bra.*

A large tear came into Bridie's face. She looked pale and tired. She jerked her head towards the altar and mimed throwing up. *Sorry*, Shell mouthed again. She reached out an arm to touch Bridie's wrist, but Bridie only grimaced and shook her off. Dad's hand gripped Shell's shoulder. Shell thrust the note into the hymn book and started praying mad.

The Stations done, Father Carroll gave a sermon on the awful pains of Christ. Father Rose sat by, his face wrapped in holy abstraction. Was he at the cross's side? Shell wondered. Or back with his brother Michael as a child? Or in the car again, with herself, looking down on the rainbow bay?

As she pondered, a movement to Father Rose's side distracted her. It was Declan. He was half-winking at her, with his fingers intertwined, as if in prayer. Only his forefingers were wriggling together, like fat worms, all muddled up. *Two bodies naked in Duggans' field.* When he saw he'd caught her eye, he rolled his tongue out a tiny way, another fat worm, and flipped it up and down.

She was sure the worms he wriggled had somehow got inside her.

At the end of the long service, Jesus was laid in the tomb. Everybody went up to the rails to kiss the true cross. When St Helena found the cross of Christ, Father Carroll said, they'd ground it up into tiny crumbs so that every parish in the world could have a portion. In Coolbar the morsel – a mere speck – was contained in a bauble of glass set into the top of a brass crucifix. The speck was there, he assured them, only so small you couldn't see it. The people of Coolbar queued to kiss the bauble. The priest wiped it clean after each kiss and took it to the next person's lips. Every five or so people, Father Rose took over the job, then swapped it back to Father Carroll.

Shell prayed to be in Father Rose's batch. He took the cross from Father Carroll when there were only two people ahead of her. But just as she stepped forward, Father Carroll seized the cross back from Father Rose and held it out to her instead.

Shell kissed the place, expecting a rush of holiness. None came.

The service being concluded soon after, they left the church. Jesus had died, but there was no tempest. The dead did not arise and appear to many. Instead, a quiet evening of misting rain lay around them. Dad darted off – to do a message or two, he said. He headed fast down the street towards Stack's pub. She saw Bridie retreating up the hill, shaking rain off her hair, putting up her see-through umbrella. She nearly launched after her, wanting to make up, but Declan

Ronan came up behind her and pulled her back by the ponytail.

'Shell,' he said. 'Sweet Shell.' His fingers tickled the back of her neck.

'What d'*you* want?' Shell said.

'I saw you looking at me in church,' he teased.

'Leave off.'

'I did. You were ogling.'

'I was not.'

'You were. Ogling and gogling away. Either at me or Father Rose.'

'Give over.' She grabbed Trix's hand and started to yank her down the hill. Jimmy followed. 'You're romancing, Declan.'

'Am I?' He wouldn't leave off walking beside her.

'You are.' She looked up at him. He grinned at her. His hand darted forward and pinched her cheek.

'This is a holy day, Declan Ronan.'

He guffawed. 'All that stuff. It's a load of sexual sublimation.'

'Don't listen to him, Trix. He's blaspheming.'

Declan grabbed her collar to stop her in her tracks. He leaned over and whispered in her ear. 'Shell. Don't be cross. Meet me in Duggans' field, won't you? One morning soon. Just for a kiss. One kiss, like last time.'

She felt the worms wriggling inside her again. She shrugged.

'I'll wait for you,' he urged. 'Early on Easter morning. However long it takes.'

'You're insane, Declan Ronan.'

'You're a walking sex-bomb, Shell Talent.'

She jabbed him in the rib, and Trix leaped up on his back, but he extracted his long, lanky body with a laugh and made his way off up the avenue.

'Toodlepip,' he called.

'Tarala,' Trix shouted.

'Whisht, the pair of you,' Shell said. But she couldn't help smiling.

Mrs Duggan pulled over as they continued on through the village. Her two boys stared out from the back, pulling faces at Jimmy.

'Shell,' she called, 'is your dad with you?'

'He's doing some messages, Mrs Duggan.'

'Is he now?'

Shell nodded.

'Squeeze in, the three of you, out of the rain. John and Liam, bunch up there and make some space. I'll give you your tea, if you like. I've tarts made.'

She drove them over to the Duggans' farm. It was where Trix and Jimmy often used to go to play, back in the days when Dad worked there. Since he'd stopped the work, they'd been over less often, but still went in the school holidays. Mrs Duggan had been Mam's best friend from the days of their youth. There was a photo of the two of them at eighteen, in slender dresses from the 1960s, at a dance in Castlerock.

'Dr Fallon told me you were sick, Jimmy?'

Jimmy pulled up his sleeve to show off the cut, dark and thin now, with the anger gone from it.

She tutted and tousled his head and gave him an extra slice of tart.

Afterwards Shell helped clear away. Mr Duggan

fetched the younger ones out to help feed the calves.

'Shell,' Mrs Duggan said as they dried the plates, 'you're more like your mam every day.'

The words were sweet and sad, like the taste of bitter lemon Father Rose had given her the other day. 'Am I, Mrs Duggan?'

'With your figure coming out and the colour of your hair, you are. Your mouth's the image of hers. Only your eyes are different. Lighter than your mam's, I'd say.'

When the job was done, she gave Shell the loan of her bike so that she could cycle down to the strand. Shell pedalled down the quiet roads. The weather had cleared. She was soon out on Goat Island, with the Atlantic before her. There was no one there but herself. Near the cliffs, the sands shifted, wrinkling in the wind. The water's edge meandered on a pancake surface. She took off her shoes and socks and, like a child, tucked her skirt into her underwear. The cold bit into her bones as she paddled. '*The sea has made the sand a mirror which my two feet destroy,*' she muttered as she walked. It was the start of a ditty she and Mam had made up together, long ago. She squinted into the low sun, and there was a figure, a candle flame, drifting away from her: just like Mam, taking one of her beloved lone walks down to the end of the strand. Surely that was her olive-green scarf tied over her ears? Her hands were planted in her pockets, her head was down to the wind in just that familiar way. Shell blinked. The figure vanished.

Shell's heart had a purple cover over it.

When Jesus dies, she thought, you die a little too.

Sixteen

Holy Saturday was a nothing-day. The tomb was sealed, the world was quiet.

Trix and Jimmy walked with Shell across the fields carrying their spades of red and blue. They picked the lemon daffodils on the grass slope and piled them in Jimmy's bucket. They sat on a fallen tree and watched the smoke of Coolbar writhing, white on white. The lambs mewed and bounded. Jimmy found grubs under the trunk. He collected some on his spade and transported them downhill, arms flapping.

'Where are you going?' Shell called.

'I'm the plane. We're off to America,' he said.

Trix practised balancing.

Dad didn't appear from his room all day. They hadn't seen him since the Stations. There was a holiday in their hearts.

The long day passed.

Trix and Jimmy had a second tart Mrs Duggan had given them for tea. Shell was fasting until the time of Jesus' rising. She was determined to stay awake all night in a vigil of waiting and prayer. Having nothing nicer to wear, she risked putting on Mam's dress of seamless pink. She tied her hair back in a neat green ribbon.

After Trix and Jimmy were safe in bed, she heard a stir from Dad's room: a floorboard creaking, a curse. She took herself out the door as fast as she could and ran behind the cairn in the back field.

Only just in time: he came from the house, with the braces down around his pants and no shirt on. He'd a look on his face as if to say, *Where's my tea?* He shouted Shell's name once or twice, then gave up and went inside. She waited. Twenty minutes later he reappeared, a new shirt on him and the jacket of his best-but-one suit. He took himself down the road, the change jangling in his pocket.

Once he was out of sight, she gave a long, contented breath. She sat on the hill and looked down on the squat grey bungalow that had always been her home. There'd been a time when Dad had promised to raise the roof and build an upstairs floor. But it had never happened. The moon floated up like a perfect dandelion fluff over the wooded horizon. She yawned. She'd been up since early morning, doing any number of jobs. *I'll just lie down an hour,* she thought.

In the bedroom, Trix and Jimmy were sleeping sound. She lay on top of her own bed in her pink dress and without meaning to drifted off to sleep . . .

. . . In her dream, she was in the village. There was little sound. She was gliding between the houses, glimpsing cracks of light through curtains. The eaves were all crooked, and television aerials askew, stabbing the low fast clouds of a stormy night. She stole a look through the window of Stack's pub. Dad and Mr McGrath were within, with Father Carroll trying to get some life out of the broken jukebox. Tom Stack the barman was pulling the pints. By the fire three dogs slept in a tangled heap.

She tried the door of the church. Locked. She sat in the porch and waited, for what she didn't know. The temptations of the devil visited her in her watch. Before she knew it, she was halfway along the street, up the avenue to the Ronans' big pink house, and knocking on the door. Declan answered and took her out for a night on the fields. His hand was bony and hard, his wicked tongue was in her ear, the clothes were mumbo-jumbo between them, they rolled from the coastal dunes to the mountaintop and down the other side. But Father Rose walked over the brow of the hill, appearing from the copse. Declan fizzled away. She was neat and trim again in pink and ribbon-green. He came and sat beside her in her vigil. They were back at the fallen tree where Trix, Jimmy and she had sat earlier. Not a muscle moved, no words were spoken. Even the grubs were sleeping. But love coursed between them, a different love from Declan's, a love beyond flesh and bone, a love you took with you to the grave. His tears fell from him as he sat beside her. Shell prayed that they might cease, but he only shook his head, as if to say, *Shell* – in that way of his – *the tears are part of it, didn't you know?* The night of waiting became a hundred nights, but with him by her side, Shell didn't mind. *To thee do I send my sighs,* she heard Father Rose praying in his head. She answered him: *Mourning and weeping in this vale of tears.* Waiting was life itself. In the waiting she saw the sweetness, as when she'd mixed the scones and put them on and could smell their fragrance growing as they cooked. She hugged her ankles and looked out over the jumbled headstones to the one that marked her mother's place. First light arrived. She could see the headstones now: it was time. Father Rose and she left their place of waiting. Together they walked into the garden of serried tombs.

Father Rose must have been sore afraid, as the apostles had been. He vanished. Shell was on her own. She was Mary Magdalene, waiting.

The half-light was eerier than darkness. She stopped by her mam's grave. She couldn't see the lettering, only the bright specks of the daffodils she'd planted the previous autumn.

She sat down on the grass and waited some more.

From somewhere up the hill, a voice started. First it was a tuneful murmur, like birdsong. Then it was like crows in a fluttering tree. The sound came closer, right over by the church gate. It took shape as human song. She couldn't hear the words, only the notes. They rose and fell, like shining bubbles, forming a pattern of loveliness. They were so beautiful, Shell wanted to cry. For by now she'd recognized the voice. It was Mam's. It seemed like she hadn't heard her sing in a lifetime. She smiled and relaxed, trying to make out the tune.

A door opened and the song grew louder. Her mother was coming in from the yard, as she'd done countless times, ever since Shell could remember. She's in the kitchen now, Shell thought. A tap gushed on. A broom clattered on the floor. Was she singing the one about the lassie that dies a day before her wedding? She strained to hear the words, but she couldn't catch them.

Long vowels curled their way towards her, through the bedroom door. The cadences grew closer, as if her mam was coming to check up on her, to see that she was all right. She was back at the time she'd had a fever, three years ago. Trix and Jimmy were at school, it was just Mam and herself in the house, with Mam in and out of her bedroom several times a day with the thermometer and hot lemon drinks, stopping to feel her cheeks. The floorboard on the other side of the door creaked in its familiar way. Shell couldn't wait to see her.

The song paused, just for a fraction. Shell held her breath.

When the voice resumed, something had changed. A terrible sadness had crept in. Perhaps the lassie was saying one last thing to her lover before she died. Or perhaps the man was explaining why he had to leave. A high note soared swiftly up to a sustained 'O', bringing the song to its climax. But instead of dropping back to a conclusion, the note stuck at the top, spinning like a coin, unbearably pure. The note turned into a fierce and piercing cry.

The door handle turned, just as Shell remembered the truth.

Mam was supposed to be dead. Her singing couldn't be coming from inside the house. It was coming from her grave. They'd buried her alive by some terrible accident and she wasn't singing, she was choking to death.

Shell was her mam by then. She was penned under the ground, frantic, unable to breathe, pushing against the soft white padding of her coffin. She tried to jolt upright, back in the present. Her fingers kneaded the blanket. Velvet darkness pressed all around . . .

. . . She woke up.

She couldn't tell where she was at first. In a coffin, or a field? By the gravestone of her mam? No. She was in her own bed. Mam's fingers had surely just fluttered past her face.

'Moira.' A voice, familiar. *Him* again. She froze.

The curtains were ajar. Moonlight toppled in over the counterpanes. Her father loomed at the foot of the bed, swaying on the spot. Only he'd no clothes on. His nakedness was appalling. She'd forgotten to bolt the door.

Her heart hammered. Her breath came sharp and fast. He was fumbling towards her.

'Moira.'

His voice was slurred. There was a sizzling in her ears.

One of his hands pawed at the hem of her dress.

94

The other came up to her hair, pulling at the ribbon. His eyes were half shut, half open. His breath was stale and old. The flab on his pale arms wobbled as he groped.

Jimmy murmured something in his sleep.

The sound he made unfroze her. She knew what she had to do.

She rolled swiftly off the edge of her bed, too quick for Dad to catch.

His hands wondered over the sheets, shifting a pillow as if in search of her.

She crouched on her hands and knees and began to move away.

He sat on the bed rummaging, muttering. It was hard to tell if he was asleep or awake.

She crossed the floor as soft and supple as a cat.

She reached the door. She heard him groaning, stretching out on the bed. 'Moira. Don't turn away, lovey, turn to me.'

Shell's belly heaved. Jimmy tossed and sighed, Trix breathed smoothly.

She slunk through the door. Then closed it firmly behind her.

In the kitchen, she huddled on the chair. *God in heaven.* Her breathing returned to normal as the darkness thinned. He'd have passed out by now. She waited until the birdsong started, for real this time, not in the dream. Then she went to the window and looked out. The grass blades were grey. Dawn slunk across the back field.

'Oh, Mam,' she said out loud.

The sound fell back, dead, into her ribcage. Tears

pricked at her and when they fell, she didn't bother to wipe them dry.

'Why did you have to die?'

There was no answer, only the fridge's fretful hum. Maybe the man from Galilee hadn't risen as he should. Maybe he was still cold in the grave, stone dead, just like her mam. An aching chasm yawned inside her, a white-cold loneliness like a distant star. She touched the keys of the piano, pressing them down softly so that they did not play.

'Oh, Mam.'

She heard the bed in the room beyond creak. Dad must have turned in his drunken slumber.

The house pressed in on her. She opened the front door and breathed the dawn air. It was cool and fresh. The copse beckoned at the top of the hill. For want of anything better to do, she started up towards it. The exercise brought a flush back to her cheeks. She drifted through the demure and thoughtful trees. A starling called a downward scale, like a sigh.

She emerged out onto Duggans' field.

A figure was walking up it, coming towards her from Coolbar. As it approached, it grew first darker, then white and grey.

She remembered Mary Magdalene at the tomb and how she'd thought the man she met there was the gardener.

She waited.

Father Rose? she thought when the man's height became clear. Her heart leaped. Light was playing in his hair.

Three startled rabbits bounded away from him as he drew nearer. She recognized him then. It wasn't Father Rose. It was Declan.

'Shell,' he said. He smiled straight into her eyes. He didn't seem to notice she'd been crying. He stretched out his arms to her. 'I knew you'd come.'

Part II
AUTUMN

Seventeen

The sun came down hard overhead. The heat was close and still.

'Who d'you like, Declan? Who d'you like most in the world? Tell me.'

Declan didn't answer. Instead he started tickling her, snapping a stalk of barley and swishing it back and forth over her belly as they lay naked in Duggans' field. The fuzzy prickles made her squirm and giggle. He pinned her down, laying his strong arm across her shoulders, and tickled her harder. She fisted him on the back.

'Stop!' she screeched.

'I'll stop – if you pass me a fag.'

Shell hunted round the ground for the packet of Majors. She eased one out and popped it in Declan's mouth. Then she found his lighter and lit it. Declan took a long drag and crinkled his fingers through her hair. He rolled her onto her side and curled up behind her, fitting his knees snug into the backs of hers. Their assignations were top secret; he'd made her promise to keep them that way. *Declan and me, a private club*, she thought. The tall ears of crop hid them from the world.

'You haven't answered my question,' she reminded him.

'Hmm,' he murmured in her ear. 'You haven't answered mine.'

'You didn't *ask* me a question.'

'I'm asking it now.'

'What then?'

'Who *d'you* like most? In the whole wide world?'

'That was my question.'

'Is it Kevin Dunne in Year Five? Has he his eye on you, the stinky devil?'

She didn't move.

'He's a squint and a case of pimples – but he's forever mouthing off about the girlfriends.'

She shook her head.

'Not Kevin Dunne, so. Is it Mick McGrath?'

'Mick *McGrath*?'

'The son, not the father.'

'He's over in Cashel, boarding, isn't he?'

'He might have had a go in the holidays.'

She shrugged. 'Hardly see him.'

'Not telling then?'

She shook her head.

'If I promise to buy you a present, will you tell me?'

'What present?'

'Whatever you like.'

'Anything?'

'Any whole thing, Shell Talent.'

'Would you buy me a new bra?'

He laughed. 'What size?'

'Dunno. I was thirty-six C before. Think I've grown since.'

'I'd say so. You're a D, if ever I saw one. Or two.'

'Would you give me the money then – if I tell you – who I like most?'

'I would.'

'Promise?'

'Promise.'

She lay still and thought. Then she turned round and whispered in his ear.

'What?' he said. 'Didn't catch it.'

'It's true,' she said out loud. 'He's the one.'

'But I didn't get the name. Whisper it again.'

She leaned over his ear and whispered louder: '*Pistols and Shuttlecocks.*'

'That was nonsense – shocking nonsense, Miss Talent.'

'You weren't listening. I'm not telling again.'

'You're as close as a thicket.'

'You owe me a bra, Declan Ronan.'

'You cheated.'

'You promised.'

'OK, OK. I'll give you a fiver and you can buy one for yourself in town. On one condition.'

'What?'

'You say: *Declan Ronan, I like you more than any whole soul in the whole wide world.* And, you come back here on Thursday for another go.'

'That's two conditions.'

'OK, two conditions. 'S all or nothing.'

She said the words, then she ran her hands over his good, hard bones and flat belly. He'd slithered up onto her before another second passed and gave her a slow kiss.

'And it's a deal,' she murmured. 'About Thursday.'

Afterwards they pulled on their clothes. Declan ruffled her hair and blew on her cheek.

'You're a funny one,' he said. 'You're like a cat that's been dragged backwards through a hedge. You've bits of grass all over.'

'So've you. Only worse. You're like a bird that's had a dust-bath.'

He picked up his jacket and flung it over his shoulder, grinning.

'Don't forget your promise,' she said.

He groaned, but rummaged in his jacket pocket and found the money. 'Make sure it's big enough,' he said, handing it over. 'You're popping out all over in that yoke.'

She folded the money up into a tight cylinder and put it down her front. He laughed and pinched her arm and went on his way. She watched as his tall, raunchy silhouette receded down the summer field, into the fold of slope.

It was only when he'd gone that she realized he'd made her say what he wanted, but had said no such thing to her. She walked along the top of the field and into the copse. The nettles were dying back, and the leaves were brown-edged. Blackberries twinkled in the hedge. They'd been going together for more than four months and he never once said any of the things she wanted to hear. She shook her head, worldly-wise, and patted the place where she'd put his fiver. She smiled. That, she supposed, was the way of boys the world over.

Eighteen

She collected Jimmy and Trix from where they'd spent the day at Duggans' farm. Mrs Duggan was hot and cross, not in her usual humour. She scooted them out of the kitchen. Trix had lost her spade and was bawling mad, but Shell found it for her in the milking parlour. She'd dropped it there when they'd been playing Dead Soldiers on the high bars where the cows were penned in as they were milked. Shell remembered teaching them the game herself. It was her own invention. You hopped up on the bar, one leg in front, one behind. You curled your front ankle around the back knee. You balanced straight and tall. When somebody on another bar winked at you, you went flat over, dead, as if you'd been shot at close range. You stayed upside down, swinging, until all the other soldiers were down and dead like you. You lolled out your tongue and stared like a dead mackerel. If you caught somebody's eye, you could still wink up at them and kill them, even though you were dead yourself.

Trix said the red spade must have dropped from under her arm when Jimmy'd killed her. She slapped

Jimmy's backside with it all the way over the fields. Every time she struck, Jimmy squealed like a pig, jumping in the air dementedly, making Trix laugh. Shell's head pounded with the two of them.

There was nobody in when they got back. Dad had gone to the city the day before. He was into the city with his collecting tins most of the week these days, and often stayed overnight. Where, she did not know. He'd been due back two nights ago but still hadn't come.

She fixed tea. She'd rashers in the freezer compartment. She didn't wait for them to defrost, but fried them up along with slabs off the pan loaf.

Perhaps the bus he'd gone in had keeled over on a sharp bend, killing all aboard.

Perhaps he'd thrown himself in the river Lee.

Perhaps a thief had knocked him out and when he'd come round, he'd forgotten who he was.

Perhaps he'd run away, leaving them, and was on the boat over to Swansea.

She smiled at the thoughts, munching her tea. She was hungry. Jimmy and Trix peeled off their rinds and she ate both. When they'd finished, Trix said, good as gold, 'Can I be excused, Shell?'

'You can, both of you.'

They were out of the door like arrows for their evening games.

She cleared up, humming the song her mam had liked, the one about the soldier who promises the girl he'll marry her 'when broken shells make wedding bells'. Shell thought it a romantic idea, that of a bride and groom, and a great wedding party, walking up the avenue to Coolbar church to the tune of jingling shells. She swept the floor, washed the plates, and put everything away. She left the fat in the pan in case Dad turned up.

When everything was done, she sat herself down in his chair to dream of Declan. It was the only armchair in the house. She only ever dared sit there when Dad was far away.

Her arms lay on the rests and she shut her eyes.

Declan was with her again, blowing into her fringe. She hugged herself, eyes shut, imagining every little motion. *You're my love*, he was saying. *We'll get married, Shell, as soon as we've made the bells.*

Four months or more, and nobody knew.

Then a cold needle threaded its way through her insides.

The bad thing she tried not to think about from one end of the day to the other came back. It would rush up to her like a bad smell when she wasn't prepared. She'd be crossing the road and freeze in front of an on-coming car. Or she'd be making the scones and realize she'd beaten the dough to glue. And she'd be caught in the middle of the thought like a fly on sticky paper.

The curse hadn't come. Not in ages.

She knew all about the curse. Mam had told her about it a couple of years before she died. Then it started one wet winter day, when her mam was already poorly. She remembered being doubled over, walking in the rain, coming back from school, as the strange pains filled up her belly. She'd shivered. Her legs had felt as if they'd drop off. It was as if a great lump of dough was expanding inside her, giving her a great, dull ache. Her mam had given her pills and supplies and told her what to do. She remembered what her mam had said.

It feels funny, Shell. But it's normal. It's your body, hoping every month for a baby to grow inside of you. I remember Sister Assumpta at my convent school – how we laughed at her behind her back! – calling it 'the tears of a disappointed uterus'. When the baby doesn't happen, your body gives up and lets go. Then it starts over the next month, hoping all over again.

What if the baby does happen? Shell had asked.

The curse doesn't come. It stays up inside of you, making a nice warm lining for your baby to lie in. It's a blessing of nature, Shell. Not something fearful.

Then why's it called the curse? Shell had asked. Mam had tousled her hair.

It's just the way we women like to dramatize things, Shell. We'd a joke at our school: 'What's worse, the curse or no curse?' and the answer was 'Depends if you're married, of curse.'

Shell couldn't remember when her last one was. She scrunched up her face and squeezed tight her eyes. She went back over the summer holidays, the jobs in the week, the Mass-days, the dinners she'd made, the shopping days. She went back through the previous summer term. Sports day. Exam days. The Sacred Heart of Jesus holiday, when they'd had tomato sandwiches and biscuits out on the lawn as a treat at school. Bridie Quinn had gone off to have hers with Theresa Sheehy, ignoring her like she'd done since

Easter. She didn't even sit near her on the bus and she'd rebuffed Shell's every effort to make up. The school days had been slow and empty without her. Shell shrugged and cast back her mind through May, then it blurred.

No curse days could she remember.

In the heat of the evening, she listened to the house. Flies buzzed around the flypaper. The far cries of Jimmy and Trix came in from the back field. The clock on the sill ticked. She wished the old Bridie, knowing and pert, could materialize at her side to whisk away her worries. *You're romancing,* she imagined Bridie saying. *You're no more up the spout than Mother Theresa.*

She looked over to the holy calendar on the wall. It was open in May because nobody had remembered to turn the pages since. Our Lady of Lourdes was in the grotto with stars forming a coronet floating over her head, and arms reaching forward, lovingly. Drapes of blue robe spilled from her, around the rocks. St Bernadette was kneeling off to the side, in a peasant dress of green and red. A spring of water bubbled up by her side.

Mam had wanted to go to Lourdes for a cure. Dad had not allowed it.

She leaped up from the chair at the sound of a car pulling up outside. A door slammed. She heard Dad saying, 'Thank you, Father.' She stole a look through the window and saw Father Carroll wave and pull out onto the Coolbar road.

Her father stood on the path a second, dressed in

110

his best suit. He'd unwrapped it some months back from the polythene and put it on for his city trips. The jacket hung open now; the shirt was two days old. He was looking at Trix and Jimmy, running across the top of the back field, heading for the copse, perhaps trying to get away from him. She saw her dad's shoulders sag, his head droop. Father Carroll's car vanished around the turn.

'Shell,' he called. She could tell he wasn't in good humour. But he wasn't drunk either.

She switched on an electric ring to warm the pan.

Nineteen

With Dad back, they'd to get up and do the stones again. The morning was the first of autumn. A dew was on the grass, a smell of vitality in the yard. The cairn was taller than Shell and wider than the length of Trix.

Trix and Jimmy went ahead of her while Shell put the cereal and jam back in the press. She wiped over the plastic cover on the table while her father jangled change in his pocket, impatient.

'Get a move on,' he said.

She rinsed off the crumbs from the sponge.

She pushed the chairs back in under the table.

She opened the window to air the room.

He tutted.

'Dad,' she said, hanging the tea cloth over the back of one of the dining chairs. 'There are no more stones to pick up.'

The room went quiet. She could see his lips pucker, his brows come down.

'We've picked up every last stone in that back field.'

'Check over it, then. Inch by inch.'

'But *why*, Dad? 'S too late to plough it this year. Unless you've a plan to sell it?'

He blew out through his nose and got up. She saw his palm flatten, as if to strike. He raised it, walked forward, then stopped. She did not move.

His hand dropped back to his side. He breathed out, hard and long. 'Maybe I have. Maybe I haven't. But get out of the house, Shell. Scram.'

She shrugged and left.

When she got out, she saw Trix and Jimmy over by the cairn. Jimmy had his arms up, aeroplane-wise, Trix was hopscotching. Instead of joining them, she tiptoed around to the front of the house and crouched by the window she'd deliberately left open.

She could hear him moving around. A piece of furniture – a chair? – was being dragged across the floor. She brought her eyes up level to the sill and peered through.

It was the armchair he'd moved. He'd brought it forward, so as to clear the space in front of the piano. Then she saw him rummaging under the keyboard. He eased off the panel of wood above the pedals. She'd forgotten it came apart like that. It hadn't been done since well before Mam died, when the piano tuner last called over. She ducked again when Dad stood upright, lifting the panel away. She came up for another peek; he'd rested it by the table and was crouched again by the piano. He retrieved from the inside a bottle of whiskey and a big old tea caddy she hadn't seen in ages and brought them over to the table. He sat down with it, his back to her. She couldn't see what he was doing, but she saw him take little frequent nods of the head, as if he were counting. And she saw him taking a few gulps of whiskey straight from the bottle.

She scooted back around to the back field, half smiling.

Dad. Hunting them out so he could booze in secret at eight in the morning. Dad. A man on the social who didn't dare put his dishonest earnings from charity collecting into a bank account.

Later that day, when he'd gone off out for his Wednesday session, she opened the piano herself after Trix and Jimmy were in bed.

She found the caddy. There were two bottles of whiskey along with it, one half empty. She unscrewed the cap on the open bottle and smelled it. It was like lemon and sugar at once. She remembered Father Rose's bottle of bitter lemon and smiled. Then she opened the caddy. It was chock-a-block with paper money. She counted it.

There was a fortune. Hundreds and hundreds of notes, and no coins at all.

She measured out a small tot of the whiskey and knocked it back. Her stomach turned. The burning fluid nearly came back up her throat. What, she wondered, was the attraction? It didn't taste sweet. It didn't fizz. It was luke-warm then mad-hot. It tasted of burned hay. She coughed and her stomach tossed again. For a second she thought she'd be sick. She quickly put the bottle back in the piano. She wasn't touching that stuff again.

She turned to the caddy. She itched to take the money, or some of it. She imagined herself with Bridie in the lingerie section of Meehans' stores, trying on the wafting gowns and lacy tops and buying them all, instead of having to steal them. Then the two of them were down the amusement arcade over in Castlerock, flinging in coin after coin with oceans of coins spilling out around their feet. Then they were on the boat to England, on the run, with a sea wind in their hair, as free as the wheeling gulls.

She sighed. He'd probably counted it down to the last single note. And Bridie wasn't even talking to her. She put the lid on the caddy again and replaced it. As quietly as she could, she put the piano back together again.

Twenty

The mobile library came to town on a Friday afternoon.

Shell had never used it before, but she'd often noticed it drawn up by the parkland at the head of the pier on her way home from school. She was doing the messages as usual and trudging back to the bus stop when she saw it again. It was a great white van, with green writing on the side and light aluminium steps going up to it.

On a whim she climbed inside.

There was a woman within, sorting around shelves of books. She was hardly larger than Jimmy with short dark hair, and she wore a baggy white boiler suit. She'd a radio playing the latest hit in the background which she was humming along to. It was the beat of another place.

'H'lo,' she said without turning round.

Shell stopped on the top step, not daring to go further.

The librarian peered over her shoulder. She'd a narrow chin and brown eyes, with a crease of laughter around them, a little like Mam's had been. 'Come in and look around, if you want to,' she offered.

'Can I?'

'You can.' She broke out into the words of the pop song and jiggled her hips: '*No need to ask, he's a smooth operator, smooth operator . . .*' She trailed off and shrugged as Shell still lingered at the door. 'I don't bite.'

'I thought you had to be old,' Shell said.

'Old?'

Shell nodded. 'To come in here.'

The librarian smiled. 'Why so?'

'I've only ever seen old folk step in. Grey heads.'

'We have all kinds of heads coming in here. Grey. White. Red. Black. Thick. Hot.'

Shell laughed. 'What's that song they're playing?'

'It's just out in England. It's about a guy who breaks hearts all across America.'

''S not bad.'

'Come on inside,' the librarian urged. 'I'll show you what we've got.'

Shell stepped in. The librarian pointed out picture books, story books, nature books and how things were divided up in sections. One side was fiction, she said, the other non-fiction. 'The only thing we don't do in the van,' she said, 'is poetry. You've to come into the branch for that. D'you like poetry?'

'No,' said Shell. 'Only songs.'

'Songs *are* poetry, aren't they?'

Shell shrugged. 'Dunno.' She thought of all her mother's old songs about broken hearts and missed chances. '*Coast to coast, LA to Chicago . . .*' went the woman's voice on the radio. 'Some, maybe.'

'Was there anything in particular you were after?'

Shell swallowed. 'No. Nothing.'

'But you'd like a browse?'

Shell nodded.

The librarian smiled. 'You browse away. I'm off down the pier for a quick fag. You can hold the fort for me, can't you?'

Shell nodded again and watched the librarian move away, down the steps and out along the pier. The tide was in. She seemed so dainty against the great bounding blue that Shell wondered how her feet ever reached down to the pedals of the van. The song on the radio died away to be replaced by chatter.

She turned to the books. Through the radio din, she could hear Mam's voice talking in her head. *It's a blessing of nature, Shell.* She went to the nature section. She'd noticed a book of trees and shrubs. She put her finger out and ran over the titles. *Whales and other Sea Mammals . . . Fungi and Lichens of Our Land . . . Ireland Goes Wild . . . Brucellosis: Prevention and Treatment.* Then she found something closer. *Doyle's A–Z of the Human Body.* It was thick and large, too awkward, surely, to drop into her shopping. She looked nervously down the pier. The librarian was at the far end. Her heart pounded. The radio crackled.

She started turning the pages. Illnesses and body parts darted out at her. Ataxia. Carotid artery. Glandular fever. Shingles. Thyroid. She flipped back to the beginning, looking for the contents. Instead, she found herself back in the As. She read a couple of entries. They had nothing to do with her. Her eyes glazed over, and she was reading without knowing what it was she read. *Amenorrhoea: An abnormal lack of the menses in women* . . . What the hell did that mean? She slapped it shut, closed her eyes. She breathed out long and hard through her lips. She opened it again at the back index and hunted under 'P'.

The word 'Pregnancy' was there. A long entry. Pages 368–404.

She turned to page 368 and began to read.

She'd just turned to page 369 when she remembered where she was. She darted a quick look down the pier. The librarian was walking back. She'd be here any minute. She withdrew into the back of the van and tried to tear out the pages. They were too tough and too many. Her hands shook. Panicking, she stuffed the book to the bottom of her shopping, flanking it with tins and cartons. She rearranged the books on the shelf to hide the gap the vast tome had left behind. She grabbed another book from nearby and plunged her head into it just as the steps rattled.

'H'lo again,' the librarian said. 'Found anything?'

Shell looked up. Her cheekbones were on fire, her throat hoarse. 'Um,' she said. 'This.' Another song started up on the radio, a shrill man's voice. Shell couldn't make out the words.

'What is it?'

Shell looked at the book herself. *An Affectionate History of Pigeon Carriers.*

The librarian looked at it, then looked at Shell. She guffawed. 'I'd never've taken you for a pigeon-fancier,' she said, turning off the radio in mid-song.

Shell blinked in the silence. She shrugged her shoulders and put the book back.

'You can have it out, if you want,' the librarian offered.

'I've no ticket.'

'You can join today. All I need is your address and date of birth.'

'I've no time. The ice cream's melting. In the shopping.' There was no ice cream in the shopping, but the librarian wasn't to know. 'I've to get it home.'

'Another time maybe?' the librarian said.

Shell nodded. She picked up the shopping and shuffled out of the door. 'Bye now.' She started down the steps.

'Can I help you with that? You've quite a load there.'

''S fine. I can manage.'

'Bye, then.'

She could feel the librarian's eyes boring into her back as she walked away. 'Hey, there. Before you go.'

She'd only gone a few paces. She froze, then turned. 'What?'

'Pigeons are great. My small cousin Timmy keeps them.'

Shell stared. The librarian nodded. 'When he went over to England last year, he brought his best homing bird with him. In a cage, with the cloth over. A white and grey fellow, swanky out, with a fluffy collar. And when the boat pulls in on the other side, Timmy lets him off. At the harbour in Fishguard. Hundreds of miles away. And d'you know what?'

Shell looked at the librarian's smiling eyes, her heart hammering in her ribs. 'What?'

'When they got back from holiday a week later, guess who was waiting on the eave of their roof?' The librarian nodded even though Shell didn't say anything. 'You guessed right. Your man. That same fluffy-collared homing bird.'

Shell managed a smile.

'D'you want to know the name of that bird of Timmy's?' the librarian asked.

Shell shrugged. 'What?'

'Boomerang.'

Shell managed a polite titter.

'Now, *that's* what I'd call poetry,' the librarian said.

Twenty-one

Shell lugged the shopping onto the bus. It set her down at the top of the village. The sun shone hard on the red berries on the browning trees and on the parting of her hair. She felt sweat on her back as she walked. Her palms ached from the way the handles on the laden shopping bag dug into them.

She walked through the village in the midday lull. The priests' house had no cars outside it. The dogs from Stack's pub were sunning themselves on the pavement. McGraths' was shut for lunch, with the venetian blind down. She was just about to turn off before the bridge into the fields, when she heard a strange spurting and rumbling from round the bend. It was like a plane in the cinema, when the engine keeps cutting in and out and you know the pilot's in big trouble. She stopped. She knew that sound by now.

Father Rose's purple car jerked over the bridge. The engine failed just as he saw her and the car stopped dead.

He sat with his hands on the wheel, staring down the length of the bonnet, expressionless. The side window was open and she could see his sideburns, fuzzy and rough, and his mouth, closed and tight.

He hadn't said so much as a hello to her in months. The most she got from him these days was a polite, distant nod.

She'd sat through any number of his Masses. But the spark had gone out of them. Something had shifted, gone slack. He read the words in that same even tone but the pictures had evaporated from his sentences. His eyes were fixed, always, on some distant place as he spoke. It wasn't heaven and it wasn't here: it was somewhere in between, a limbo.

She walked towards him. 'Father Rose?' she said. 'Is the car dead?'

He didn't answer, but slowly turned his head to her. 'Hello, Shell,' he said. His lips went up at the corners a fraction. He nodded. 'Not so much dead as resting. The engine's overheated. It will go again soon.'

'She's being bold again, is she? Jezebel?'

He half laughed, half grunted. 'I've a good mind to flog her,' he said. He tapped the steering wheel. 'You've a lot of shopping there, Shell.'

She hugged the bag to herself and felt her cheeks grow hot. It was as if everybody could see through the plastic to the big book that lurked within. 'Only the usual amount,' she muttered.

'I'd give you a lift home – only . . .' He raised his hands off the steering wheel and flopped them down on it again.

She knew what he meant. It wasn't the resting car. It was as if they could both still hear the echo of Father

Carroll's voice whirling around the church sanctuary last Spy Wednesday. *We've no cause to be driving around with unaccompanied females, Gabriel.*

'Don't worry,' Shell said. 'I can manage fine.'

'S'long then, Shell.'

'S'long, Father.' She turned into the field.

'And Shell?'

She looked back.

He was looking at her in that old way, the eyes hitting straight into hers like meteorites. She felt as if her sins, Declan, the book, the kissing and everything else were emblazoned on her forehead. She was more naked than she'd ever been in Duggans' field.

She couldn't hold his gaze and shifted her eyes off over his shoulder, biting her lip.

'What?' she managed.

'God bless.'

She nodded. The two simple words went to the heart of her, finding a home deep inside. She flushed, and turned to hide the smile his kindness brought to her face. She nodded at him and walked on up the hill.

Halfway up she heard the choke of his engine, burbling, dying, then starting again. She paused as the sound of his car carried on its way through the village, growing smaller, then dying away in the distance. She put down the bag. *God bless.* His voice was like smoke rising inside her, curling its way along her limbs, up to her head. She stared up to the copse. The trees were turning. The sun shone quiet and gold on their tops. She sat down on the track. The last grasshoppers sang. A sparrowhawk fluttered motionless overhead. In her mind she was up there with him, floating, looking down from a great height on the mundanities of the world.

Twenty-two

Over the next days, Shell spent many hours in the copse reading *Doyle's A–Z of the Human Body*. She kept the book in a plastic bag and hid it under some stones at the edge of the cairn. She took it out in the quiet times of day and read it on the fallen log, close to some timber shavings. That way, if anyone came along suddenly, she could plunge it into the shavings as a temporary hiding place. But nobody ever came. She read all the entries she could find to do with having babies. She looked at the pictures of foetuses, bulging in bellies like young salmon-trout. Then they grew noses and eyes and fists and fingers and slouched backwards, like a map of Ireland. She'd look at the pictures and look at her belly. She couldn't believe any such creature was growing inside her. Her belly was tougher than usual, less spongy. But apart from that it wasn't sticking out in the way the pictures made out. She found the entry again on amenorrhoea. She learned that sometimes the curse didn't come for other reasons. *That's what I have,* she decided. *I've a small dose of amenorrhoea.*

A chat with Mrs Duggan a week later almost convinced her. She'd come to pick up Trix and Jimmy of a Saturday, after they'd been to play. Mrs Duggan was slumped in a chair, her feet on a stool. She told Shell to sit down by her.

'I'm not a well woman, Shell,' she said. 'Trix and Jimmy are getting too much for me these days.'

'I'm sorry, Mrs Duggan. What's wrong with you?'

Mrs Duggan gave a strange smile that was not a smile. 'I'm expecting again. A baby. That's why I'm so tired and sick. Usually a woman gets sick in the first ten weeks or so. Then it goes. But I'm much more far gone, and still as sick as ever.' She grimaced and shuffled on her seat.

'You're *pregnant*, Mrs Duggan?'

She nodded. 'For my sins. I am.' She sighed.

They sat in silence. Shell looked around the kitchen. It wasn't as clean as usual, and Shell realized there'd been no home-made tarts made in ages. Then she looked at Mrs Duggan's belly and realized it was vast. Why had she not noticed before?

'Dr Fallon's told me to rest up to keep the blood pressure down, Shell. I've to ask you not to bring Trix and Jimmy over for now. They're too much on top of my two. Just at present.'

Shell nodded. 'They're terrible for the fighting,' she suggested.

Mrs Duggan gave a limp smile. Her eyes shut, as if she might nod off.

'Mrs Duggan?' Shell asked. 'Can I ask you something?'

'What, Shell?'

'When you're expecting. How can you tell?'

'Don't they teach you biology at school these days?'

Shell shrugged. 'Sort of.'

'I'll tell you how I know, Shell. Every time, without fail, within days, I go right off smoked salmon. Usually it's my favourite treat. We have it Christmas and Easter, or with guests. Jack gets it oak-smoked, from the fisheries the other side of town. But when I'm expecting, the mere thought of the shrivelled pink flesh makes my palms sweat. The smell makes me gag.' She laughed, and tousled Shell's hair. 'It's a sure-fire test. Put a scrap of smoked salmon under my nose and I'll know right off.'

She shut her eyes again, smiling.

Shell stood up. 'Bye now, Mrs Duggan,' she said.

'Bye, Shell. Sorry about Trix and Jimmy.'

'Never worry, Mrs Duggan. They're back to school tomorrow, anyhow.'

She put Mrs Duggan's theory to the test the next day after leaving Trix and Jimmy off at school. She'd stolen some coins from her dad's spare pants and headed into town, where she bought the smallest packet of smoked salmon she could find. She cut open the packet as soon as she got home and smelled it. Then she lay a pink ribbon on a cut of bread and butter and munched on it.

She cut another slice and munched on some more. Then some more until the whole pack was gone. She'd never enjoyed a snack so much.

She threw away the wrapping at the bottom of the

rubbish and washed her hands so nobody would smell it off her. Then she sat back on her dad's armchair and breathed out long and hard. She heard Bridie laughing in her head: *Told you so. You're no more pregnant than Mother Theresa.* She saw the calendar, stuck still on May, and got up and turned the pages four months on to September. There was a picture of Jesus on the mountain, feeding the masses with the loaves and fishes. She rehung it and sat back with a smile, hugging herself. The thin needle of fear threaded its way deep into the back of her thoughts again, like an earthworm disappearing into the soil.

Twenty-three

The next day was Thursday. She'd been due back at school for the autumn term two days ago, but instead she mitched off again to meet Declan at the top of Duggans' field. A shock awaited her. The barley had been cut. The field was empty and open, exposed to view all round. Of Declan there was no sign.

She sat by the edge of the copse and waited. A half-hour passed. She picked a Michaelmas daisy and pulled out its petals. She scratched her kneecaps with the long grass ends. She wished she'd brought her body book to while away the time. Just as she thought he wasn't coming, she heard a car hooting from the road. She ran back over the back field to the gate. Declan was inside his dad's new French hatchback.

'Hop in, my lady,' he said, flourishing an arm.

She stared. 'Didn't know you drove,' she said.

'I've the provisional licence this past month,' he said. 'I've been out in it loads of times.'

'Your dad – does he know?'

'Hop in, or I'll drive off without you.' He reached over and opened the passenger door.

She grinned and got in. The seats were of soft grey cloth, the bonnet gleamed navy. It was as pristine and clean as Father Rose's had been jumbled and jaded. Declan pressed a switch to lower the windows and zoomed off. The wind whipped up her hair and coursed past her face. She scrunched up her eyes into the sun. She felt his hand squeeze the top of her knee. Her heart surged. They shot round the bends as if their lives depended on it.

He drove the back roads to Goat Island, the rocky peninsula where sheep grazed. He went down a narrow track to its hidden beach: a strip of colourful shingle, giving way in the middle to fine, pale sand. At the far end, boulders sprawled, fronting a tumble-down cliff.

The cocklers had been and gone. The schools were back. The place was deserted.

'Fancy a dip?' Declan said, changing where he sat. He'd his pants off already.

'Not me,' said Shell. ''S cold.'

'Go on. Just 'cos it's September, doesn't mean it's frozen.'

Shell shivered. 'I've no costume.'

'Go in starkers, then. There's nobody about.'

'I'll put my toe in.'

Declan laughed. He clouted her with his T-shirt, and ran straight from the car to the surf. She watched him striding in through the shallows, going '*Hoo-ha-ha-hoo*' as the breakers slapped up against him. She clapped as he took a nose-dive.

Suddenly something flip-flopped inside her. Like

a leaf falling from a tree. Or a guitar chord hovering after it's been strummed. She grabbed her belly.

What the hell was that?

Declan's head bobbed up. 'C'm in, Shell. It's gorgeous.'

She couldn't breathe. Something was twitching under her hands. *God Almighty. What's happening?*

She tore off her clothes and ran down to the sea, naked. She screamed as the cold water banged up against her and plunged headlong into a wave.

Her scalp stung. Her jaw was like ice. She could feel nothing.

Declan had her by the ankles and was dragging her in further. She splashed her arms as hard as she could. Anything so as not to think. The numbness spread from head to toe.

They had a seaweed fight. Then a game of Float-the-waves. But soon they got cold. They came out and dried off on Declan's towel. Shell shivered back into her clothes. They walked over to the cliff and crawled into a cave through a crack only the locals knew of. Haggerty's Hellhole, it was called. He pinched her behind as she led the way on all fours. She yelped.

'You're like a ewe on heat,' he said.

'You're like a bull with its horns stuck, Declan.'

'Stuck where?'

'Dunno. In a gate. No, a thornbush.'

He pinched her again.

There were four lager tins and cigarette butts left from the last occupants.

'Haven't been here in years,' she said, standing up

in the silent dimness. 'I remember Mam showing it to me when I was little.'

'We boys used to bring victims in here for torturing,' Declan recalled. 'Girls. D'you remember?'

'No. You never caught me. I was always too fast for you.'

'You still are.'

'Give over. You're the fast one.' She shivered. 'What did you do to them when you got them in here? The girls you did catch?'

'Not much. We tied them up and left them to the mercy of the waves. We called it "the Abattoir".'

'The Abattoir? What's that?'

'You know. A butcher's place. Where they slaughter the animals.'

Shell's stomach heaved at the thought of dead meat hanging from hooks. 'Ugh.'

'Now it's where all the girls go to fornicate. Didn't you know?'

Shell shook her head. *Did you take Bridie here, so?* she couldn't help wondering. She pushed away the stray thought and peered around. 'Ugh. It's smaller than I remember. Colder. Mam said it was beautiful. A place the wind and water made over a thousand years or more. She'd sing her songs in here.'

Shell sat down. Seaweed squelched, the black pockets popping under her. She folded her arms around her knees and began to sing the one her mam'd liked, about the blacksmith who writes a letter and makes a promise, then marries someone else. The notes flew around the walls, colliding with each other in lovely clashes.

Midway through the third verse, Declan stopped her, kissing her hard on the mouth.

Before she could say a word, he was at it again, going for broke, flat out, his head down under her chin. She shut her eyes tight, the notes of the rest of her song still fizzing in her ears. Then she was back in the laundromat, where she'd taken the clothes earlier. She was watching them sloshing back and forth, jumping and flopping in the foam. Next, she was the sparrow-hawk, beating its wings high above the field, poised in the blue soup of sky. As it plunged down, it turned into the fluffy-collared homing bird, flying across the Irish Sea, darting in and out of the spray in the wake of a returning ferry. Anything not to think about the strange twitching she'd felt inside her on the strand. *I was imagining it.* The sea mumbled outside, distant, uneasy. A drop of water from the ceiling kept kataplunking on a shelf of rock above her ear. A yawning nothingness seeped into her. She opened her eyes.

Declan's curls were pressed in below her shoulder, and beyond were the ridges of the encrusted wall. *Mam, why did you have to go and die?* Muffled and mysterious, she heard a toll of a far-off bell. The Coolbar church, ringing out the midday Angelus. One, two, three. *Pray for us, o Holy Mother of God.* What would Dad say if he saw her now? The bell sounds rolled away with the wind and drifted back again. Six, seven, eight. *That we may be made worthy of the promises of Christ.* She remembered Mam's record player, its needle bouncing across the black ridges of the old LPs, crackling with the golden voice of John McCormack, Ireland's legendary tenor.

'*Will ye bury me on the mountain, with my face to God's rising sun.*' Eleven, twelve. A sudden heart-catching climax, the swift pure cry, her mam singing along, soaring to the high note, peeling the spuds, hand-washing the woollens, turning to smile at Shell as she wiped her hands.

Declan's knuckle dug into her back. The record player and records had all gone. Dad sold them soon after she'd died. '*Hoo-ha-ha-hoo,*' Declan yelped, as if another sharp wave had slapped up against him. He rolled off her, panting softly.

She didn't move.

'Pass me a fag, Shell,' he said after a while.

She passed one over and waited as he lit and smoked it. He offered her a drag, but she'd gone off them. He squeezed her wet hair as he puffed.

'Know what, Shell?' he said, more to the cave ceiling than to her.

'What?'

'This cave. Haggerty's Hellhole. It really is a hellhole. Like the whole of Ireland.'

'Is it?'

'It is. The Black Hole of Calcutta's nothing to it. A load of shite. Only worse.' He stubbed out the fag, then lit another. 'All Ireland's a black hole. A great big bloody black hole. D'you wanna hear my latest poem?' Before she could reply, he started:

'*Put Munster in the dumpster*
Feed Connaught to the dog
Tie Leinster up in Limericks
And flush it down the bog.'

135

He spat out the words at the walls, so they rebounded back on themselves. 'What d'you think?'

''S not bad. What about Ulster?'

'Ulster's an ulcer, of course. Perforated. 'S not part of Ireland, thanks be to God. The Brits are welcome.'

Shell giggled. 'They'd shoot you in Derry, Declan, for saying that.'

'More fool them.'

'As Ireland goes, Coolbar's not bad,' Shell suggested, thinking of the copse, the fold of slope, the wild things all around.

'Coolbar's pathetic. The worst of the lot. My family moved in twenty years ago from the other side of Castlerock, but as far as the neighbours are concerned we're still blow-ins.'

On the phrase 'blow-ins' an eerie gust of wind hissed through the cave, making her shiver. 'Let's get out of here,' she said.

Declan nodded. 'OK.'

They scrambled into their clothes. It was a relief to get back out onto the beach. The sun had gone in, the waves were closer to the shore. She looked out to sea and sniffed the air. A sheep baa-ed behind her. She turned and spotted it, caught halfway up the cliff on an outcrop of rock. How had it ever got there? She imagined it stranded for all time or jumping off in desperation to the rocks below.

'C'mon,' Declan said, pulling her by the arm.

He drove her back as far as the cross above the village, saying little. She sang the rest of the black-smith song as they passed over the rough country roads, but his eyes stayed on the road ahead, staring at the tarmac broken into two halves by grass growing up the middle.

'You'd best get out now,' he said, stopping.

She nodded. 'OK. Bye then, Declan.' She opened the door and started to climb out.

'Bye, Shell.' He caught her wrist. 'Shell—' he said.

'What?'

He wriggled his hand round so that they were palm to palm. Then his fingers interlocked with hers.

Shell's heart missed a beat. He'd never done that before.

'What?' she said, smiling.

'You're—' He stopped.

She waited.

She felt him squeeze her hand.

'What?'

'You're top of the class,' he said.

Shell thought of her dismal marks at school, her failed examinations. She grinned. 'Don't be daft,' she said. 'You're the one with all the points.' Everyone knew Declan had got enough points in the Leaving Cert. to go to college twice over. He'd won a place to study the law at university, but he'd said he wasn't going, whatever his family wanted. Shell didn't understand his objection. She thought he'd make a good lawyer with his quick tongue and eye for the main chance.

'OK. You're not top of the class. You're . . .' He considered. 'You're in a class of your own.'

She smiled. He still had her gripped by the hand.

She leaned back into the car and pecked him on the cheek.

'Tarala,' she said.

'Toodletits,' he said.

'See you Thursday?'

He looked away from her and through the windscreen, withdrawing his hand. His lips flattened.

'Thursday, is it? Declan?'

He started the engine. 'S'pose. P'raps.'

'In the field? Or down Goat Island?'

'Dunno.' He let down the handbrake. 'Wherever.' The car rolled forward. 'Over the hills and far away, Shell.'

'Bye so. Till then.'

He nodded, then shrugged. He pulled out and drove on. She saw him look in the rear-view mirror as he started down the hill, into the fold of slope. He waved. 'S'long, Shell. *Au revoir*,' he called back through the open window. The words hung in the hedges after him, then burst like bubbles as the navy hatchback glittered one last time and vanished round a bend. The last she saw of him was his dark curly-top, slightly off to one side, like a pigeon considering its next move.

She shook her head and smiled. *As daft as two left feet.* Another movement, a murmur, fluttered inside her: like a moth this time, stirring out of its chrysalis, soft and hesitant. She grabbed herself, staring blindly down the empty road.

She knew then.

Doyle's A–Z or no. Amenorrhoea it was not.

She'd a baby growing inside her.

She turned off and went up the hill, passing into the back field without knowing where she trod. One foot after the other, she went around like a robot for the rest of the day. Her brain turned inward, onto the thing moving around in her middle.

The following evening, Jimmy brought home news from the younger Ronan boy, Seamus, who was in his class at school. Mr and Mrs Ronan were hopping mad. They'd got up that morning to find a note scrawled from Declan on the kitchen table. He was off to America, he said, leaving his family and college place behind him. His friend Jerry Conlan had a job lined up in Manhattan, he said, where he could earn a hundred dollars a day straight off, so no one was to worry about him. In the PS he'd written a final rhyme:

Back soon —
When it snows in June.

Twenty-four

On Monday she went back to school in her winter uniform. The pleated skirt was tight, where last spring it had been baggy. Her shirt fitted, but only because it had been two sizes too big before. She fastened the top half of her cardigan buttons and left the bottom ones undone. She'd a notion it made her skinnier like that.

Out on the playground nobody came over to her. Bridie Quinn was nowhere to be seen. Declan was thousands of miles away.

She sat behind the hut. She shut her eyes, to see where her mind would take her. *Declan, walking up to her through the early ground mist on Duggans' field. Father Rose, making a bridge for her with his arm, saying 'There but for the grace of God, Shell . . .'*

'Shell.' She looked up. It was Theresa Sheehy, the girl Bridie had gone off with last term.

'What is it?'

'You've got fat.'

'Have not.'

'Have too. A stone at least.'

'Well. So what?'

'You should go on the banana diet. 'S great. You lose five pounds in five days.'

'What do you eat?'

'Bananas.'

'That all?'

'And boiled eggs.'

'Ugh.' The thought of a boiled egg made Shell's stomach turn. She'd been off eggs for months, she realized, just like Mrs Duggan was off smoked salmon.

'Works, honest,' Theresa said. 'I've tried it.'

Shell shrugged. 'Seen Bridie?'

'She's not talking to you.'

'I know. But is she here?'

'Nah.'

'Where is she?'

'How'd I know?'

'Was she here last week?'

'Not a sign of her. They say she's gone off to her aunt in Kilbran.' Theresa came up close. 'I know better, though.'

'What?'

'She told me something over the summer. A secret.'

'What?'

'She said she was going to run away from home. From Ireland. Maybe she's already gone.'

'No.'

''S true. Know what I think?'

'What?'

'She and Declan.' Theresa Sheehy nodded, as if it were obvious.

141

'What about them?'

'Maybe they've run off. *Together.*'

Shell stared. She shook her head. 'To America? No!'

'Why not?'

'They stopped going months back. Bridie told me.'

Theresa smirked. 'That's old news.'

'What d'you mean?'

'They got together again. In the summer. At a dance in Castlerock.'

Shell's mouth opened. No words came out.

'I saw them. On the disco floor. Jiving and squirming. Like two cats on a case.'

'You're lying.'

'Am not.' Theresa shook her head and looked down her long red nose. 'Don't know what you two saw in him. The dirty devil.'

She turned and walked off.

The bell rang.

Shell didn't move. She watched as the maroon ants filed into the school in long lines. When the playground was deserted, she got to her feet and dusted down her skirt. She walked to the back entrance where the deliveries came in and slipped out.

She drifted her way through town. At the pier the librarian had walked down she paused, then turned onto it and strolled down to the end. *A pier is a disappointed bridge*, Mam used to say as they'd often walked down it, hand in hand. *It's trying to get somewhere, but it runs out of faith.*

She imagined Declan and Bridie, skipping down

the streets of Manhattan, among dustbins and sky-scrapers, crazed Americans, glittering limousines. Lights flashed, sirens blared, the great city pulsed with life. They were gone, leaving her behind. Forgotten. A Coke can rolled at her feet. She stamped on it, squashing it flat. She picked it up and threw it out as far as she could into the sea. *Perhaps it's not true*, she thought. But perhaps it was. Bridie had always gone on about how one day she'd run off to Hollywood and become a star. With her dirty blonde hair, she'd fancied herself as a cross between Marilyn Monroe and Meryl Streep. Maybe she was halfway across America by now, heading for California and endless sun. The next thing Shell would hear of her, she'd be starring in the pictures at the Castlerock Palace.

The crushed can bobbed jauntily, floating further out from the tip of the pier into the open water. She leaned on the railing, watching it. It would take its time, but eventually it would get to the mouth of the harbour and reach the open sea.

Then she knew what she had to do.

Twenty-five

Dad was in Cork again that day, so she had a clear field. She went home from town on the eleven o'clock bus and packed the holdall she, Trix and Jimmy had used to pick up the stones in the back field. She put in her jeans and T-shirts, her spare bra – the old one Bridie had stolen for her – her underwear, her one Sunday dress. She changed out of her uniform into Mam's pink dress, which she hadn't worn since Easter-time.

She'd no passport, but she didn't need one where she was going. She took her bus pass just in case it came in handy as ID.

She packed a sandwich and a drink.

She popped in her toothbrush with its splayed, old bristles.

She put in her little bag of crocheted powder-blue, the one Mam had given her for church.

She tried the weight of the holdall. '*Light as a feather*,' she said out loud. She smiled. *No. Light as a shell.*

She picked up Nelly Quirke the dog. It had been hers once. Mam had given it to her when she was small. Shell swore she could remember opening it as a present on her birthday, aged two. It was Trix's now, but Shell itched to take it. She nursed its worn ear, and stroked its snub black nose and soft white whiskers. Then she tucked it into Trix's bed, with the sheets folded daintily around its neck.

The piano panel came apart easily now she'd the knack. She reached in for the caddy and took out every last note. She counted it. Then she tucked it into the powder-blue mass-bag and hung it from her wrist.

She put the piano back together again.

A brisk wind blew round the bungalow, whistling in the guttering.

Should she write a note, like Declan had? She paused, then shook her head. He had gone west; she was going east, and they'd be gone for different reasons.

She walked out of the house, put the holdall down and closed the door behind her. She had a key in her hand and was about to lock it, before remembering Jimmy and Trix. When nobody came to pick them up from school, somebody – a teacher maybe – would take them home. It was better for all concerned that the door was open.

But *she* wouldn't need a key any more. She stepped back inside and left the key on the kitchen table. It would do instead of a note. She laid it tidily in one of the navy blue squares of the checked plastic cloth. She looked around one last time.

The fridge door was open. She was sure she'd shut it when she'd put back the cheese she'd used for her sandwich.

She shut it again.

She paused, listening.

The fridge did its song, low and deep. The house settled onto its foundations. There was a creak, then a tap, like a floorboard being depressed or a door closing. She could hear her own breathing and her blood pumping around her ears.

'Mam?' she said.

There was no reply.

From somewhere close came a sharp clatter. Shell froze. *Dad's room.*

She darted through the hallway and opened his door. A strong breeze pushed past her face. The curtains billowed.

A bottle of aftershave belonging to Dad had fallen over on the dressing table. That was all.

She breathed out. She righted it and closed the window. She bit her lip. The three mirrors were begging her to sit down for a last game of Eternity. She ran her finger over the top of the panels, collecting dust. 'I'm too old for that now,' she said out loud. The words bounced back at her, making her jump.

She fled the room and dashed down the hall to the front door. She slammed it behind her and sighed with relief. Whatever ghost was in there, it wouldn't follow her out. Retrieving the holdall, she marched up the back field to the copse. She would circuit the village and hitch a ride on the main road from a long-distance lorry. Nobody would know where she'd gone. She thought of Mary Magdalene, landing in France. She imagined the whistling dunes and the small toddler, a child of Jesus, struggling to keep up with its mam, its hand in hers. There'd be no small child in her case. She'd be landing in Fishguard Harbour, with the gulls and waves behind her, and she wouldn't be coming back. She'd be first on the night-train to London, then first queuing up at whatever hospital it was the Irish girls went to for the abortions. Wherever it was, she'd find it.

She rounded the copse, then sat on the fallen tree to look down on the fold of slope a last time. She stared at the church steeple, the slate roofs, the swaying elms, the tired fields. She dumped the bag down at her feet. She took out the money and ran her hands over the notes.

The ghost had followed her.

She remembered Mam's voice, singing to her that Easter night from beyond the grave.

She thought of Nelly Quirke, the dog, and the way Jimmy had been when he was sick last spring, with the white freckles standing out on his narrow face, asking for a spade.

She thought of Trix, with her paper dollies and strange chants, cuddling up for another Angie Goodie adventure.

They won't know to bolt the bedroom door at night.

She remembered the night the owl had spoken to her, telling her to *wa-ai-ai-t*.

The morning ticked by.

At the end of it, she picked up her bag. The Angelus started ringing yet again, like a broken record. She didn't bother to count the peals. She trudged back down the back field to the house and unpacked all her things. She undid the piano, replaced the money in the caddy and put the piano back together again.

She ate the sandwich she'd made. Then she turned the oven on and started on some scones.

Twenty-six

Twenty-six

The willow leaves blew ghost-white in the wind. The red hawthorn berries dropped in the frost. Shell turned sixteen. She told Dad one day she'd finished with school; he nodded, as if he understood.

He was only home nowadays on weekends. The money in the tea caddy slowly shrank. She'd given up counting it, but she could tell.

He'd sit in his chair by the electric-bar fire most Saturdays, staring into space, jangling the change in his pocket. It was as if he'd nothing to do until Stack's opening time. There was something preying on his mind, but she didn't know what. He'd look at her sometimes, then look away. He'd clasp his hands as if in prayer, but the fingers kept kneading the knuckles, as if the prayer wouldn't come.

She wasn't frightened of him any more.

At night she lay in bed, listening to the sing-song breathing of Jimmy and Trix asleep. Her hands went roving over her belly. She was sure the button was about to pop right out. She could hear Declan, doing a recitation -

Shell's belly
'S like solid jelly . . .

But she'd get stuck. Declan would have ended it somehow, more cleverly than she'd started it. Then she remembered he'd fled without a word, with Bridie in tow most probably. *You're in a class of your own, Shell.* The class with the school's worst dunce: that was her class. She grabbed her pillow and curled up round it, wishing she could grab Declan Ronan by his long dark curls and throw him in a cowpat. She smiled at the thought of him head first in green ooze, and sat up straight in the dark room, nodding her head. Then she shook it. No. For some reason she didn't wish that. Not quite. *You're in a class of your own, Shell.* New York was five hours earlier; he'd still be out on the town, drinking the beers down in an Irish bar, reciting his poems. He'd be eyeing out the main chance, going for broke.

Go, Declan, go, she thought. He wasn't like the blacksmith in Mam's old song. Unlike him, he'd never made any promises. He'd never written a letter. He was maybe a heart-breaking smooth operator, like in the song the librarian had played, but he'd never pretended anything else.

Then she had it:

Shell's belly
'S like solid jelly
The button's inside out
She's up the pole, without a doubt.

She could almost hear Bridie cackling at it and went to sleep soon after.

One Saturday morning in late October, she woke to find Trix and Nelly Quirke in bed with her. Trix was lying on her back, singing her nonsense words to the ceiling.

'Trix – what are you doing here?'

'You were crying, Shell. In your sleep. So I came in with you.'

Shell stroked Trix's hair. 'Silly Shelly, crying in her sleep,' she muttered.

Trix wriggled onto her front. 'Finger-pictures, Shell!'

'Not again.'

'*Please.*'

Shell dipped her forefinger in an imaginary pot of paint. She drew a big tree, with branches going up to Trix's neck and shoulders, and roots growing into the small of her back.

''S easy. A tree.'

Shell always started with a tree. Next she drew Nelly Quirke, right down to the chewed-up ear.

'Dunno. Draw it again.'

'Again?' She drew it a second time. Trix guessed it. She'd known all along, Shell knew, only she'd wanted the finger-drawing to go on longer.

'My turn now,' Shell said, turning so her back faced Trix.

Jimmy sat up in his bed and watched. 'Do a cement mixer,' he suggested.

Trix began a long tracing that went round and round in spirals, right up under her arms, then down around her waist.

'A cement mixer?' Shell tried.

'No.' Trix kept spiralling.

'She's making it up as she goes along,' Jimmy pronounced.

'You're tickling, Trix! Stop!'

'Guess. What is it?'

'Dunno. Ocean waves?'

'No. 'S load of snakes.' Trix's little hands reached right round Shell's stomach, tickling as they went. They stopped when they got to the middle of the bump. 'What's *that*?'

'Whisht, Trix. 'S nothing. Just me.'

'It's huge.'

'It's just the way I'm lying.'

''S like Mrs Duggan was. Before she went to hospital.'

'No, it isn't, Trix. Whisht up.'

Jimmy hurled himself on top of them both. He yanked back the bedclothes. 'Let's see!' he shrieked.

'Get off, the two of you. Get off.' She clouted her fists at them.

''S like a football in there.'

Shell curled up tight and sobbed. 'Get off. Both of you.' She felt them withdraw. 'You'll wake Dad.'

Then she lay still, not moving.

'Shell. You alive?' said Trix.

Shell opened her eyes. Trix was on one side of the bed, Jimmy on the other, staring.

'It's a secret, right? My belly. A secret. You're not to tell anybody, right?'

Trix nodded. Jimmy nodded.

'If you tell anybody, Dad will kill me. D'you understand? He'll kill me.'

They nodded again. 'He'll kill you,' Trix repeated.

Jimmy's freckled face went off to one side. 'Shouldn't you be in hospital, Shell? Like Mrs Duggan? Isn't that where you go to have the baby pulled out?'

She'd no idea where he'd got that from.

She sighed and shook her head. 'Any old fool can pull a baby out,' she said. 'You can do it yourself. You see, it pops out. When it's done.'

Jimmy's eyes opened wide. 'Like toast? In a toaster?' he asked.

Shell wiped off the last of her tears. 'Yes, Jimmy. Just like toast.'

Twenty-seven

Jimmy found an old jumper, dumped on a fence near school. It was black, thick and long. He brought it home for Shell. She washed it out and put it on. It went a third of the way down her thighs and covered up the lump.

In the mornings Trix and Jimmy took it in turns to feel the wriggling under her skin. Jimmy said it was a caught frog. Trix said it was a sparrow wing.

Dad came and went, drunk and sober, Fridays to Mondays. Shell didn't think he noticed. He never seemed to look at her or anyone else any more. He was always staring into the middle distance, as if his doom floated there in the invisible air.

On All Souls' Day he had them kneeling at six sharp as usual for the rosary. It was the turn of the first joyful mystery, the Annunciation, when the Angel Gabriel comes to tell Mary that she is with child. Today, Shell could see only its doleful side. Who would ever have believed in an immaculate conception, then any more than today? The plain people of Nazareth, she supposed, were no different from those of County

Cork. As they rattled through the first 'Our Father', she thought of Mary's simple boudoir, a kneeler, a prayer book, flowers, a golden halo; and then the window, open to the bright sky, full of white angel. And the face of Gabriel was that of Father Rose. Dad led them on as they started on the ten 'Hail Mary's.

'Hail Mary, full of grace,
The Lord is with thee.
Blessed art thou among women
And blessed is the fruit of thy womb . . .'

His voice tapered off. Trix and Jimmy rattled on to the end of the prayer. They stared at each other nervously, wondering why he'd gone quiet. He'd never done so before. Trix started on another 'Hail Mary' but faltered on the word 'grace'. They knelt in silence. Something was wrong. They waited for him to explode. But instead he got to his feet and wandered into the hallway without a word. They heard him go out into the night and he didn't come back before they'd gone to bed.

After that, there were no more evening rosaries.

A Sunday came when Shell couldn't get into her usual mass dress. It was a long-sleeved green corduroy, zipped at the back, gathered at the waist. The zip wouldn't go, not with Trix's tugging, nor with Jimmy's. She changed back into her jeans, which these days she kept up with a belt, covered over with the long, black jumper. She went out into the kitchen.

'Dad,' she said. 'Can't go church today. I'm sick.'

She tried to look pale and feeble. But she knew her cheeks were glowing.

He looked up from his chair. He'd been stooping over to do his shoelaces.

His eyes scooted off her onto the wall.

'Sick?'

'I've a pain, Dad. A headache.'

He nodded. 'Stay at home, so. You can mind the dinner.'

Every Sunday after that she said the same thing to him, and he made the same reply.

During the weekdays she borrowed his rain mac whenever she went out. It hung round her, reaching halfway to her ankles. She fetched Jimmy and Trix from school, did the messages at McGraths' and nobody said a word. Miss Donoghue did stare at her once when the weather was fine.

'Don't you like looking on the bright side, Shell?' she asked kindly.

Shell frowned, confused.

Miss Donoghue's firm hand caught a fold of her voluminous mac and shook it. 'There's not a drop of rain in sight, my dear.'

'Oh.' Shell shrugged. '*That.* The forecast isn't good, Miss Donoghue.'

'No?'

'No.'

Miss Donoghue looked dubious.

'There's a storm moving in,' Shell suggested. 'From the Atlantic.'

'That's the first I've heard of it.'

'It was on the radio, Miss Donoghue.' She rushed away as fast as she could.

Another day, she was lingering in McGraths' shop. She'd change in her pocket and wanted a treat. The front with its counters was empty, the door to the back of the house left ajar. She could hear voices from beyond, Mrs McGrath giving out about something, Mr McGrath defending himself. Her fingers itched to pinch a bag of liquorice all-sorts, a penny more than she had, but she stopped herself. The door opened and Mrs McGrath stood at the till with a face like thunder.

'Shell Talent,' she said. 'Only you. I thought I heard that jingle-jangle bell. What are you after?'

Shell drew the mac around herself. No chance of Mrs McGrath taking a penny off anything.

'I'll just take these,' she said, choosing some cheaper fruit gums.

She paid for them.

'D'you want a bag?' Mrs McGrath minced.

'No, 's all right.' She put the pack of gums into one of the mac pockets.

Mrs McGrath stared. Her flabby lips went crooked, her tiny eyes were sharp as pinheads. 'Why've you that big old coat on?' she said.

'There's heavy rain forecast, Mrs McGrath,' Shell said.

Mrs McGrath peered. 'I'd say.'

'I'd best be off before it starts.'

'Before what starts?'

'The rain, Mrs McGrath. 'S due any minute.' She edged towards the door.

Mrs McGrath came from behind the counter, as if she was going to pounce. 'It's a fine day, Shell. Not a cloud in sight.'

Shell whisked herself through the door, closing it behind her with an almighty jingle-jangle. She could feel Mrs McGrath's pinhead eyes digging in between her shoulder blades as she strode off down the street. She'd not got far when, like an answer to a prophecy, rain came, even though the sun still shone. It plastered down, a freak deluge. She scrambled up the muddy hill, munching the gums as she went, laughing out loud as droplets trickled down her hair and neck.

That'll show you, Mrs McGrath, she thought. *Cabbage-face.*

Twenty-eight

December arrived, misty and cool. Trix hung up the advent calendar from two years ago, the last one Mam had bought them, on the wall again. Shell had re-shut the doors with sellotape and every morning, Trix and Jimmy took turns to open one with the nail scissors. They counted down the days to Christmas.

'Are the presents bought, Shell?' Trix asked.

Shell blinked. 'Presents?'

'Last year we had chocolate money. And bath cubes.'

Shell remembered how Dad had surprised them on Christmas morning with some last-minute gifts. There was no chance of him doing the same this year, going by his current doom-laden looks. If there were any presents to be bought – or stolen – she'd have to do it.

'Santa will surely bring something,' she promised.

'Huh.' Trix shook her head. 'Santa's stupid.'

'Who says?'

'Jimmy says. He says only stupid people believe in him. Or flying reindeer. Or God.'

'Does he?'

'Yeh. He says they're all pretend.'

Shell looked at the angel peaking out from behind a cloud through the advent calendar window. The angel, Santa, Jesus and the Virgin Mary all seemed to float away to the land of fairy tales.

'Is he right, Shell?' Trix eyed her challengingly.

Shell pinched her chin. 'Dunno, Trix. All I know is, there's nothing wrong with being stupid. Stupid people are sometimes right.'

Trix frowned, considering. Then she put her hand out to touch Shell's belly.

'Will *it* come for Christmas, Shell? Our secret? Like Jesus did?' Her eyes glistened.

'Dunno, Trix. Don't think so. January, more prob'ly.'

'January?'

Shell nodded.

'*January?*' Trix turned away, her lips wobbling. ''S ages away.'

Shell stroked her neck. 'Whist, Trix. Santa will have something else for you before then, wait and see.'

Every morning she walked Trix and Jimmy to school, climbing up the back field, around the copse, and down the side of Duggans' field. Jimmy went first, Trix next and Shell last, hugging her vast middle. They were like the three kings with no star to follow. Shell was winded by the top of the copse, and in the frosty air her breath came out in white balloons. At the turn-off to the village, she shooed them on to the last lap without her.

Dad stayed away in Cork, mostly. Shell had a notion he'd a woman there. One morning, while spying in his wardrobe, she'd found lipstick on his shirt collar.

The money in the piano had shrunk down to the last hundred.

One day, she thought, he'll go off to the city and never come back.

In the day time she'd go into town for messages. She'd take the bus from the stop beyond the village, going in at lunch time, when no one was about. Then she'd come home, sweep the floor and maybe bake something if the humour was on her. In the dim afternoons she'd shuffle out of her shoes and sit on the armchair. She lit the electric-bar fire, listening to the fizz as the metal elements glowed red, then orange.

The baby jostled when she was still.

Kevin. Hughie. Paul. She shook her head. *No. Gabriel.* She smiled.

What if it was a girl?

Her mind went blank. Then she had it. *Rose.*

'Shell,' Jimmy said that evening.

'Get on with your homework, Jimmy.'

He threw his pen down. ''S done.'

'Don't believe you.'

Jimmy poked his cheek out, tent-like, with his tongue. 'Mr Duggan's first cow's calved.'

'Already?'

Jimmy nodded. 'It was early. Too early, Mr Duggan says.'

Shell stared.

'Saw it coming out, Shell. After school. Mr Duggan let me and Liam watch.'

'And?'

'It came out the cow's bottom.'

Trix stared up from her work, open-mouthed.

'So?' said Shell. 'Where else would it come out from?'

'Mr Duggan had some twine. He wrapped it round the small hooves and yanked it.'

'Ugh,' said Trix.

'Didn't *pop* out, Shell. Not like toast.'

'No?'

'Least, not at first. Once it started, then the rest slid out. Kind of.'

'There then.'

'Didn't look nice,' Jimmy said.

Shell tutted. 'That was one unlucky cow,' she said. 'Usually they just drop.'

'And Shell—'

'Get back to that homework, Jimmy. You too, Trix.'

'There was all this stuff came out too.'

'Stuff? What stuff?'

'Muck.'

Trix grimaced. 'Ick.'

'What kind of muck?'

'Brown lumps. Ooze. Jelly, like. Mr Duggan said it was the afters. And know what?'

'What?'

'The cow tried to eat it. And she licked all the goo off the calf too.'

Shell shuddered. 'Get back to that work. Now.'

Jimmy picked up his pencil. Trix turned a page. The fridge hummed.

'A cow's a cow,' Shell said. 'Babies come out soft and white. You'll see.'

A terrible hunger came on her as they got on with their work. She went through the larder to find something to eat, but every last cut of bread had gone.

'Shell,' Jimmy resumed.

'*What?*'

'When – you know what . . .' He pointed at her lump and rolled his hand around.

She frowned. '*Yes?*'

'What are you going to *do* with it?'

She stared at him.

'She's going to hide it. Aren't you, Shell?' Trix piped up.

Shell's lips pursed.

'Where?' scoffed Jimmy.

'She could put it in a drawer,' Trix mused. 'Or under the bed.'

'Dad'd hear it crying, stupid,' Jimmy said.

'No, he wouldn't.'

'Yes, he would.'

'Would.'

'Wouldn't.'

'Shush, the pair of you,' Shell shouted. She clapped her hands over her ears.

Jimmy chewed his pencil end. 'Well? What *are* you going to do?' he called out.

Shell thought of Mary and Joseph fleeing to Egypt from King Herod's rage. She thought of baby Moses, floating down the river in his basket. She took her hands off her ears. 'Don't you worry about that, Jimmy,' she said. 'You'll see. I've it all worked out.'

Twenty-nine

But she hadn't.

She read and re-read the body book until she knew the birth section by heart. The words contractions, dilations, amniotic fluids, caesareans, episiotomies swam before her eyes, muddling themselves up into a labyrinth of normal and abnormal, dos and don'ts, befores and afters. She slammed it shut, thinking, *You just get down on your knees and push and hope. And push some more.*

Then the what-ifs started.

What if . . . ? She sat in the armchair on the darkening afternoons, with the wind howling around the guttering and the rain slanting in from the west. *What if . . . ?* No. She hadn't it all worked out. She didn't know what to do. She bit her lip. She needed somebody. Somebody other than Trix and Jimmy. Somebody she could go and tell. If only Bridie'd been around. She'd have thought up some madcap plan, which was better than no plan at all. She looked at the holy calendar. The December picture was of Mary and Child. The Virgin's blue robe rippled over her front and knees, the baby sat up straight and blessed the world. *Madonna with child plus a thirty-three J Wonderbra,* she heard Declan quip. Who had Mary told? she wondered. Her own mother, probably. Then her mother had told her father. Then her father had told Joseph. Soon everybody'd known. Everybody'd understood.

Her eyes fastened on the piano. The lid was up. Jimmy'd been playing the night before, as usual. She pictured her own mam on the stool, her right foot poised over the pedal, her fingers trawling over the notes, bringing out the light, soft tunes. 'Mam, I've something to tell you,' she tried out loud. The figure at the piano slowly turned, her eyes a question. A faint smile hung on her lips. *'What, Shell?'* The notes on the piano dangled, the tune hovered. Shell couldn't bring herself to go on. ''S nothing, Mam. Sorry. Go on.' But instead of turning to play on, the figure dissolved, leaving a great gap behind. Shell got up and shut the lid down to hide the keys.

Then Shell thought of Mrs Duggan, Mam's best friend: she was the obvious person to tell. But she was in the regional hospital. She'd gone there before her own baby came and hadn't come back yet. They'd said there'd been a complication, but nobody knew what.

Her only other friend was Bridie Quinn. Shell couldn't see what use she'd be, even if she wasn't up in Kilbran, as her family made out, or in America, as Theresa Sheehy claimed.

There was nobody.

Then she thought of Father Rose.

She remembered him making a bridge for her with his arm. *God Bless, Shell. Are you happy, Shell? Trust me, Shell. As I came up the hill, Shell, I saw you.* His words swirled around her head, his eyes looked at her across the shafts of church light. In haste, before she could change her mind, she grabbed Dad's big mac and dashed out. In the driving rain, she clambered up the back field and down to the village. Her head bent into the wind, her hands went numb from cold. The rain blew hard, turning to sleet. The puddles rippled iron-grey.

The village was quiet, with no life or soul to it. It was Tuesday, the usual afternoon for church confessions. She'd not been to confession for ages, not since Lent, when Father Carroll had absolved her of the usual rigmarole of sins she'd concocted. *Arguing with my brother. Not doing what Dad says. Missing class.* She said the same three sins every time, and if he noticed, he never said. Today, Father Rose might be hearing confessions instead. If so, she could go into the box and tell him everything. It'd be dark, with the metal grid between them, making his face a silhouette. He'd be bound by the vow of silence. He'd listen to her. He'd tell her what to do.

She let herself into the church. She'd not been there in weeks.

It was deserted. The wind chased itself around the four walls. The statues stared blankly down the aisles.

She put her fingers in the font and blessed herself through force of habit. She bobbed her right knee down and walked softly to the confessional box. The sinner's door was ajar. Over the priest's door was the sign.

FATHER ROSE. She stepped into the sinner's cubicle. With difficulty she knelt down.

'Father?' she said. There was no reply.

'Father Rose?'

Nothing. She was on her own. There was no shape on the other side of the grid. Perhaps they'd changed the times of the confessions in her months of absence. Perhaps he'd given up waiting for sinners and gone off for his tea.

She rested her head on the damp sleeves of her mac and spoke.

'Bless me, Father,' she stumbled. 'For I have sinned. I've stolen two bras from Meehans'. I've gone naked in Duggans' field with Declan Ronan. Now I'm up the pole and don't know what to do.'

Ah, Shell, she seemed to hear in reply. *That's a litany of sins, all right. But nothing God won't forgive. If you say three 'Hail Mary's, and a 'Glory Be' and try not to do those things again, you'll be right as rain and on the road to heaven.*

She felt her shoulders shaking; she was half giggling, half crying. *Jimmy's right. Only stupid people would believe in it.* She got up from the kneeler and struggled out of the box. *The whole church is a show.* Laughter threatened to erupt from her throat. She swallowed to choke it back. She didn't genuflect before the altar, but rushed down the aisle towards the door, desperate to get out. The vague incense smell, the dark shadows and eerie silent statues rushed in around her like crowds of bats. Just as she reached the back of the church, she heard the vestry door open and a brisk tread at the other end. She froze.

'Hello there. Have you come for confession?'

It was Father Rose's voice, calling out in the dark, strange and flat in the empty space.

She paused by the side door. 'No, Father,' she said without turning.

'Is that Shell, by any chance?'

A warmth had crept into the words now, the familiar *I-know-just-what-you-feel* tone he'd always had for her. She looked over her shoulder, digging her hands deep into the mac. She saw him a long way down the aisle, standing, arms folded, in a dark cassock. She couldn't make his face out in the dimness of the unlit church.

'It's been a while.'

She gave a fragile smile. 'Yes, Father. 'S only me.'

'Did you come here to pray?' he suggested, taking a step towards her.

She bit her lip. 'Pray?' She faltered as if she didn't know the word.

'Or maybe just to shelter. From the rain?'

She nodded. 'The rain. That was it.'

'Churches, Shell,' he said. His right hand flipped through the air, as if drawing back an invisible curtain. She heard him sigh. His hand dropped back to his side. 'They at least have *that* use.' The sentence rolled down the aisle towards her, with the words twisting around each other, cutting faith to ribbons. Something had slipped from him, like a mooring rope or a firm banister, just as it had slipped from her. It was as if they'd both been stranded, left in the same dark and hopeless place. She reached for the door, blindly. She couldn't turn, or he'd see what she'd turned into; she could never have lived with the shame. She fumbled for the handle.

'They do, Father,' she cried. 'They do have that use.' She hardly knew what she said or meant, but before he could answer, she'd let herself back out into the relentless cold of the day. She half ran back through the village. Nobody was about. She breathed out in relief as she climbed up the blustery hill.

The rain eased. She bent over halfway up, exhausted suddenly. When she stood upright, a pain unfolded, heavy and half-remembered. *The curse, back again.* Lemon clouds parted. A feeble sun filtered through. Her ears were hot. She panted, enjoying the last of the drizzle on her forehead. The pain curled up in a ball in the small of her back and faded away. She continued up the hill. *There is nothing he could have done*, she thought. *I'm on my own.*

The wind carried a loud whooping up to her ears. She turned back. Trix and Jimmy were running towards her, waving their arms like whirling windmills. They were out already from school. She'd no idea where the time had gone. She waited for them by the copse, shivering in her mac. *I'm on my own, apart from Trix and Jimmy*, she thought. *We three. We're in this together.*

Thirty

Jimmy had the air of 'We Three Kings of Orient Are' picked out on the piano. He sat there, doodling on the keys most of the evening, while Trix and Shell made some angel wings out of an old cornflakes box.

The dull pain came and went. The rain started up again. Shell lit the second bar of the electric fire even though Dad had forbidden it. It was Tuesday; there was small chance of him appearing before Friday, so he wouldn't know. She laid his mac across the kitchen door to keep out the draught and pressed the curtains up against the windowsill with oddments from around the house. Her hands were ice-cold even so.

She warmed oxtail soup, two tins of it, for tea. She drank her bowl quickly, feeling it scald her gullet as it went down. She was shivering again.

The pain came again, stabbing and definite. She leaped to her feet with it. Her chair toppled to the floor.

Trix and Jimmy stared. 'What's wrong, Shell?' Jimmy said.

She didn't answer. Her eyes seized on the holy calendar above the piano, fastening on the drapes of the Virgin's robe, following the creases.

'What's wrong, Shell?' Trix said.

She grabbed the table. 'Nothing.' She picked up her chair and sat down again, grabbing her middle. 'Nothing's wrong.'

'Nothing?'

'Nothing. Just remembered something I forgot. That's all.'

She got up and walked around the room.

'What was it?' asked Trix.

'What was what?'

'The thing you forgot?'

'What thing I forgot?'

Jimmy tapped two fingers on his forehead. 'She's gone doolally,' he told Trix in a loud whisper.

'Hurry up with that soup,' Shell said. 'It's bed time.'

'No it isn't. It's only seven.'

'If I say bed time then it's—' She stopped and dropped to her haunches. 'Bed time.'

'What about my wings?' Trix said.

'You can finish them in the morning.' The pain subsided. 'Or maybe now, if you're fast.'

Trix and Jimmy drank down their soup. They clattered the bowls into the sink while Shell cleared the table. Trix got her wings out and opened her paint box up. She filled a mug with water and dipped in the brush. Jimmy went back to the piano. He'd 'Jingle Bells' going now as well.

Shell got out the broom and started sweeping.

'You swept the floor earlier,' Jimmy said, without turning round.

'It's all crumbs again, with the two of you,' she snapped. She launched the bristles around his feet, darting them between the piano-stool legs and pedals. 'I'll sweep you up if you're not quiet.' She moved over towards the sink.

The lights flickered, grew dim and came on strong again. The wind got up hard and shrill. Time passed. *Jingle, jingle* went the piano keys, needling away on the same old note.

Holy God, it's coming again.

She dropped the broom. 'Keep playing, Jimmy.' She rushed into the bedroom and lay flat on her bed and panted. But the pain came on regardless. She drew her knees up to her chin and rocked. *Jingle bells, jingle bells, jingle all the way.* The oxtail stew flew up her throat but just on time she swallowed it back down. A hiss was in her ears and yellow streaks across her eyes. *Oh what fun it is to ride on a one-horse open sleigh – heh – jingle bells . . .*

'Shell?' Jimmy and Trix were standing over the bed, looking down on her.

She blinked. The pain exploded inside her into smithereens scattering into her bloodstream, then softened. 'What?'

'You all right?' Jimmy said.

Trix's lips wobbled. 'You're acting funny, Shell.'

Shell sat up. 'I'm fine.' She got up. She fluffed up Trix's hair. 'Just wanted a quick lie-down.' She went back out to the kitchen. 'Finish up those wings, Trix. Here, give me a brush.'

They did a mix of orange, white and yellow. But the green of the cornflakes packet still showed through, so they did a blue splurge over that part. They painted the grey insides bright red. Shell made a hole with a skewer and threaded through two lengths of twine in hoops for fixing the wings up to the shoulders. Trix tried them on.

Jimmy looked up from the piano. He was back on 'We Three Kings'. 'They flop.'

'They don't,' Trix said. She fluttered round the kitchen waving her fingertips.

'They do. The tips point to the floor. If you were a real angel, you'd crash.'

'Would not.'

'Would.'

'Would not.'

'Would. Crash, bang, wallop.'

'*Whisht!*' Shell screamed. It was back, hard and vicious. Her hand shot out blindly, knocking the mug of water and paintbrushes over across the kitchen table. She grabbed the back of a chair. The coloured water oozed across the neat checks of the plastic tablecloth.

She got to the sink just in time. There was no holding the oxtail soup back now.

'Ick,' said Trix.

Shell ran the taps hard, and dropped in a squat. *Ooerooooo*, she moaned from deep in her throat.

Jimmy came over from the piano stool and watched. 'She sounds just like Mr Duggan's cow,' he mused.

The pain ran off her again, like water. But she was left cold and shaken.

'Trix,' she whispered. 'Clear up that mess of paint, won't you?'

She picked up the mac from across the bottom of the door and put it on.

'Where are you going?' Jimmy asked.

'Out. Need some air.'

''S pouring.'

'Don't care.'

She got out the door and marched around the house, five times and counting. All she could see was the light on the concrete path from the kitchen windows, back and front, and the gutters and drains, sloshing the rain away into the earth.

Another one came on the ninth go round. She vomited again, into the wind. *She* was the goat coughing by the gatepost now, not Dad. Eventually the pain went.

She went back in.

'Run a bath, Trix.'

''S not bath night, Shell.'

'Doesn't matter. I'm having a bath.'

Trix ran off to do it.

'Keep playing that piano, Jimmy.'

Jimmy shrugged. He played *Star of wonder, star of night* in the gruff notes at the bottom of the piano. In the bath, the water came right up to the rim of grime that wouldn't come off. It wasn't mad-hot, but warm enough. She stopped shivering once she'd got in. Her hands and feet tingled. Trix sat on the toilet seat, watching her, as she often liked to do.

'You're wicked funny tonight, Shell,' she pronounced.

'How funny?'

'You keep starting and stopping. 'S funny.'

Contractions, dilations, dos and don'ts, befores and afters.

'I'm distracted with the pair of you.'

She rubbed under her arms with the soap-bar. 'Pass the flannel over, Trix.'

'If you punched another hole, Shell . . .'

'Huh?'

'In my wings. And put another string through. And a knot round my middle . . .'

'We'll try it later,' Shell promised. 'Out you go. Scram.'

The next pain had her in its vice the moment Trix left. *Star with royal beauty bright.* She turned in the bath onto her knees and pressed her head up against the enamel. *Oooeroooo,* she went. The sound bellowed round her ears, deep, strong. She was sure Mr Duggan's cow had joined her in the bath. It wasn't her doing the moans but it. *Oooooeroooo . . .*

She'd topped up the bath twice but now there was no warm water left in the tank. The towels were damp and grubby, but she dried herself as best she could and pulled her clothes back on.

Back in the kitchen, there was a surprise. Jimmy and Trix had cleared away the paint things. On the table lay a ball of twine, a pair of scissors, a plastic bin-bag and a set of Trix's old doll's clothes. In the middle was a small cardboard box, a little bigger than a shoebox. It was lidless and thickly lined with cotton wool.

'We've got everything ready, Shell,' Jimmy said.

Shell stared. 'Ready?'

'For the baby.'

'The baby?'

'What else?'

Trix grinned. '*Told* you it would come for Christmas.'

Jimmy patted his own belly. 'That's why you sound like Mr Duggan's cow. The baby's coming out. Isn't it?'

Shell nodded. 'I think so,' she admitted. She went up to the table and looked at their offerings. She picked up the twine and scissors and shuddered. *What if . . . episiotomies and caesareans . . .*

'Doubt we'll need these,' she said. She put them down and examined the plastic bin-bag. 'What's *that* for?'

''S to catch the goo. The afters.'

Shell shook her head. She picked up the shoebox and prodded the cotton wool lining. 'That's nice,' she said.

'It's a manger, Shell,' Trix said. 'I made it. I put cotton wool in, not straw.'

Shell nodded. 'Much better than straw,' she agreed, bending over.

'She's off again,' Jimmy said.

The pain came up this time like a juggernaut, mowing her over, rolling her flat on the tarmac. In the middle of it came a hot gushing between her legs.

''S coming!' she yelped. But after the pain grumbled away, all that was left was a puddle on the floor.

Jimmy got the mop out.

'What is it?' Trix asked, peering down. ''S a funny colour.'

'It's bath water,' Shell said. Her teeth chattered.

'Never.'

'It is.'

'Ick.'

'Get rid of it.'

Jimmy mopped it up.

'I'm all wet.' Suddenly Shell was sobbing and she couldn't stop. 'I'm frozen. I'm wet through.'

Jimmy put the mop away. He put his hand on her elbow. 'C'mon, Shell,' he coaxed.

They led her into the bedroom. Trix helped her into her nightdress. They tucked her in and heaped their own blankets on top of her.

'Jimmy?' she croaked.

'What?'

'Would you get me a bowl. The plastic washing-up bowl.'

'Why?'

'Gonna be sick.'

He came in with the bowl. Trix followed with a cup of tea and a Marie Rose biscuit. Instead of being sick she ate the biscuit and drank down the tea. For a moment she felt nearly normal. Then the next pain came on, and the next, and the one after that, until they were lining up like monsters, grabbing at her as they passed, munching on her insides, tearing her limb from limb.

She remembered coming out of a tunnel, wanting to know the time. Jimmy was saying something. Two o'clock. How could it be two? It was pitch-dark outside. 'You should be at school, the two of you. What are you doing here?'

''S two at *night*, Shell.'

''S coming, 's coming.'

'You said that last time.'

''S really coming. Jesus.' She was on the floor, crawling towards the kitchen. 'God help me.' Her knees flew apart. Her hair was down around the boards in matted folds.

'Get the bin-bag, Trix. The twine. The scissors,' she heard somebody say. It was like the voice of a torturer. He was going to carve her in two. She hollered as loud as she could, but there was nobody to hear her for miles around. A knife was in her gut with a fiery blade, savaging her.

'No! Spare me,' she screamed. 'I didn't mean to do wrong. Please.'

She was Angie Goodie on the steeple. The lightning was striking her, not the wand, again and again, cutting her to ribbons.

The room went white and silent. She brought her head up and looked around. It was cloudy and quiet, with a warm current of air on her face. She was everywhere and nowhere. She was a spirit. The monster had killed her. There was a piano playing, from far away, then the sea rolling in and out, like the waves on Goat Island. The whiteness turned to cream, then to fine yellow, like sand. The wind made it ripple, and suddenly her mam was on it, walking towards her, her olive scarf tightly knotted under the chin, the wind blowing her tweed coat. *Shell*, she called. *My own Shell. There you are. I've been looking for you all day but I couldn't find you. Where did you run off to, naughty girl?* She came up close and placed a hand on each of her shoulders. She was stooping down over her, looking into her eyes. Shell looked back into hers. She saw her own face in both of them, translucent, bobbing. Off to the side were Mam's laughter lines, crinkling up around like broken smiles, just like the librarian's had. Mam's hand was on her forehead, smoothing out a damp tress of hair. *You've a temperature, Shell. You shouldn't be out in this high wind. Come with me, Shell. I'll take you home.* Mam's cool palm was in her left hand, then it was in her right hand; maybe there were two Mams, one on either side. Shell was turning in both directions, straining to see Mam's face again, but the whiteness had come back. *Mam,* she screamed. *Don't go. Don't leave me. Please don't go. Please.*

'Shell . . . Shell . . .'

The words got softer, further. Shell . . . Something was flying away from her. Mam's soul. It fell away like a stone rolling down a cliff, sliding down the side, gathering speed. Now it was the lost sheep stuck on the outcrop of rock, falling, going round and round, head over heels, dashing down to its death below. *No,* she called out after it. *No. Come back, sheep, come back.*

The rocks, the sea, the sheep vanished. She felt a hand on the back of her neck. She was in the kitchen, crouched in the middle of a blanket. Her nightie was rolled up around her hips. Her forearms were dug into the seat of the armchair. Under her knees was black plastic. On the black plastic was a lump. It was red and blue and brown and white. Jimmy was touching it. He'd a damp flannel and was stroking it clean.

'You did it, Shell,' he gasped. 'You got it out.'

As he wiped, a face appeared. Two button-blue eyes. A tiny nose. Little, pursed lips.

'I did it?' she gasped.

Its arms were curled around its chest, ending in tiny fingers, like a doll's.

There was something caught around its neck.

'What's that – what's that thing there?' she whispered.

Jimmy was doing something, pulling at it, yanking at it, slipping it over the baby's head.

'Don't take it off – it's—'

She shook her head, touching it. It was whitish-grey, like a strange necklace.

'Is it twine? You didn't pull it out with twine?'

'No,' Jimmy said. 'Didn't use the twine. It came out like you said. On its own.'

He got the scissors out and cut the round thickness of the thing in two. It oozed round the baby, a long, truncated worm.

'Ick,' said Trix. ''S horrid.'

One bit of it ended in the baby's belly button. Jimmy did another snip to cut it away. The other bit dangled from between Shell's legs. She remembered what it was now, from the body book: the umbilical cord.

Jimmy went on wiping the baby.

'Is it a boy or girl, Jimmy?' Trix said.

'A girl, silly. Any fool can tell that.'

'A girl?' Shell breathed. 'Give her over, Jimmy. Let me hold her.'

Shell reached out and touched the strange, alien creature. Minutes past, silent and still.

A gloop tickled her thighs. 'It's the afters,' Jimmy yelled.

A purple sludge, liverish and dark, came out. Shell didn't care. She hardly noticed. By now, she had the little girl picked up, and was holding her like cut-glass, hunched on her kneecaps, smiling. The little face blurred, then sharpened again. She touched the head. It was soft, like apple skin. There were tiny purple veins inside it, and no hair on top of it. Her heart missed a beat, then a surge of warmth flooded over her. '*Rosie*,' she whispered. '*My Rosie, love.*' She touched the little nose. '*Is it really you? Did I do this?*' She started to hum her mam's favourite hymn. '*Love divine, all loves excelling, joy of heaven to earth come down.*' The little baby, daintily creased, lay in her arms asleep, making not a sound.

Thirty-one

Jimmy and Trix tried to take the child away but she wouldn't let them. She went to bed with her, singing her the hymn. She wrapped her in a soft flannel sheet, and laid her on a pillow at her side.

She must have slept.

She woke late next day. Panicking, she searched for the baby. She was where she'd left her, rolled on the side, hugged into Shell's shoulder by the pillow, with her head under Shell's armpit. Shell picked her up and sang some more. Slowly she got to her feet. Soreness stung from her stomach to her knees. She hobbled out of the bedroom, through the kitchen and made it to the bathroom. She ran another bath. She stepped in, carrying the baby with her, scooping the water over the little wrinkles on the forehead. '*I baptize thee Rose*,' she said. The child was cold through, however hard she tried to warm her. Milk dribbled from her breasts but the baby was too tired to drink.

She got out and wrapped her up warm in a towel. She put her in Trix's cardboard box, in the snug cotton-wool lining. She folded up some clean socks to support her precious head. Then she made the breakfast.

Trix and Jimmy woke up. It was well gone school time, but she didn't scold them.

'You can stay home from school,' Shell said. 'Just for today.'

She drew back the curtains, putting the oddments back. She hummed the hymn. '*Joy of heaven to earth come down, fix in us thy humble dwelling . . .*' The morning light shafted in. Fast clouds skimmed the sky. A feeble sun snuck low across the field. ''S fine today,' she said. She went to touch the baby's cheek and smiled.

'Rosie,' she murmured.

''S that what she's called?' Trix said.

Shell nodded. 'Like it?'

''S pretty.' Trix's lips wobbled. ''S very pretty, Shell.'

'What's wrong with you, Trix? What's there to cry about?'

Trix said nothing, but bawled out loud, tears streaming down her cheeks.

'You're worried about what Dad will say – when he gets back?'

Trix shook her head. Then nodded.

'Don't worry. We'll think of something. Maybe he won't mind after all.' Shell went on humming.

Jimmy threw down his spoon.

'Shell,' he said.

'What?'

'You know Mr Duggan's cow?'

'God in heaven. If you'd ever stop going on about that bloody cow.'

'The one I told you about. That had the early calf.'

'What of it?'

'It came out dead.'

'Dead?'

Jimmy nodded. 'Didn't tell you before.'

Shell stared.

'Didn't want to scare you.'

'Oh.' Shell's fingers went to her neck, shaking and cold. 'That poor cow. And her licking the calf.' Her teeth chattered. 'And the calf dead.'

'She didn't know, Shell. She didn't know the calf was dead.'

''Spect not. The poor cow.'

Shell picked up the baby-box. She sat on the armchair, cradling the box on her lap. The baby was still asleep.

She stared across the room to where the sunshine came in through the window.

She tried to hum the hymn but the notes wouldn't come.

A great lid slammed down in her heart.

She made herself look down at what was in her lap. The baby was blue and stiff. It was dead.

They found the lid to the box and put it on, covering the small child. Shell tried to cry but her eyes were dry. Jimmy took the spade of ocean blue and Trix the spade of ladybird red. Shell carried the tiny coffin in her arms. They processed out of the door into the sun.

She, Jimmy and Trix were like sentinels, walking up the field in a silent row. In the middle they dug a hole in the earth. The ground was soft and heavy after the rain. There were no stones. Jimmy put the box in at the bottom and Shell cut off a strand of her own hair and curled it on top of the cardboard lid. Trix added a sprig of holly. They crossed themselves. Then they filled in the hole and surrounded it with a ring of small, round stones, taken from the cairn.

Part III
WINTER

Thirty-two

Dad got back from Cork at the end of the week.

He had his supper quietly and sat in his chair. He didn't say anything.

Shell noticed him following her round the room with his eyes as she put the things away.

'So, Shell?' he said.

'So what, Dad?' she said.

'You're all right, are you, Shell?'

'Fine, Dad.'

'Your headaches. Have they been plaguing you while I've been away?'

'They did a bit. But now they've gone, Dad. All gone.'

He nodded. 'Good.' He got up and paced the room, jangling change in his pocket. He looked at her oddly, with one eye scrunched up small, the other large and round. He kept starting to say something then changing his mind. Finally he said, 'Right, I'm off.' He left the house, even though Stack's would have scarcely opened.

Days slipped by. Milk dripped from her breasts.

Sister Assumpta, the nun who'd taught her mam, would have called them 'Tears of a Disappointed Mammary Gland'. She'd to stuff tissues in her bra the whole time. She didn't cry. Instead a hardness grew in her like black ice. It froze her numb. Every minute seemed a week. Rosie's little hands, the light sketchy veins under her skin, floated around in Shell's head, but no tears came. In the mornings she stood by the ring of stones. She looked ahead into the copse at the harsh spokes of tree. Her mind was empty.

Dad stayed home. Perhaps he'd done with the city and the lipsticked mistress. Shell didn't care. She went into town. She managed to steal a bangle for Trix's wrist from Meehans', then a pair of bright yellow and green football socks for Jimmy. The man serving was only a stone's throw away, chatting to somebody, and she didn't care if she was caught. Finally she stole a sheet of wrapping paper, pale blue with embossed silver angels, blaring trumpets. When she got home, she wrapped up the presents and hid them under her bed. She found the body book there, collecting dust, bea... 's neatly folded. She took and the pink dress of Mam the body book out and put it in the rubbish bin. She didn't care any more if anyone found it.

School ended. The final run-up to Christmas started. Mrs Duggan came home from hospital with a baby boy. He'd a hole in his heart, they said, but he would live. Jimmy and Trix were mad to go and see him, but Shell didn't want to know. On Christmas Eve she gave into their pleadings and let them go. She stayed behind to cook the dinner.

While they were gone, a knock came at the door. She and Dad had just sat down to eat. Dad humphed, but got up to see who it was.

He returned to the kitchen with Sergeant Liskard from the garda station in town behind him.

Shell froze. *The socks and bangle. How did they find me out? How?*

The sergeant stood at the window. The tip of his boot drew squiggles on the kitchen floor. He'd a frown on his face.

'So, Tom. What's new?' Dad said. 'Are you collecting for Christmas, or what is it?'

''S not that,' the sergeant said. He sucked in his lips then blew out. 'We've found a baby, Joe.'

'A baby?'

The sergeant nodded. 'A baby.'

Shell stared. Her hand went to her throat without her knowing. She'd been out in the field as usual that morning. The stones were in a ring where they'd been placed. Nothing had been disturbed.

'A baby?' she whispered.

The sergeant nodded. 'Over on Goat Island. On the strand.'

'On the strand?' Shell said.

'In the cave up there. You know the place?'

Shell nodded.

'The baby was left in there.'

'In the cave?'

'Mrs Duggan's small lad is doing fine. I've just checked,' the sergeant said.

They stood in the small kitchen, waiting for what

came next. The world dropped away from beneath Shell's feet.

'A baby,' she repeated.

'Yes,' the sergeant said. 'And the baby's . . . dead.'

The word was a dagger. It hurt so that the tears came. The little fingers and pursed blue lips. The thundering silence of the cry that never came. 'Dead,' she sobbed. '*Dead?*'

''Fraid so.'

Dad's hand fastened on her arm. 'Get a grip on yourself, Shell.'

'I've got no choice, Joe,' the sergeant continued. 'I'm sorry. I'm acting under orders. I'm instructed to bring the two of you in for questioning.'

Shell looked at Dad. He was looking beyond her, staring at the piano, transfixed, as if somebody or something was coming straight at him. He shook his head and started. 'What's that you said, Tom?'

'You've to come with me.'

'Where to?'

'To the station, Joe, for questioning. I'm sorry.'

'Right so. I'll get the coats.'

Shell shook, her knees like jelly. *Dead.* Dad put a coat around her shoulder. His hand was on the small of her back, propelling her to the door. His thumb and fingers dug in hard. *Dead.* His voice was in her ear, the syllables spitting fast and hushed.

'Don't you say anything, Shell, understand? Don't – you – say – a – word.'

She nodded and couldn't stop nodding. *Dead.* She was still nodding as Dad led her to the back of the sergeant's car and got in the other side. Her fingers clasped and unclasped each other. She didn't bother to wipe the tears. The Coolbar fields floated away, hedgerows trammelled on either side. She didn't know where they were taking her. The only thing she could hear was the word *dead* clanging in her brain, over and over like an Angelus bell.

Thirty-three

Don't say a word.

They'd left her in a room, waiting.

Outside, a naked tree tapped the windowpane. The rain was incessant. *Don't you say a word.*

She'd said nothing. The questions had rolled around her ears, loud then soft, like waves. She was underwater. The sound kept breaking up. The woman with the spiky hair had gone away. Before going, she'd spoken, in between passing her the tissues. Whatever it was she'd said, Shell didn't hear. The baby on the strand. The baby in the cave. The baby in the field. Dead, all dead. *Don't say anything.*

They'd taken Dad away, to another room.

She stood up and walked to the window to watch the dancing branches. The chimneys and aerials of Castlerock sprouted below her, dropping down in tiers to a murky sea. She hugged herself, gripping her elbows, thinking of the box lined with cotton wool. She began to sing.

> '*Now the holly bears a berry*
> *As red as any blood . . .*'

The doctor they'd warned her about interrupted her. He hurried in, breathless, balding on top, with flushed cheeks. He asked her things in rapid fire. She nodded yes or no, or shrugged for 'don't know'. Then he examined her from top to toe.

He left ten minutes later, saying that was all and nothing more.

They came to move her to a different room. They took her down an echoing stairwell, along a corridor, through a door, the last on the left. This room was smaller, with peeling yellow paint. The window was frosted over. You couldn't see out.

The spiky-haired lady came in. She said her name was Sergeant Cochran, and coaxed Shell into a chair on one side of the table, while she sat on the other. There was a third chair beside her, vacant. They waited.

'You can tell me, Michelle,' she said, breaking the silence. 'You can tell me about it. If you want.'

Shell looked up. *Is it me she's talking to?*

'Yes, Michelle. You can trust me.'

Don't say a word. Shell tried to speak, but the words were like stones, stuck in her gullet. She shook her head. *No good.*

'Silence then?'

Shell nodded. Silence.

'It is your right.' The spiky woman smiled. The word 'right' seemed to stay like an upturned card on the table, staring up at the two of them. Minutes passed.

The door opened. A man came in. He stopped short, hand on handle. She could hear his tongue click against his teeth, *tut-tipper-tup.*

'This her?' he drawled. Shell stared. He was looking away to the side as if he'd a squint, or she'd a face too awful to look at. He was grey-suited with a shirt of immaculate white. There was a restlessness to him, as if the room were too small to contain him. His hair was sandy and straight, oiled back. His straggling eyebrows were the only untidy bit of him.

'Yes, sir,' the woman said, sitting upright. 'This is Michelle. Michelle Talent.'

'I've just done the father. They're typing his statement up now.'

Sergeant Cochran nodded. 'She's only sixteen, you know.'

'And the medical report?'

'It's been done.'

'I know that. But was it *conclusive*?'

'Yes, sir.'

'Good. We're nearly through, so.'

The woman shrugged.

He strode into the room and dumped a buff file on the table, right on the place where Shell's imaginary card with the word 'right' had lain. He sat down and pattered his fingertips on the top. 'Grand,' he said. 'Let's get cracking. Tape on.'

The woman reached up to a shelf and started a recorder. Shell heard the soft hiss as it wound from one spool to another. The man leaned back in his chair and waited. Then he cleared his throat and spoke a time, a date, a place. Then his name, Superintendent Garda Dermot Molloy. He pattered his fingertips again.

'*Your* name, now,' he said. 'Can you confirm it? Just for the tape?'

Shell lifted her gaze to his. His eyes were like razor blades. She looked away, nodded.

'Can you say that louder?'

She pulled at the fluff on her old jumper.

'Sorry? Didn't catch.'

His words were in her head, hunting around, prising out her thoughts.

'I'm Michelle,' she whispered. 'Like you said.'

'Good.' He got something from his pocket: a packet of cigarettes. He tapped it on the file then opened it.

'Mind if I smoke, Michelle?'

She shook her head.

'Perhaps you'd like one too?' He offered her the packet, jostling the fags around. 'I was younger than you when I started. Molloy's the name, Michelle. Just call me Molloy.'

She looked at him again. He was smiling. Or at least, the corners of his lips were turned up. The skin around his eyes was hard and flat.

She shook her head. *No. Not from you.*

'You've had a baby, haven't you, Michelle?'

She started. The word 'baby' seemed odd coming from him, robbed of its small, sweet grace. She swallowed and looked at her lap.

Molloy tapped the file. 'It's in here. In note form. Your father's told us everything.'

Dad? Everything? So he's known all along? She thought of him over the past weeks, staring at her, then at the floor, frowning, acting as if in a dream.

'His statement's being typed up as we speak,' Molloy continued. 'Know what it will be then, Michelle?'

She shook her head.

'It will be fact. Provable, undeniable fact.' He lit his cigarette and exhaled, blowing three wavering rings across the table. They hung between them and rose, breaking up as they swelled out. 'Facts are funny things, Michelle,' he mused. 'There's gossip, rumour, suspicion. Then there's fact. Facts are the business we're in here. We're the gardaí and we're here to get the facts. If people lie to us – or don't tell us the facts – know what happens?'

'No,' she whispered.

'They go to jail, Michelle.'

'Jail?'

'Jail. Without fail. Pass me the ashtray, Cochran.'

The woman reached up to the shelf and brought down a tin ashtray crammed with dog-ends. Molloy tapped away some ash.

'So, tell me, Michelle. Just say yes. Or nod. You did have a baby, didn't you?'

Shell nodded. Her eyes filled. She struggled to squeeze the tears back, but they wouldn't go.

'Miss Talent nods,' Molloy intoned to the tape. 'A babby,' he said, as if trying out the finer possibilities of the word. The Bs collided, rough and harsh. 'A babby that you didn't want. Isn't that so?'

He might as well have pulled a knife. *Didn't. Want.* Two stab wounds below her ribs. Shell thought of how she'd wanted amenorrhoea instead. Then of how she'd planned to get the boat over for the abortion.

Then of the black plastic bin-liner, the white-grey cord, the gunk, with Jimmy washing it away, so that under it appeared the glass-blue eyes and button nose, the minute hands and veins.

She shook her head.

'Miss Talent shakes her head. So you agree: you didn't want it?'

She shook her head again. She started rocking on her chair. The air in the room pressed on her lungs like lead. The rocking grew harder. *The tracery of veins, the smooth, cool scalp, hairless and helpless.*

'Say it, Michelle. Say it. You didn't want it, did you?'

The smoke was in her face. The words seeped into her skull, mocking her. She rocked, shuddering. The tape spool hissed.

'All you have to do is say it. Then we'll leave you be.'

She closed her eyes. She was St Peter at the Tribunal. The cock was about to crow. He was on the verge of denying Jesus. If the cock would only crow before she spoke, she'd pass the trial. The prediction wouldn't come true. SAY IT, SAY IT. *Don't say a word, Shell.* Molloy's words and Dad's, fighting in close combat. She panted, her hands pressed to her eardrums. It was worse than childbirth.

'Say it, Miss Talent. You'll feel better for it. They always do.'

She opened her eyes. The competing voices screamed in her head but she disobeyed them. She spoke. Not the words the man wanted. Her own. The words nearly killed her, breaking her apart, but she said them. 'I loved my baby,' she sobbed. 'I loved her. Loved her.'

The words crashed about the room, like toppling chairs. She was head down, arms splayed on the table. The file was prised from under her. The tape was turned off.

Somewhere in another world, a door closed.

Thirty-four

Later.

Molloy and Cochran were talking in whispers.

She'd been in the field by the ring of stones. Now she was back in the room with the window of frosted glass. She could hear rain gusting against it and the man and woman by the door, muttering. She did not raise her head from the table. They didn't realize she could hear.

She listened.

'She's confused, sir.'

'No. I think I know her game, Cochran.'

'What?'

'She wanted a girl. That's what she wanted.'

'You mean—?'

'She's in denial. It came out a boy and she couldn't face it.'

'But—'

'So she kills it. I knew it. All along.' Molloy's voice, low, staccato.

'Knew what, sir?'

'That she's the one. The father's lying.'

'Lying?'

'Lying to protect her. I can always tell.'

It's me they're talking about.

Shell raised her head. The man and woman looked up towards her.

'Michelle,' the woman said. 'Can I get you something? A cup of tea? Water?'

'No,' she said.

'Do you want to see your father?'

'No.' Her voice sounded loud in the tiny room. The last person she wanted to see was Dad. 'No,' she repeated, softer. 'I'm all right.'

'Good.'

'I want to make a statement.' She nodded towards the woman.

'You do?'

'Yes. I want to make a statement to *you.*'

The man's nostrils twitched; his lips flickered from Shell to the woman. He looked at his watch. 'I'll give you twenty minutes. I want this wrapped up by the day's end.'

He left the room, closing the door behind him.

'Are you sure you're ready to talk, Michelle?' Sergeant Cochran said.

'Yes.'

'Will it be the truth?'

Shell nodded. 'The truth.'

Sergeant Cochran put the tape back on. She stated the names, the dates and the times.

The ghost-hiss filled the room.

The wind chased itself around the outer walls.

Shell began to speak.

She started with the body book, how she'd stolen it from the mobile library. The sentences came, one after another, as if she were reading a script that she'd learned by heart. The words were dull and quiet, with no gloss to them. It might have been another time, another place, another person: somebody else's story. She only cried when she got to the bit about Jimmy cutting the grey-white cord. She remembered now what the body book had said: you were supposed to clamp it in two places and cut it in between. Jimmy hadn't done that. She'd forgotten to tell him. *Is that what went wrong? Is that why the baby died? Or was she dead already?* She finished with the ring of stones in the back field.

Sergeant Cochran didn't interrupt. After Shell stopped, the ghost-hiss came back into the room along with the moans of the wind.

'I've just a couple more questions, Michelle,' Sergeant Cochran said after a spell. 'Can you answer them, do you think?'

Shell nodded.

'Where was your father in all this?'

'He was in Cork. As far as I know.'

'In Cork?'

'He goes in during the week to do the collections.'

'Collections?'

'For charity.'

'I see.' The woman looked nonplussed. She didn't see. 'You mean he wasn't there?'

'No, miss. He wasn't there. I didn't tell him. It was just me, Jimmy and Trix. The three of us.'

'And you buried the baby in the field?'

'Yes. In the middle of the field. The field behind the house.'

'So how did it end up in the cave, Shell? The cave down on Goat Island?'

Shell looked up. 'The cave?' she said.

'That's right. You said you knew the place?'

Shell nodded. Haggerty's Hellhole. The Abattoir. She shivered. *We'd tie them up and leave them there to the mercy of the waves.*

'How did it get there? Did you put it there?'

'No. As far as I know, the baby's still in the field. Unless—'

'Unless what?'

Shell's voice dropped. 'Unless somebody dug it up. And put the stones back. And the earth. Just as they were.' She felt the table lurching, the knots in the wooden surface swinging around. She shut her eyes and swallowed. *But who would want to do that?* She shook her head and opened her eyes. *Not Jimmy. Not Trix. No.*

'So that's your story?'

Shell nodded.

'One last question, Michelle.' The woman clasped her hands on the table and leaned forward. 'Who was the baby's father?'

A vice closed on Shell's throat. Declan was drinking in the night bars of Manhattan. He was chasing the break of day down with the pints. *You're in a class of your own, Shell,* he said, his eyes laughing. The barley stalk went *swish-swish* over her belly, then he was face-down in a cowpat. Sergeant Cochran was waiting. It was none of her business.

'Nobody,' she replied.

'Nobody?'

Shell shook her head.

'That's not possible, Shell. There are no virgin births these days. Not so far as I'm aware.'

'Nobody important, so.'

'Is that all you've to say?'

Shell nodded. 'Yes.'

Sergeant Cochran sighed. She switched off the tape. She sat back, casting her hand over the machine. 'Is this the truth, Michelle?'

'The truth?' Shell smiled, remembering one of Mam's songs from the carol book:

This is the truth, sent from above,
The truth of God, the God of love;
Therefore don't turn me from your door,
But harken all, both rich and poor.

The sweet sadness was in the notes, with her mam's eyes far away as she sang them, looking out of the window, over the fields, and Christmas was everywhere in the house with the sound of her voice. Perhaps Molloy was right. You did feel better when you spoke.

'Yes,' Shell said. 'It's the truth.'

Sergeant Cochran put her hands on the table and rubbed her knuckles. Her eyes were cool and sad beneath the spiky hair. 'You *say* it's the truth,' she sighed. 'But it doesn't make sense.' She shook her head. 'You know what Superintendent Molloy's going to say?'

'No.'

'He's going to say: it doesn't accord with the *facts*.'

Thirty-five

The door opened. The man of facts returned, brandishing a typed statement.

'It's from your father,' Molloy said, needling her with his eyes. He folded the paper in half and put it in his jacket pocket.

Sergeant Cochran leaned over and whispered something to him.

Shell stood up and turned away. Nobody stopped her. She stepped towards the pane of frosted glass. She ran her hand over its reticulations, imagining the storm-tossed day that lay beyond. The whispers went on, fierce and urgent. She heard the tape being rewound, the ghost-hiss again, then her own words, sounding lighter, disembodied; higher-pitched than how she thought she sounded. The thin reediness of her voice was like straw, something the slightest breeze could blow away. She wanted to block her ears off, but in this tiny room, there was no escape.

'Come back here, Miss Talent.' Molloy's voice was piercing, a metallic hook.

She sat back on the chair. Slowly she looked up at

him. His mouth was open and frozen, the upper lip stretched off to the left, so that she could see a large front tooth, a small tip of tongue. She averted her eyes.

'Bollocks,' he said. His fist crashed onto the tabletop. 'Bloody bollocks, isn't it?'

She drew in her breath.

'Well? Isn't it?'

She let out her breath. 'No.' But it was so quietly said, he didn't hear.

'You expect me to believe this crap?'

She squeezed shut her eyes.

'Babies being delivered by little brothers? Little sisters making cots from old boxes? Babies being buried in back fields? Miss Talent. You know, I know. It beggars belief.' He thumped the table again. 'Top marks, Miss Talent, for fiction. Bottom marks, Miss Talent, for truth.'

He sat back. *Tut-tipper-tup* his tongue went against his teeth. He gave an elaborate sigh. Sergeant Cochran sat at his side, but by now she'd dropped off the edge of the scene, an irrelevance.

'The facts, Miss Talent. I want the facts.' He tapped his fingernails on the tabletop, accordion-like. He retrieved the typed statement from his breast pocket. Gingerly, he unfolded it on the table, making the page lie straight. A minute ticked by. He did not move. 'I'm not a patient man,' he observed in a confessional-box hiss. 'Sergeant Cochran here will tell you. You'd better wake up, young lady, if you don't want me to *really* lose my temper. Because it's not a pretty sight, is it, Sergeant Cochran?'

His voice grew louder.

'I have here three versions of events. First, I have solid evidence: the baby found in the cave, along with the doctor's report on how it met its death. Second, I have this' – he tapped the statement – 'the version that your father's given us. And third, I have that' – he brushed his hand against the tape machine – '*your* story. Now listen, Michelle. Number one version is true. Nobody can deny it. A dead baby was found this morning by a woman walking her dog on the strand. The dog went sniffing into the cave and wouldn't come when called. So she went in – and found, in a carrycot, skimpily clad – a baby. Stone dead from cold. She called the gardaí. When we got there we confirmed what she found. The pathologist is still preparing his report. But there is no doubt in his mind that the baby was born recently and was brought there by a person or persons unknown, and cruelly left there to die. Brutally, deliberately exposed to the elements. Do you know about exposure, Miss Talent?'

'No,' Shell whispered.

'I'm told they did it in Roman times. And in China. Who knows where else? Exposure is a way to kill a child as sure as dashing out its brains. Or smothering it with a pillow. Or plunging a knife into its heart. But exposure, Michelle, is the coward's way of killing. The person maybe thinks it's not as bad as actively murdering the thing. Let the cold do the trick, they think, and I'll have nothing on my conscience. But the child, Michelle. See it from the child's point of view. It suffers more. Just think how that little babby felt, alone in that strange, damp cave. With the sound of the tide, ebbing and flowing outside. The cold in its fingertips. Think how it must have cried, Miss Talent, cried as hard as its little lungs could manage. But no good. All to no good. Think, Miss Talent, think. Then tell me the truth.'

Shell sat in her chair, her gullet frozen, mesmerized. Haggerty's Hellhole. The encrusted black walls. The cold sand and stones. The groan of the wind in the hidden crevices. The tiny white flesh, wriggling to keep warm. A terrible place to die. Voices, loud and demented, rang in her head: *Brightly shone the moon that night, though the frost was cruel.*

'That's right, Michelle. You're seeing sense now, aren't you?'

She could feel his thoughts, moving inside her brain, shifting, restless, hurting her skull. He wanted her to say she did it. Why not say it? What did it matter? Her baby was dead, her insides were dead, everything was dead.

'Mr Molloy,' she said. She swallowed.

He leaned forward eagerly. 'Yes, Michelle?' he coaxed.

'Mr Molloy,' she repeated. She shut her eyes and breathed out. 'I *didn't* do it.'

He acted as if she'd said nothing. 'Was it the crying you couldn't stand?' he pursued. 'Was that it, Michelle? The crying? Was that why you put the babby away in the dark place with the thick rock walls? So you couldn't hear the crying any more?'

She opened her eyes. 'The crying?' she muttered.

She shook her head and bit her lip. 'The crying?' That was just it. 'My baby – my baby *never* cried. Not once. I never heard her cry. Never. I only ever heard her cry in here.' She put a hand to her head. 'In my thoughts. In here she cried. She's crying still. But out there – no, she never cried.'

Shell rested her elbows on the table and pressed her knuckles to her eyes, so that her lids streaked yellow. She could hear the man opposite breathing in and out through his nostrils. Like the sound of the tide outside, rumbling back and forth. The Abattoir. Dead meat hanging from hooks. *This cave, Shell. It's a hellhole. Like the whole of Ireland.* The baby cried for its mother and the waves didn't listen. The Angelus bell pounded, drowning out the sound.

'I've never heard of a baby that didn't cry,' Molloy hissed. His mouth was right by her ear.

'I've told you. She didn't cry. Because she was dead. I didn't realize. Not at first. But she was dead from the start. She came out that way.'

'I know the baby's dead, Michelle. You don't need to tell me that. I've seen it. You haven't. D'you know what death looks like, Michelle?'

Shell took her fists from her eyes and stared at the statement on the table. *I, Joseph Mortimer Talent of Coolbar Road, County Cork, state that the following is the truth . . .*

'Do you, Michelle? Because it isn't pretty. The skin goes funny. The body starts to smell—'

Shell was back with Mam at the laying-out, with the waxen face and the yellow hands clasping the milk-white rosary. She put her hands over her ears. 'No.'

'You listen to me, young woman. You just listen.'

'No.'

'Listen. Death is final, Michelle. Murder is a mortal sin. And your baby – for once and for all – was not a girl, but a *boy*.'

Shell got to her feet. She had her hands over her ears. She was the bird caught by the sparrowhawk. She opened her mouth to scream but no sound came out. She stood in the room of frosted glass and silently screeched. *The tracery of veins. The dark, encrusted walls.* Then the dead arose and appeared unto many. Two pale spots of light flickered on the peeling wall, hovering: the souls of the departed. Mam and baby Rosie had come together, not to haunt her but to save her. As they bobbed on the corner of her vision, she knew she was safe. Their angel wings shone around her. The man would never get her.

Thirty-six

The noiseless screaming worked where the truth hadn't.

Molloy went away.

Sergeant Cochran took her back to the room with the clear glass. She sat her down, and put an arm around her shoulders. She said kind things, but Shell didn't listen. She left to fetch a cup of tea.

The moment she'd gone, Shell went over to the window. The whirling atoms in her brain slowed down. She breathed in deep. The layers of aerials and chimneypots below faded away to early dark. The wind was loud but the rain had passed. She leaned her forehead on the pane and thought of Christmas: the presents she'd wrapped for Trix and Jimmy. *Where are they now? Who's looking after them?* She could see a necklace of yellow dots, swinging far away: fairy lights along the harbour front. Something settled deep inside. *I loved my baby. Loved her.* She hummed another of Mam's songs, the one she'd sung while washing out the woollens:

*'Green grows the lily
And soft falls the dew.
Sad was my heart
When I parted from you . . .'*

It was about a lover who hadn't proved true, a song for the man with an eye on the main chance. A man like Declan, maybe. A smooth operator. Would he be homesick now, on the Manhattan streets? She doubted it. He'd landed her in this mess and he didn't even know it. He'd be having a roaring all-night party of a time. She blew on the glass, and dabbed her finger in the patch of breath, drawing a star with five sharp points. *You're like a ewe on heat, Shell. You're like a bull with its horns stuck.*

The door opened. Sergeant Cochran re-entered with a mug and put it on the table. Shell glanced round from the window, then glanced out again, ignoring her.

'Michelle,' Sergeant Cochran said. 'Your father wants to see you.'

She drew on the window again. A crooked Christmas tree. She hoped its needles were sharp.

'Did you hear me?'

Beyond the chain of fairy lights, the dark ocean shifted. 'Yes.'

'It's your right, Michelle. To have him with you, as your parent. You should have had him with you all along, but Superintendent Molloy insisted we question you separately. As two suspects.'

'Are you going to let me go?' Shell whispered.

Sergeant Cochran paused. 'In your case, I should think so. You're a minor, according to the law. But we've to know where to send you. We can't send you home on your own.'

'But I *want* to go home,' Shell said. 'With Jimmy. And Trix.' She put a hand up to the cold glass. 'Where are they? What's happened to them?'

'Jimmy and Trix are still with the Duggans, as far as we know.'

'Can't I fetch them and go home then?'

'Shell. Your father's going to be held tonight. You see, he's confessed.'

'Confessed? To what?'

'To killing your baby.'

Don't you say anything, Shell. Don't you say a word. The typed statement. The facts. She made an 'O' with her lips and blew on the glass. But this time she didn't draw a picture. She watched the patch of mist shrink to the size of a coin, her heart seesawing. He confessed. He lied. Confessed. Lied.

'I've told you,' she said, teeth gritted. 'Nobody killed my baby. My baby died. Jimmy, Trix and me, we buried her. In the field.' She turned round. 'My baby was a girl.'

Sergeant Cochran sighed. 'That's what you say, Michelle. I know. But against that we have what your father's told us. And what we found in the cave.'

'I don't want to see him,' Shell said. 'I don't care what he says. I just want to go home. I want to see Trix. And Jimmy.'

There was a knock on the door. A guard put his

head round and Sergeant Cochran went over to talk to him. They whispered.

'It seems you've a visitor, Michelle,' Sergeant Cochran said out loud. 'Somebody who insists on seeing you.'

'Dad, is it?'

'No. A Father Rose.'

Shell's jaw dropped. *Father Rose?* Her fingers fluttered to her neck, then ran through her hair. *Father Rose?* She thought of the Virgin Mary at prayer, curtains billowing from the window, bright streaks of light, the beating of holy wings. She stumbled to the table, eyes wide.

'Will you see him?'

'I – I—' She flopped on the chair.

'Is that a yes?'

The shepherds crouched in the field, sore afraid. She grabbed the tea. 'Yes,' she said. 'S'pose.'

Sergeant Cochran left to fetch him.

The room was silent, the wind hushed.

She drank the tea without knowing what she did.

He'd know by now. Know everything. He'd think her the worst of sinners, lost beyond recall, fallen into the molten core. *The car's not so much dead as resting, Shell. God bless. Did you come here to pray, Shell? Or just to shelter? From the rain?* He'd walk through the door and she'd dissolve to nothing with the shame. She wished she'd refused to see him. She wished it was Dad instead. She wished—

The door opened. It was him.

He'd jeans on, and a brown leather jacket with a

216

lambswool collar, hanging loose. He'd the same unshaven look he always had when the day grew late.

'Shell,' he said. 'There you are.' It was as if he'd just come across her in the village, outside McGraths' shop maybe, or on a stroll by the strand. He looked more ordinary than she remembered. He turned to the guard who'd accompanied him. 'I'd prefer to see her on my own.'

The guard looked uncertain.

'One on one,' Father Rose said. He tapped his watch. 'Five minutes? You can stay outside the door, if you want.' The guard hesitated. 'It is her *right*. That's if she asks for it. Do you ask for it, Shell?'

'I do, Father.'

'There. She does.'

The guard shrugged, then retreated. 'Five minutes,' he said. 'And I'm right outside.'

The door closed. Father Rose took the other chair, plunged his hands in his jacket pockets and blew through pursed lips. Then he chuckled.

'I've no idea of the law, Shell. I just made that last bit up.'

'Did you?'

'I did. For my sins.' He smiled.

Shell smiled back.

'I do know one thing. They can't hold you overnight. Not at your age. I asked my lawyer friend in Dublin.'

'So they'll let me go?'

'Unless they're going to charge you. Are they going to charge you?'

'Dunno. They keep saying things. That man. Molloy—' Her lips wobbled, she shuddered.

'What? What has he done?'

'Nothing. Only I told him the truth. And he won't believe me. It's Dad they believe,' she whispered. 'I think they're going to charge *him*. You see – he's confessed.'

'My God.' Father Rose put his hands flat on the table, the fingers splayed. 'What's been going on? What's the man done?'

Shell pushed the mug of tea to one side and put her hands on the table, one over the other, cupped and calm. 'Father Rose,' she said. She swallowed. *It has been six months since my last confession and these are my sins.* 'It wasn't like that. It wasn't Dad. It wasn't what everyone thinks. There's been a muddle. I don't understand what's going on.'

'Try me, Shell. Maybe together we'll un-muddle it.'

She took a deep breath. In two more minutes, she'd told him, like she'd told the tape: the body book, the birth, the burial. But it was easier this time without the ghost-hiss and the narrow eyes watching. He listened. As she spoke, his hands moved across the table towards hers.

'My God,' he whispered when she'd finished. His right hand landed on hers. 'We let you down. Every last one of us in Coolbar. We let you down.' His left hand went to his forehead, covering his eyes. 'The other day, in the church,' he said. 'Did you come to ask my help?'

'I – I—'

'You did, didn't you? And I didn't see. With the two eyes in my head, I didn't see. I was too caught up in my own stupid state of grace. Or lack of it.' He paused, his head shaking back and forth. 'One last question, Shell. I have to ask this.' His voice dropped. 'Who was the father?'

Shell bit her lip.

'Who was he, Shell? He wasn't somebody close to you?'

'Close?'

'I mean, somebody in Coolbar – or even closer?'

Shell thought of Declan on the aeroplane, chasing the day to another continent, downing the free drinks, gazing at clouds. *We're still only blow-ins, Shell.* 'No, Father Rose,' she whispered. 'Nobody in Coolbar. Least not now. It was—' But somehow the name 'Declan Ronan' wouldn't come, just as Bridie's name hadn't come that other time when they'd been fighting.

Father Rose's brows knitted. 'Whoever he is, he doesn't deserve your—'

The door opened. 'Time's up,' the guard called.

Father Rose stood up. He reached a hand over to Shell's shoulder and sighed. 'Don't worry for now, Shell. Let's get you out of here. Mrs Duggan's a bed made up for you, she said to tell you. You hang on and I'll sort Molloy out. I'll be back to fetch you sooner than soon. Don't worry.'

The door closed behind him. A hollow opened in the space he'd left, silent and chill, as if the room had turned from a kitchen to a larder. She went to the window again and saw the last of the day, a thin line, on the horizon. She rubbed out her earlier pictures.

> *Then a poor man came in sight*
> *Gathering winter fuel . . .*

Jimmy was at the piano, finding the notes, the bells were jingling and the reindeer flying. The fleece collar, the shining leather, and lights along the harbour. The hollow filled. *Don't worry.* She blew on the glass a last time and drew a chimney, with smoke curling from it.

When the door opened again, she saw he'd kept his promise. On his lips was a smile of triumph. The fleece collar was turned up, ready for outdoors, the night drive was in his tread. 'Shell,' he said. 'We're out of here. Hurry. Jezebel's getting cold with the waiting.'

Thirty-seven

They drove the coast road. The low glimmer receded out to sea. Father Rose asked no more questions. Shell shuffled in the seat, looking at the debris. Licence. Crisp packets. No chewing-gum wrappers. She sniffed.

'You're smoking again, Father,' she said. 'I can tell.'

'How?'

'You're off the gum. Plus I can smell.'

He groaned. 'Trust you to find me out. There's a pack in the glove compartment. Would you ever pass me one?'

She opened the compartment up and rooted around. She found a stray stick of chewing gum and a packet of Majors, the same brand Declan had smoked.

'Can I?' she said, pointing to the fags, with a sly face.

'No, Shell!'

'Only joking. I'll stick to the hard stuff.'

She brandished the gum and unwrapped it. Then she passed him a fag. He lit it with the car lighter. She chewed and he puffed in companionable silence. They turned off the main road. The eyes of a feral cat glittered from the hedgerow. An owl flapped up from a branch. There was no traffic. The night was dark and quiet. The headlamps picked out a few yards of tarmacadam gliding around them, warm and round, a halo. Beyond, thin wraiths of dark trees loomed, their branches reaching towards them. On either side, the silent presence of the hedgerows brooded. It was home, Coolbar. She felt as if she'd been away a lifetime.

'Father,' she said, 'can we stop at the house?'

'Your place? Isn't it locked up?'

'There's a spare key under the mat. I've Christmas presents to fetch. For Jimmy and Trix. Besides—'

'Besides what?'

She crossed her hands on her lap, looked down. 'Could I show you the grave? Where I buried her? Could I?' He turned towards her, slowed the car. 'I thought maybe you'd bless it. Bless the grave. Bless her. Would you, Father?' Her voice shrank to a pinprick.

'Don't worry, Shell.' His hand was on her arm. 'Of course we'll stop.' He climbed the hill towards Duggans' farm, but turned off earlier, for Shell's house. 'There's a torch on the back seat,' he said.

They got out and she let them in. She switched on every last light. The house was frozen, echoless. He waited in the kitchen while she fetched the presents out from under her bed. Together they cleared the remains of the dinner she'd made that day. The plates, half full, were where they'd been abandoned on the table.

When they'd finished clearing, Father Rose went

over to the piano and touched the wood. He opened the lid and gazed at the ivory keys.

'Do you play?' he asked.

'No. D'you?'

'Not much. My brother Michael was the musical one.' He played a chord. It filled the empty house, breaking the hush. 'C major,' he said. 'That much I do remember.' The notes lingered, a trail of hope.

''S nice,' smiled Shell. 'Jimmy plays too. He's Mam's touch.'

Father Rose closed the piano and took the torch. 'You lead the way, Shell.'

They walked out into the back field and climbed the hill. The mud sucked at their shoes. Shell nearly slipped. He put a hand on her arm to save her and left it there. Even in the dark, she'd no trouble finding the place. It was like a magnet, pulling her to itself. He picked out the ring of stones with the torchlight. They'd not been disturbed since they were lain. She was sure of it now.

'This is it,' she whispered. 'Untouched. I knew she was safe. Knew it.'

She dropped to her haunches, hugging herself in the torch's penumbra. The night breeze curled around her, murmuring from the copse. Father Rose's hand was crossing the air. Through her tears she heard his voice, like a shimmering C-major chord. *May perpetual light shine on her, o Lord,* he prayed. An owl hooted, as if to join in the prayer. *And grant unto her eternal rest.*

Thirty-eight

He drove over the hill and dropped her off at the Duggans' farm. The three dogs sniffed round her and Mrs Duggan came to the door, the smell of a fry behind her.

'Shell,' she said, reaching out and hugging her. 'What are those stupid guards saying about you? Come in and have your tea.'

The kitchen was warm and bright. From above, stairs pounded. Trix and Jimmy burst in. 'Shell!' Trix yelped, flinging herself forward. Jimmy punched the air, then himself.

'Shush,' Mrs Duggan smiled. 'You'll wake him.' She nodded over towards the hot press. A pram was parked there. 'He's only just gone off.'

It was Mrs Duggan's new baby boy, the one with the hole in his heart. Shell had forgotten all about him. Her heart stopped. *My God.* The hustle around her froze.

On the range, fat spat.

Everybody was staring at her. *Child murderer.*

She took a step towards the pram. *I'll look at the*

covers, not the face. It was expected of her, she could tell. *I'll say, 'He's only gorgeous, Mrs Duggan,' and that'll be that. I'll never have to look again. Never.* She glanced down and examined the plastic animals dangling from the bar, a lemon blanket with pinprick holes in the weave. At the bottom, a knitted rabbit was strewn in a heap. Trix barged up.

'He's blowing a bubble again,' she shouted. 'With the spit.'

'Whisht, Trix,' Shell said. But too late. She'd already looked. There was the glob, collapsing on a wrinkled lip. He'd chipmunk cheeks and dark, quivering lids. Mam's lines of music rose and fell, floating before her. The baby in the cave, the baby in the field. The living and the dead. His body was full of tiny movement, where hers had been still. She gripped the handle of the pram. She righted the rabbit. 'He's sound, Mrs Duggan,' she managed.

Rest. Eternal. The warmth of the press, the sheets of tiredness, the smell of the food. The sound was breaking up, the colours had smudged. The bottom was surely falling from the world. *Light per-petuuuu-aaal,* the owl yodelled. Somebody was holding her, taking her up the stairs. 'He's sound, Mrs Duggan, sound,' she said. The baby was in her arms and she was walking, struggling. Up the hill, to the copse. The owl was gone, the trees were bare. Blankets came up and over her. At last. She put the baby down, somewhere in the great field, among the swinging barley.

Thirty-nine

They let her stay in bed all Christmas. In her mind, strange things moved. The face of Molloy. The ring of stones. The baby in the cave. Twelve rounds of the Angelus. Blackberries winking in the hedge. *Did you come to shelter or to pray, Shell? To pray or shelter?* The white reticulations of frosted glass, the wraith-like trees. *Confess, lie, kiss or die, Miss Talent. Wa-ai-ai-t,* the owl said, flapping in a bowl of light. *I hate this place.* Declan waving a valediction from the wound-down window.

Trix was in the bed with her, drawing snakes on her back that turned into Christmas streamers. Jimmy bounded on the camp-bed by the window in his socks of yellow and green. *We didn't need the twine, Shell. It came out on its own. Honest.* They gave her a present, wrapped up in red paper. A bottle of scent called *Je Reviens,* the one Mam used to wear on Sundays.

She fell asleep again. Lie. Confess. Die. Dad in a cell. No Christmas lights, only a naked bulb. He'd lied to save her, she knew that now. He was back in the kitchen, looking past her shoulder, with Sergeant Liskard waiting. Eyes frozen, locked into the face at the piano. Mam. Her eyes steady, commanding. The bars, the frosted glass, the iron door. No whiskey in the piano where he was now. What would he do without it?

She woke up. Mrs Duggan had come in with breakfast. She laid her baby down near Shell while she made up Jimmy's camp-bed. A hush was in the room. The small mouth champed at nothing. Shell put her little finger to his fist. His fingers curled around it like a lock to a key.

Outside, a miracle started. Snowflakes floated past her window, a rarity in Ireland's south.

'Are you well enough to get up?' Mrs Duggan said.

Shell nodded. 'Think so.' She emerged from the bedclothes and tiptoed over to the casement. She could see through the white specks over to the copse, and beyond that, a heavy sky with more snow in it.

'Where's Dad?' she asked.

'He's still inside, at the station. The gardaí are holding him.'

'Mrs Duggan,' she whispered. 'I've to see him. I've to talk to him.'

'Yes, Shell,' Mrs Duggan said. 'You can go tomorrow. When you're stronger. Father Rose will take you.' She joined Shell at the window, rubbing her hand around baby Padraig's back as she spoke, winding him. 'Your dad rang yesterday, Shell. While you were sleeping. He said they'd given him some turkey with the white sauce. And to tell you Happy Christmas.'

The youngest Duggan dog streaked out across the yard, chasing a stray flake with its snout and jaws. No sound came from him. The world was a silent film.

Happy Christmas, Shell. The snow gusted upwards as if somebody'd put every whole thing into a souvenir scene in a glass bauble and shaken it upside down. Between the flakes came a flash of a happier past. Dad in the white spray, standing by her in the breakers, his pants rolled up. They were jumping together when the waves tipped, making snow from foam. Mam walked past, her cardigan knotted round her middle, skirting the tide. She stooped to splash them with her hand, then ran away laughing when Dad kicked squalls of water up and over her. Shell, only small, clung to his forearm to keep her balance. She stamped and hopped and hooted Dad's old rhyme, *Ice cream, a penny a lump, the more you eat the more you jump.* Mam ran back in, lassoing them both with seaweed ribbons.

Mrs Duggan's hand was on her shoulder. The snow settled on the car roof. 'You'll be a mother again, Shell,' she whispered. 'One day. You wait and see.'

Forty

'Dad,' she said. 'It's me.'

Father Rose had taken her to the garda station in Castlerock, but she hadn't wanted him in the visiting room with her. She and Dad were alone in the room with frosted glass. A guard stood outside the door. She could hardly bear to look. Her father across from her was a shrunken man, withered and slight. His face was thin, grey-tinged. His hand drifted over the table towards her, hovering like a butterfly.

'Shell. My own girl.' His lips were trembling. She could swear a tear glistened in his eye before he dropped his face. With a finger he traced a figure of eight upon the table, in and out.

'You all right, Dad?'

He shrugged.

'Mrs Duggan said you rang. For Christmas.'

'Did I?'

She nodded. 'They gave you dinner, Dad, didn't they? Turkey? With the sauce?'

He frowned, then smiled, drawing a wider loop. 'I'd a grand time in here, Shell. We'd a party.'

'But Dad, you needn't be here at all.'

He shook his head as if she'd never understand.

'Why did you confess?' she burst out. 'Why?'

The shape he traced changed to sharp zigzags.

'Dad. Why? Answer me.'

'The baby's dead, Shell. Thanks be to God. No need to talk about it now. But I'd to explain it to them. I'd to explain it somehow.'

'But Dad, the baby in the cave. You don't understand. It wasn't mine.'

He didn't seem to hear. His finger went up-down on the knots of wood.

'Mine's above in the field,' she nearly shouted.

He looked up, smiled grimly. 'I did this to you, Shell. God forgive me. I did all this. I knew all along the state you were in.'

'You didn't, Dad. Did you?' She remembered how he'd stared at her that time in the midst of the rosary.

'I tried not to see, but I knew. I did all this.'

'You didn't, Dad. You didn't do anything.'

He blocked off his ears. 'I'm a mortal sinner. The worst kind.' He thumped his fist to his breast three times as if he were up at the church pulpit, leading a round of the confession: *Through my fault, through my fault, through my own most grievous fault.* 'It was hell, hell in a glass. You don't have to die to go to hell, Shell. Any devil will take you there, any time. And the devil that came was the image of her. Moira. My Moira. Out of my league, living or dead. She'd never let you catch her. And when I woke, I didn't know where I was. The house was empty. The morning come. You, Trix, Jimmy, gone. Moira. All gone.'

His teeth chattered. He wasn't making any sense.

'You cold, Dad?'

'Cold? No, I'm roasted, Shell. Roasting.' His teeth chattered harder.

'Will I get some help? You're not well—'

'Shush! Don't draw them on us. Don't, Shell.'

'Dad.' She leaned forward. She put a hand on his to stop the shaky tracing. 'You must retract. Retract the confession. Father Rose says so. It's not true. You must tell them.'

He shook her hand off his. His forefinger tapped the wood, then moved in a wavering line from one end of the table to the other. 'I confessed in my mind, before the Almighty. But it won't save me, Shell. Not now. It's too late.' He made the sign of the cross, but halfway through his shivering hand stopped, then dropped back to the tabletop. 'When I was young,' he mused, 'I'd a mighty appetite for the venal sins.' He chuckled and began again on the tracing, bringing his face down, inches from a particular knot of wood at the table's edge. 'The fairs. The lads. The pints. We'd a mighty appetite then.' He cackled and wheezed to himself as if on his own.

The guard opened the door. 'Time's up,' he announced.

Shell sighed, relieved. 'Dad. I've to go.'

He looked up. 'When did *you* get here?'

'I've been here fifteen minutes, Dad. We've been talking.'

'Talking?'

231

'Don't you remember? About your confession? Your statement to the guards?'

He grimaced, more like himself. 'Oh, that.'

'Retract it, Dad. It's not true.'

He smiled. In the redness of his eyes, she saw him harden. 'I had it coming, Shell. Your man, Molloy: he's the right idea.'

She stood up. 'Trix and Jimmy send their love,' she said. It was a lie, but she said it anyway.

He gazed blearily, as if he'd never heard of them. Then he nodded. 'Tell them to be good,' he said. He wrapped his hands around himself, holding onto the fabric of his shirt at either elbow as if he were strait-jacketed. He bit hard into his bottom lip.

'I'll tell them, Dad. Bye now.'

'You off? Already?'

'I'll be back soon. Promise.'

But Dad beckoned her over. Reluctantly, she approached him. He was whispering something.

'What, Dad?'

'When you come next. If you can manage it,' he hissed, grabbing her elbow.

'What?'

'Just a drop. A miniature would do.'

'Oh. That.' She laughed. 'The *whiskey*, you mean?'

'Shush, Shell!' He looked murderous. She wriggled from his grasp.

'Time's up,' the guard repeated. As he ushered Shell from the room, Dad's hands began thumping the table. He hurled a stream of curses at her back. The noise stopped abruptly when the door shut.

'Don't mind him,' the guard said. 'He doesn't mean it. It's the drink talking. Or rather the lack of it.' He threw a wink and laughed. 'This is the driest Christmas he's had in years, I'd say.'

Shell looked away to the dingy walls of corridor. *Hilarious. Delirious.* Dad married to the drink, not her mam. And for so long now, hardly anybody could remember the man he'd been without it. Jimmy and Trix, never. And for her, it was the time in the breakers; then years of nothing.

Forty-one

Father Rose was waiting at reception. Molloy also was there, immaculate and frowning. He'd arranged to see her again but this time Father Rose would be with her. Molloy led them into his office. They passed other guards, secretaries and a cleaner along the way. Everywhere Molloy walked, a well of silence followed.

His office was bare and bleak, with dingy cabinets of files and wired-glass windows. It smelled of furniture polish. He beckoned them to hard chairs on one side of his sparse desk and sat down on a revolving chair of black leather on the other. He rested his chin on his linked hands.

Shell stared at the lino: speckled reds and blues on grey. The two men spoke. She only half listened. She couldn't get Dad and his butterfly hands out of her mind. *The baby's dead, Shell. Thanks be to God.*

'You've only her word for it,' Molloy was saying, as if she wasn't there.

'We've more than that – haven't we, Shell? She's shown me the place.'

'You mean you believed her?'

'I did. I do.'

'It's baloney. Two babies? In one small place like Coolbar?' The man snorted, like a horse after a tough jump.

'It's the truth. I know it.'

The words went back and forth. In her mind Dad's hands and lips trembled for the whiskey in the piano, the smell of the night-bar, the rattle of the collection boxes. *Don't draw them on us, Shell, don't.* She pictured the main street in Castlerock, where Father Rose had led her earlier, through a morning of Christmas shoppers. The snow had melted, a light fog undulated in the chill air, dimming the lights. The ring of stones had been blessed. They couldn't be un-blessed.

Somebody asked her something.

'What do you think, Shell?' It was Father Rose.

She blinked.

'Could you bear it?' His voice was low.

'Bear what?' she whispered.

'If we disturbed her, Shell? If we dug her up? To prove what you say is true.'

She stared. 'Dug her up?' She shook her head. 'Oh no. We couldn't do that.'

'You see,' Molloy gibed. 'She's lying.'

The ring of stones. The cotton-wool lining. The tracery of veins. They had been blessed.

'I don't want to disturb her. *Please.*'

'We can bury her again, Shell,' Father Rose said. 'In consecrated ground. I can do it.'

Her teeth were gone like Dad's, chattering. 'Must we?'

'Shell, I fear we must.'

They came to the field later. Shell stood near the cairn, looking on from a distance. *What if the baby's not there? What if someone's stolen the body? What if I've been dreaming it all along?* The strange questions darted round her mind like arrows. Four men – Father Rose, Molloy and two uniformed guards – walked up the field. Molloy's face was without expression, his sharp features dividing the wind. *Why do we have to pick up the stones, Dad? Why?* Father Rose was face down, his hands clasped in front him, shoulders hunched. Mrs Duggan was on one side of her, Miss Donoghue, her old school-teacher, on the other. The men stooped at the place, looking downwards. The guards in the uniform started on the soil with trowels. *Now and at the hour of our death, Amen.* Miss Donoghue had her hand on Shell's shoulder. 'It won't take long, Shell,' she said, her voice kindness itself. 'It will be over before you know it.' They hadn't wanted her to watch but she'd insisted. The heavy earth shifted beneath her feet. The trowels started a landslide in her head. The digging stopped, then started again, slower. 'They've found something,' Mrs Duggan said. The two men who were crouched on the hillside paused. One stood up, crossing himself. The dark figure of Molloy dropped down on his haunches, his hands reaching into the hole. The third had got a camera out. In the drab light, she saw a flash, three times over.

When the box came out, she could have sworn she saw Trix's sprig of holly fall from it. She turned her back and stared at the stones in the cairn, heaped in their hundreds, the labour of endless mornings.

'It's over,' Mrs Duggan said. 'Thanks be to God, they've found her. Just as you said, Shell. It's surely over now.'

'Come away now,' Miss Donoghue said. 'We'll leave them to it.'

They led her to a waiting car. She stumbled on a stray stone and looked back a last time. Father Rose's right hand was crossing the empty air. *It's over, Shell.* Whatever about his confession, Dad would go free. Her baby would be reburied. One day soon, the moment would be a memory.

But as she watched, the camera flashed again. And again. One of the men drove some stakes into the ground and ran a yellow tape around it. She saw the silhouette of Father Rose, his hands gesturing, then flying apart. Was he praying? Or protesting?

'What are they doing?' she whispered.

'Come on, Shell. Don't watch. Whatever it is, it's surely only a formality. It's over now.'

But it wasn't.

Father Rose came back to Mrs Duggan's house. He sat at the table, his fists clenched. Strange workings crossed his face.

'Is it over, Father?' Mrs Duggan said as she got the tea things out. 'Have they gone? Will they close the case against Shell?'

Shell fiddled with the biscuits on the flat plate, arranging them in an interlocking pattern. Chocolate, plain, chocolate.

'Will they let Joe go?'

Father Rose picked up a biscuit from the plate. He brought it halfway to his mouth, then put it back. 'I overheard them talking,' he said. 'They called it a crime scene.' He laid the biscuit back higgledy-piggledy on top of the others. Shell returned it to its original place, in the gap between two chocolate ones. 'They've taken the baby away. Under Molloy's orders. For tests, they say.'

Shell thought of sums and essays, exam papers lying face down on the desk, the wall clock ticking in the silent classroom. 'Tests?' she puzzled.

Father Rose nodded. 'To see how she died, they say.'

Her insides knotted. She thought of Jimmy cutting the cord, how'd they'd forgotten to clamp it in the two places as the body book instructed. The biscuits on the plate began to twirl, a brown and cream cart-wheel, chocolate, plain, chocolate.

Miss Donoghue pressed her into a chair. Mrs Duggan put a warm cup into her palms. 'This is turning into a joke,' Miss Donoghue said to nobody in particular. She plumped herself down but didn't touch her tea. 'A bad joke.'

'I've to be down at Goat Island for five,' Father Rose muttered. He got up. 'It will be all right, Shell. It's just a formality. It'll be all right.'

After he left the kitchen grew dim. The baby slept.

Miss Donoghue, Mrs Duggan and herself sat in the half-light, forgetting to turn on the lights. Tests. She saw the grey worm-like cord slithering around the baby and Jimmy with the scissors.

They'd broken up the ring of stones.

When the lads came in, full of noise, Shell vanished upstairs to the quiet of her bed. She got under the covers with her clothes on. She put her two fists to her eyelids to make the patterns happen. *Don't draw them on us, Shell. Don't.* Yellow explosions bobbed, floating downwards like tired clouds. From far away, the phone rang. Voices, exclamations filtered up the stairwell.

She didn't want to know.

Forty-two

In the night she listened to the sing-song breath of Trix by her side and Jimmy over on the camp-bed. She listened out for the first bird of the next day but the blackness was stuck and wouldn't shift. The silence was endless. The pages of *Doyle's A–Z* floated behind her eyelids. The baby was dead. *Thanks be to God, Shell.* The ring of stones was broken and they would say she'd killed it. And maybe she had, because she'd known about the clamping of the cord in two places and hadn't done it right.

But the next day, when she woke up, Trix had her head tucked under her armpit and she knew she hadn't killed her child. Not like Molloy made out. She'd not left her in a freezing cave to die. She'd come out dead like the Duggans' early calf. So what was Molloy doing with the body? And what was the world saying about her? What had the telephone calls of last night been about?

She woke Jimmy up as soon as the house stirred and dispatched him downstairs to eavesdrop on what the Duggans were saying when the children's backs were turned. Later in the morning he reported back to her.

'Did you hear anything?' she asked.

'Nothing.'

'Nothing?'

He shook his head.

'Some spy. You're useless.'

'Mr Duggan's down with the cows. Trix has gone with him to see the calves. And Mrs Duggan's in the kitchen cooking. With the baby. The others are out the yard.'

'So?'

'So. 'S nothing to overhear. Mrs Duggan'd hardly gab to the baby, would she? She wasn't on her own with Mr Duggan for even a minute.'

He'd a look of triumph on him, so she knew he'd found out something. 'Come on. Out with it.'

He drew from behind his back a copy of the local paper. ''S this,' he said. 'Today's. Mr Duggan fetched it from the village first thing. Then I saw him bury it in the fire pile.'

She grabbed it off him. Newsprint blurred then sharpened as she read an article emblazoned across page one. It made no sense. She read it again.

MYSTERY BABIES FOUND DEAD

An unnamed sixteen-year-old girl and her father are being questioned by the Gardaí Síochána in Castlerock, County Cork, in connection with the deaths of two babies whose bodies have been found locally. One was discovered abandoned on a strand on Christmas Eve by a woman walking her dog. The other was dug up yesterday in a field in the vicinity of the girl's house, apparently on the evidence of the girl herself.

Superintendent Garda Dermot Molloy, who is in charge of the investigation, reports that the girl's father is being held in custody pending charges. He has now signed a fresh confession admitting to having killed both babies, who are believed to be twins. While the girl is said to be the twins' mother, the identity of the twins' father is yet to be divulged. 'The case has shocked this tiny community, where nothing of its kind has ever been heard of before,' said Superintendent Molloy. 'Infanticide is a terrible crime in a child-loving nation such as ours. My job is to see that the perpetrators feel the full force of the law.'

A team of top pathologists has arrived from Dublin to examine the babies. 'They will confirm that they are twins and how they died,' says Superintendent Molloy. 'And hopefully close the case.'

The strange words popped out. 'Vicinity'. 'Divulged'. 'Infanticide'. 'Perpetrators'. 'Pathologists'. She let the paper drop to the floor.

'Shell . . .' Jimmy said. 'Is it *you* they're talking about?'

She looked at his narrow white face with the freckles bobbing on it. *'On the evidence of the girl herself.'* She flopped back on her pillow, laughing. God in heaven. *'Both babies, who are believed to be twins.'* Hilarious. Delirious. She laughed some more. Soon she'd a stitch in her side.

'Jimmy,' she gasped. ''S me all right.'

He frowned then smiled, as if he wanted to join the joke but didn't know how.

'Twins!' She hooted, cackling at the ceiling. The laughter clattered round the walls.

'Shush, Shell! Mrs Duggan'll hear downstairs.'

'Don't care if the dead hear. *Twins.*' She almost choked. 'Can you pinch me?'

He pinched her.

'Harder.'

He got a good chunk of flesh on her upper arm and pinched again.

'Did one baby come out, or two, Jimmy?'

'One.'

'Sure?'

'Certain.'

'Swear?'

'I can count, can't I?'

'Can you?'

'I got nine out of ten for my last test, Shell.'

'Twins!' She howled, hugging her side.

'Don't, Shell. Don't laugh any more. Please.'

'They'll find another baby tomorrow. Then it'll be triplets.'

'Shush!'

'It's a pantomime, Jimmy. The case of the Coolbar babies. The next one will turn up in the priests' house.'

She squealed and coughed with streaming eyes. 'OK, Jimmy. I'll not laugh any more.' She swallowed and pressed her lips flat. *Twins*. Tears from the laughing had gone down her cheeks. She brushed them off and got out of bed.

''S not really funny, is it?' Jimmy said.

The baby in the field, the baby in the cave. The tide ebbing and flowing. The dark encrusted walls. Mirth left her like air from a pricked balloon. She shook her head. 'No, Jimmy.' She hunted round for her clothes. ''S not funny at all. It's that Molloy. He's after me.'

'But Shell,' Jimmy said. 'I don't understand.'

'What don't you understand?'

'If you had one baby, where did the other come from?'

'Who knows? Maybe the storks dropped it there.'

Jimmy stuck out his cheek with his tongue, tent-like. 'Huh.'

'Or maybe—'

'Maybe what?'

She didn't reply. Distracted, she pulled on jeans beneath her nightdress and brushed her hair. She sprayed *Je Reviens* behind her ears. Her brain turned over, started to life, then died again, like the engine in Father Rose's car.

'Maybe nothing,' she said. 'God knows, I don't. Jimmy, I've to visit that crazed father of ours and see what he's confessed to this time. D'you want to come?'

'What? To see Dad?' Jimmy's tongue nearly

244

popped through his cheek. His nostrils scrunched up.
'Nah.'

'Can't say I blame you. Now scoot so's I can finish dressing.'

Forty-three

Shell got out her powder-blue bag. She popped into it the miniature bottle of Powers which she'd found sitting forgotten at the back of Mrs Duggan's cupboard. *I'd a mighty appetite for the venal sins. Hell in a glass, Shell.* She'd heard of the DTs. Delirium Tremens. Declan used call them the Detox Terrors. They were the furies from hell, he said, bringing the things you most feared. He said when his uncle had had them he'd imagined snakes of vast proportions had returned to Ireland to torment him. If that's what Dad had, she thought, he'd confess to anything. Quads. Quins. Maybe a drop of whiskey would bring him round.

Rain turned to sleet as she and Mrs Duggan walked up through the town to the garda station. The wind blew the flakes forward and up, into their eyes as they walked up the main street and turned up the hill on the zigzag path. They waited in the draughty reception. The guards dropped in and out, passing her, staring, turning away. *She's the one*, she felt them thinking. *The girl in the headlines. Infanticide. Perpetrator. The force of the law.*

A guard approached, nodding. 'He agrees to see you. If you follow me.'

'Are you sure you don't want me there?' Mrs Duggan said.

Shell shook her head. 'I've to tackle him alone,' she said.

The guard led her down the stairwell, along the corridor to the last door on the left: the room of frosted glass. He showed her in.

'Call me, if you need me,' he instructed. He closed the door and stood outside to wait.

Dad's face was on the table. He didn't move as she drew near.

She turned to check the guard wasn't looking through the glass panel in the door. Then she drew the miniature from her powder-blue bag.

'Dad,' she said, 'I brought you this.' She set it down near his hand, but kept her own fingers around it.

He didn't look up at first. Then an eye fastened on the tiny bottle of lemon-brown. His fingers inched towards it. He stared shiftily around the cell. She pulled it back.

'Dad,' she said, 'I'll let you have it. If.'

'If?' His voice was a croak. 'If what?'

'If you retract your confession. About the twins.'

'*If.*' It was more of a hiss than a word. He shut his eyes. His brows bulged and she could see a vein in his forehead throb. He gave a grim *huh-huh-huh*, the laugh of a fiend. His hand darted at hers.

'Give that here.' He'd snatched it out of her hands before she could stop him.

'Dad! Only if you retract.'

'Retract?' He squeezed the bottle, shook it, turned it upside down. He brought it up to his nose, as if he could smell the whiskey through the glass. His tongue ran round his lips. He held it so hard, she thought the glass would crack.

'Git – behind – me,' he said through clenched teeth. 'Git, git, git.'

His fist pounded the table.

Shell jumped back as if he might explode.

He flung the bottle at the wall. It splashed like urine on the yellow paint.

The glass tinkled on the floor.

Shell froze. The guard didn't hear. The door was solid. 'Dad,' she gasped.

Another mask had come over his face, a look of strange beatitude. It reminded her of the pictures of the martyrs, when they'd arrows piercing their limbs and belly, or nails stuck through their wrists, and they were looking up to the sky in holy rapture.

'Shell,' he said, 'I did it.' He outstretched his arms to her. She'd no choice but to let him hug her. Her stomach shrank. Her mouth curdled. He'd not hugged her in living memory. She smelled his prison mustiness and sour breath. 'My own Shell.'

She wriggled from him as soon as she could. 'Dad. I'm sorry,' she faltered. She fed her hands around the table and sat down. *God in heaven. What devil's got him now?* His eyes settled on hers like calm lakes. 'I didn't mean to tempt you, Dad. Are you cross?'

'Cross?' His right forefinger touched his forehead, then his chest, then his two shoulders. He smiled. 'No.'

'Only you asked for the miniature. Last time.'

'Last time?'

'Don't you remember? When I visited last time?'

He waved a hand. 'All the days seem as one here, Shell. I've my rosary for counting. But time doesn't matter now.'

'You all right, Dad?'

'Never better, Shell. I'm in the hands of the Lord.'

She dropped her voice, leaned forward. 'I'm here to ask you something, Dad. Something important.'

A tiny ripple of annoyance passed over him. 'Nothing's important any more. What is it?'

'Your confession. About killing the babies. You must retract it.'

The annoyance passed. 'Oh, that.' His hand fluttered up, wafting her words away.

'But 's not true, Dad. You didn't kill them.'

'I did, Shell. I killed them all right.' He smote his chest. *Through my fault, through my fault, through my own most grievous fault.* 'Your man Molloy. He's the right idea.'

'But Dad, you didn't. You were in Cork. Doing the collections. Remember?'

'The collections?' His pupils went black and dull. They left Shell's gaze and landed on the wall, on the rectangle of light the window framed there. 'The collections?' His hand stroked the tabletop. 'After that night, the night of Holy Saturday, Shell, and the waking up in an empty house, I'd go to the city all right. I'd learned my lesson. Up and down the streets, walking, rattling the tin can. Doing the collections. Like you say. But then I'd spend it all, down at the harbour. You should see the place. It's a desolation, Shell, down by the river harbour. The women there, all kinds, all ages. Some only your age, Shell. Like that schoolfriend of yours, Bridie. As bold and brash as her. And I found a nice lady there. Peggy, she was called. A man has to have an outlet, Shell. A man like myself. But she charged me through the nose.'

She remembered the lipstick on the collars. She opened her mouth to say something. Dad and his Mary Magdalenes. It was beyond belief. No sound came out.

'It was the pink dress, Shell.'

'The pink dress?' She thought of it, folded beneath her bed. She was back at the dressing table, looking into the panel of mirrors, with the images of herself receding back into the world of spirits. *Mam.*

'Yourself wearing it. The pink dress.' He covered his eyes with his hands, digging them in like gouges. 'I should have got rid of it along with the rest. But I couldn't, Shell. It was the dress she wore the night she said she'd marry me. She'd never worn it since. It was unpolluted by the years.'

'The years?'

'The years of the drinking.'

His eyes glistened in the dingy room.

'I don't understand, Dad,' Shell whispered. 'About the drink – what's the draw of it?'

'Ah, Shell. It's not the first sip, or the second. But the third. It hums in the head. It smiles in the belly. It's like wings opening in the soul.' His gaze had an ocean of sadness in it. His voice dropped. 'After she died, Shell, everything of hers made me ill. Ill from the memory of her, watching me from the sickbed, reproaching me. She never said a word. But her eyes, Shell. They said it all. The years. The lies. The sessions. And the time I hit her. It was only the once, but I'd failed her. From that bad night to the day she died. Her eyes following me, staring up from the bottom of the pint glass. Her clothes, her records, her music books, I burned them all. You, Jimmy and Trix were at school when I did it. I had a mighty bonfire in the back field. The flames licked up to the sky, taller than me. I threw them on and watched them burn. The skirts, the slips, the pants. The lipsticks, the scarves, the Sunday hats. Gone in seconds. And the whiskey warming me as the ash flew. And the smell of her, going up in smoke. But not the pink dress. Not that.'

'You kept it back?' Shell whispered.

He nodded, eyes shut, far away. 'She danced with me in it the night she said she'd marry me. Coolbar'd won the hurling league and there was celebrating in the village. Stack's was heaving. I bought her a drink of port and lemon and I asked her. The band was tuning up, the notes like fingernails scratching the board. She took a sip. And she looked me in the eye and said *Yes*. Yes, Shell. We danced away the night. I twisted her round, rocking and rolling. Faster and faster. The walls whirling. People shouting. We danced so quick we nearly rose off the ground, with a crowd around us, cheering, clapping. There was nobody but us that night. Me, her. Her face as I swung her, Shell. Her lips pink like the dress. Her eyes like suns beaming. She was happy, Shell. I'd her two hands in mine, crossed over, wrist over wrist. I'd asked her to marry me and she'd said yes. We were happy. She. Me. Her hair spinning like ribbons. There was nobody else in the room that night. Nobody.'

His eyes were fixed on the wall where the whiskey had splashed.

'I loved your mam, Shell.'

The light in the room dimmed, as if a cloud had passed the sun. In Shell's mind, the snowflakes were falling upwards, as if going back to the place from which they'd come. Mam was leaving them with silent steps. She and Dad were on their own. The bleakness returned, heavy and still.

Dad's eyes met hers. 'I loved her, Shell.' The wreck of a life was in his face.

'I know, Dad,' Shell said. She was back at the foaming waves, kicking and romping. *Ice cream, a penny a lump.* 'I know.' A tear slid down her cheek. She reached her hand out towards his. 'But Dad, the *confession*—'

The door behind her opened. The guard came into the room. 'Molloy's orders,' he said. 'I'm sorry. Time's up.'

Dad stood up. He waved a hand over his face and shook his head. He turned away and walked to the window of frosted glass. She saw his fingers there, going over the reticulations. Up, down, side to side.

'Bye now, Shell,' he said.

The guard waited, coughed.

'Bye, Dad.' His fingers were like the butterflies again, up and down the pane of glass. She saw him nod slightly. He was miles away.

She'd no choice but to go.

Forty-four

The next morning Trix, Jimmy and Shell sat in a heap on the bed cutting up the stories. They'd mushroomed overnight and there was no hiding them in the fire pile. Dead babies littered the counterpane. *Superintendent Garda Dermot Molloy asserts . . . A source close to the family suggests . . .* Trix gathered the shreds up and tossed them over the three of them like confetti. Shell shut her eyes. Somewhere in a Cork laboratory, the babies were side by side on a slab. A man in a mask was doing things to them. She saw syringes, scissors, needles. Thread, tubes, tissues. Four eyes of button-glass blue.

Mrs Duggan had told them not to leave the house. The village was in an uproar.

The sky was clear and still. A low winter sun toppled into the room over the bedclothes.

Shell belly-flopped over the morsels of newsprint.

'Draw me something, Trix. Please. Draw something on my back.'

'What?'

'Anything. Anything you like.'

She felt Trix's fingers going round her lower back then climbing up between her shoulder blades.

'What is it?' Trix challenged. 'Guess.'

'Dunno.'

'*Guess.*'

'A tree?'

'No.'

'Snakes?'

'No. 'S more than that.'

'Dunno. What?'

'It's the sea. And fishes. And Superintendent Molloy. He's here.' Shell felt Trix's thumbnail on the small of the back. 'At the bottom. Drowned. They're nibbling him up.' Her fingers went up to the shoulder blades. 'And here's the sky. And here's Rosie, sprouting her wings.'

A door slammed below: Mrs Duggan, back from shopping in town.

Shell went downstairs to help her put away the messages. As she entered the kitchen, Mrs Duggan looked up and grimaced. Four carriers of supermarket goods overflowed on the floor.

'That Mrs McGrath,' Mrs Duggan snapped. 'I've had it with her.'

'What's she done?'

'It's not what she's done. It's what she's saying. She's like poison gas.'

A source close to the family.

'What's she saying, so?'

Mrs Duggan picked up a bag and unloaded washing powder, detergent, sponges.

'It's not fit to repeat.'

The pack of sponges fell to the floor. Shell picked them up. She opened the cupboard under the sink and put them away. 'What? What does Mrs McGrath say?'

'You sure you want to know?'

Shell nodded.

'She's boasting she spotted your trouble, ages back.'

Shell remembered the gloating, angry eyes in the dim-lit shop and the way she'd lurched at her father's old coat.

'But it's worse, Shell. She claims to know who the father is. She claims to have seen you together. In "compromising circumstances", as she puts it.'

Shell froze. *Naked in Duggans' field. Naked in the waves. Naked in the cave. When did the old crow spot us? When?* 'Really, Mrs Duggan?' She kept her voice calm and even. 'Who does she say she saw?'

Mrs Duggan put a joint of gammon in the fridge and slammed the door shut. 'Who? Huh! You won't believe. You just won't believe.'

Declan?

Mrs Duggan leaned against the fridge. 'It'd make a dog laugh.'

'Who, Mrs Duggan?'

'Father Rose. Of all people.'

Shell stared, confounded.

'"Compromising circumstances"? I ask you. She saw him giving you a spin once. On a wet day.'

'Father *Rose*?' Shell pretended to laugh. She turned away. *The slur on him. The slur on his name. The slur on his cloth.* It was like accusing Jesus of dallying with the cripple girl.

'Shell,' Mrs Duggan said, 'I don't like to pry. But don't you think . . .'

'What?'

'If only to stop the gossip. Don't you think you should say who the real father was?'

Shell stared. *Shell smells of flea balls . . .*

'I know you're trying to protect him. But Shell, think about it. Does he deserve it?'

Shell's mouth dropped open. *No, Mrs Duggan. He doesn't.* She shook her head instead and retreated up the stairs. She hounded Trix and Jimmy from the room. She cleared the newspaper shreds. She made the beds. It was lunch time and there were few about: a good time for slipping down to the village if she wanted. She could make herself invisible. The blinds would be down over McGraths', the CLOSED sign hanging on the door. She'd be halfway up the main street with nobody seeing her. Somebody might emerge from Stack's pub but she'd avert her face, and turn up the tree-lined avenue. The Ronans' big pink house would be looming at the top. She'd knock on the door.

Sorry, Mrs Ronan, can I just come in and tell you about your granddaughter, the one I buried the other day.

Mr Ronan, I just thought I'd pop round to let you know. Your son, Declan. He's the man. Not Father Rose.

Good man, young Seamus. How's school? Did you know you were nearly an uncle once?

She'd knock again. The pink house would sit

impassive and demure. She'd look at the tall hedgerows Mr Ronan had shaved into a riot of topiary. Castletops, mushroom-shaped trees, a horse's head. His daft garden leprechauns would dot the path and peep from the rockery. She remembered Declan saying how he kept swapping the fellows round when his dad wasn't looking. And how his dad always joked that the leprechauns came alive and moved of their own accord. In the chill air the place would be laughing at her. Somewhere over the western ocean Declan would be bursting his sides, like the sly fellow with the red cap peeping through the pampas grass. *Toodletits. You're in a class of your own, Shell.*

There'd be no reply. Mr Ronan would be away in Cork City doing his fancy job at the tax office. Mrs Ronan would be down the golf club with the Castlerock ladies. Even if the door had opened, they wouldn't have believed her. Their son with all the points for college, going with the likes of *her*?

She remembered Declan waving from the car window, a valediction. *Over the hills and faraway.* They were back in Duggans' field and he was tickling her with the ear of barley. *Declan and me, a private club.* He'd made her promise not to tell and she'd kept her word. But he was a man with an eye for the main chance. A smooth operator, if ever there was one. *If the gossip about Father Rose gets any worse,* she decided, *I'll tell on you, Declan. Then. Only then.*

Forty-five

That Sunday, they didn't want her to go to church, but she insisted. Mrs Duggan squashed them into the car, Shell in front, crammed up with Trix, the three boys and the baby squashed in the back. Mr Duggan walked on ahead. Shell had her crocheted bag of powder-blue slung over her wrist. She'd *Je Reviens* sprayed on her wrists and lobes. She'd not been to church in months.

They drew up outside. The bell was ringing. All Coolbar was there.

'Are you sure you want to go in?' Mrs Duggan said as the younger ones piled out. 'You'll get a few stares.'

'I'm sure,' Shell said. *If they stare, I'll stare back,* she thought. She imagined staring at Mrs McGrath so hard that her hat exploded into smithereens and the feather turned into a squawking duck. Mrs Fallon's grey rinse turned turquoise and she passed flat out on her back. Nora Canterville's home-made consommé, clear as a newborn soul, gushed from her mouth, the onion shreds dribbling from her lips.

As she entered, the harmonium music went awry.

The place fell silent. Mrs Duggan led her down the aisle to the front. She saw a hundred fork-prong eyes, noses twitching, hands fluttering: like small animals salivating. Then she heard the chattering: like starlings on a pylon. *Don't care.* She took her place and straightened her back. She scrutinized her nails. She investigated the contents of her powder-blue bag. *Don't give a monkey's.*

The music resumed with the entrance hymn. They stood. Father Carroll emerged from the side door. No sign of Father Rose. She felt his eyes latch onto her, so she averted her gaze to the statue of St Theresa. She sucked in her lips. The Mass began.

The three kings drew close to the stable, the time of their epiphany.

At Communion, Theresa Sheehy came up close in the queue, nudging her in the side with an elbow and pointing at her own belly. Shell raised her eyes to heaven and showed her teeth. She turned her head and met the eyes of Mrs McGrath. The woman glanced and looked away, her nose wrinkling up. Shell swallowed the host and sat down. The Quinns passed by, the last in the queue, all excepting Bridie. Of her there was no sign. She remembered what Theresa Sheehy'd told her. *They say she's off to her aunt in Kilbran. I'd say she's run away to America. With Declan.*

After Mass was ended, she slid past the gossiping crowds and caught up with Mrs Quinn on the road outside. She was walking away from the church fast, yanking two of her younger children along by the crooks of their arms.

'Mrs Quinn,' she called.

Bridie's mother turned and glared. 'Shell Talent. What do *you* want?'

The woman had a livid maroon scarf over her head, but her dark hair flopped out, bedraggled and damp. The young ones ran on up the hill. She looked at Shell, then looked away as if Shell didn't exist. She made as if to go.

'Mrs Quinn!' Shell touched the woman's arm. 'I just wanted to ask – how's Bridie? I heard she's been away.'

The woman looked as if she'd spit. 'You've surely heard. She's up in Kilbran with my sister May.'

'She's still there?'

'She is. They've a thriving business. Bridie's been gone since the summer, helping out with the B & Bs. It's work experience.'

'Is she well?'

Mrs Quinn sniffed. 'Quite well. We saw her over Christmas. We all went up to May's when school was finished, just for the change. And Bridie was keeping well, thank you. Never better.' The woman scowled. She drew her arm away from Shell's touch and tightened the scarf around her. 'We sent her there to get her away from the likes of you.'

'Me?'

'You're a bad influence, Michelle Talent. A bad influence on her and everyone in Coolbar. If I'd known the kind of things you two got up to. If I'd known earlier, I'd have—'

'What, Mrs Quinn?'

The woman said nothing. Her eyes bored into Shell's as if she was a fiend incarnate. Then they filled suddenly and she turned away. For a moment she stood with her back to Shell, staring at the ground as if searching for something she couldn't find. Her shoulders were hunched, her hands in her raincoat pockets. 'I've the joint to get on,' she muttered and walked away, almost stumbling. She retreated up the hill, just as Bridie had that time with her see-through umbrella. Shell stared after her, confused. Other churchgoers spilled through the gate along the pavement, jostling past her, murmuring things. She moved along the street and climbed into the Duggans' car and waited. Rain had come and gone during the Mass and sprinkled the windows. People passed, squinting in, taking a look, as if she were a prize exhibit. She pouched her lips together and gulped like a goldfish, eyes shut. She remembered Declan imitating her as she sang that time in church. It seemed an age ago. *Don't care.*

So much for how she'd imagined Bridie, hitching across America, bent on stardom. Or living it up with Declan in New York. Bridie of the 34D bra-cup. *Hickory, dickory, Bridie Quinn.* But Theresa Sheehy had been wrong. And she'd lied about the dance she'd said she seen her at in August. Bridie and Declan had never rocked and rolled like two cats on a case. It had all been false. Bridie was in Kilbran. Shell was glad. She'd be making the beds, gassing with the guests. Turning the toast, getting up the fries. She'd be bored as hell. She'd be sneaking out at night-times and be down on the main road, thumbing, with stolen notes in her bag, along with fags and gum. Lorries would hammer past. She'd be on the road to the nearest nightspot. Anywhere but Kilbran. A grey old market town if ever there was one, with no life to the place. Hardly the best place for a B & B, let alone in the middle of winter.

She frowned. Jimmy was by the yew tree, fighting with someone. She couldn't see who. Mrs McGrath was by the church gate, gossiping to Mrs Fallon. She was sure she could lip-read 'Father Rose' at the end of every sentence. Bridie faded from her mind. She was back in the garda station again. *Was it somebody in Coolbar, Shell?* Father Rose was saying. *In Coolbar, or even closer?* Then Dad, his hands quivering. *It goes back to that night. The waking up in an empty house. It was the pink dress, Shell. I'm a mortal sinner.*

She opened her eyes. *My God.* A terrible truth dawned. The village thought it was Father Rose. And Father Rose thought it was Dad. And Dad himself? *I did it, Shell. It was my doing.* He was by her bed again, groping at the sheets, his eyes half open, half shut. *Moira, my Moira.* The night of Holy Saturday. She realized then. He'd have woken up on Easter Sunday morning with no memory of the night before, to find himself in her bed. And what would he have thought?

Oh, you're drunk, you're drunk, you silly old fool,
If indeed you cannot see
Sure, that's a fine white sow
That my mother sent to me.

A lad from Jimmy's class was staring in, sticking out his tongue. She stared at him without seeing him and he scampered off. Soon afterwards, the car door opened. Jimmy got in along with Liam and John Duggan. Trix followed, huddling up close to Shell in the front.

Then Mrs Duggan. She strapped baby Padraig into his car seat, came around to the front and got in. 'There you are.' She patted Shell's arm. 'Are you all right?'

'Yes, Mrs Duggan. Fine.' *You don't have to die to go to hell, Shell. Any fool will take you there.*

Mrs Duggan sighed and turned on the ignition. 'Was that a Mass, Shell?' she said in a low voice. 'Or feeding time at the zoo?'

Forty-six

Shell visited Dad the next day, one more time, in hopes of relieving the torment in his mind. Maybe that way he'd retract. He shuffled into the room of frosted glass, taut and fidgety, and sat opposite her, glowering. The guard left them.

'The night of Holy Saturday, Dad,' she whispered.

'Shut it, Shell.'

'*Dad.*'

He grabbed her cuff. 'Couldn't you have brought a miniature. Just a drop. Like last time? Couldn't you?'

He was in a desperate mood. His eyes were like dirty coins, his lips had yellow cracks in them, his hair was dark with grease.

'You didn't want it last time, Dad. Remember?'

He snarled.

'You threw it at the wall.'

He drummed his fingers on the table. 'Don't remember. Don't remember anything. Christ, I'd murder one.'

'Dad. You must remember. You told me about it yourself. The night of Holy Saturday. You woke up in

265

an empty house, you said. Trix, Jimmy and me. We were gone, you said.'

He stood up, twitching. His fingers on the right hand scratched his left upper arm. He went to the window of frosted glass. He stood there going *scratch-scratch* as if he'd fleas. He stared at the milk-white glass as if he could see through.

'Remember, Dad? D'you remember?'

'Shut it, Shell. You're a broken record.'

She got up and walked towards him. '*Dad.*'

'Get away from me, Shell. I'm in no mood for talking.'

'D'you remember the pink dress?'

His toes were tapping now, like he'd a case of magic dancing powder in his shoes. 'Jesus. Would you ever stop?'

'The pink dress, Dad. The one you didn't burn.'

'Stop it, Shell.'

She put a hand out to stop the scratching. 'It wasn't you, Dad.'

He'd shaken her off. His hands were over his ears.

'It wasn't you,' she said louder. 'The night of Holy Saturday. It wasn't you.'

His eyes were screwed up tight, his head was jerking. He'd be speaking in tongues next. He'd be writhing on the floor.

'Dad.' He opened his eyes and she thought he was going to scream. But he didn't. The toes stopped tapping. The fingers stopped scratching. The head stopped jerking.

'What did you just say?' he whispered.

'It wasn't you, Dad.'

'The night of Holy Saturday?'

She shook her head. *The tomb was sealed, the world was quiet.* 'Nothing happened.' Mam's fingers fluttered past her face as she reached the high note of her song, the swift, pure cry. His eyes half shut, half open. His appalling nakedness. *Moira. Don't turn away, lovey, turn back to me.* 'You thought I was her, didn't you?'

His hands were at his throat. 'Her eyes, Shell. Following me everywhere.'

'You came in, Dad. Confused with the drink. *Moira,* you kept saying. You remember?'

He shook his head. 'It's a closed book.'

'It was the dress confused you, Dad.'

'The dress?'

'I'd fallen asleep in it. The pink dress.'

'God forgive me,' he whispered.

'You were like a blind man, walking in your sleep, at the foot of the bed, feeling around. But Mam woke me up. She came in a dream and woke me up. So I rolled out of bed. And you fell in. You passed out. I left you there. And that was all.'

He kneaded the skin on his gullet. 'All?'

'All.'

'Nothing – nothing more?' His fingers rose and plucked at his lips. She saw the words drifting across his eyes. *All. Nothing. All.*

'Nothing.'

'You mean it?'

'Nothing. Honest to God.'

'I didn't – touch you?'

267

'You were too far gone, Dad.'

'Praise be to God.' His nostrils quivered. He shut his eyes, nodded. He made the sign of the cross. Then one eye opened. 'I've only your word for it,' he said.

'It's true, Dad. Would I lie about a thing like that?'

'Thanks be. You're certain, Shell?'

'Certain, Dad. As God is my witness.'

A long silence fell. Shell went back to her chair.

'I loved your mam, Shell.' It was almost a squeak.

'I know, Dad.'

'The pink dress wasn't the only thing I kept.'

'No?'

'No. There was this too.' He reached into his jacket pocket. 'They tried to take it from me, but I wouldn't let them.' He held out the golden wedding band, the one Shell had seen him take from Mam's hand at the laying-out. 'They said I should leave it on her, bury her with it. But I couldn't. I took it off her before they covered her over. It wouldn't go on my littlest finger, Shell. So dainty were her hands. Slim, from all the piano-playing. The way she'd fly over the notes, up and down, like tiny birds. So I kept it in my pocket. All this time, the same pocket, by the breast. Everywhere I went. Even in here. They tried to take it from me. But I wouldn't let them.'

She stared. She thought he'd pawned it for a drink and she'd been wrong. 'Has she haunted you, Dad? Like she's haunted me?'

He nodded. 'Every second of every day, Shell. The eyes reproaching me. Telling me to pack in the drink.'

He retook his seat and put the ring down on the

knot of wood. He folded his arms, grabbing the elbows straitjacket-wise. 'The moment they let me out, Shell, I'll be down the pub. I know it. I'd sooner go to jail for the rest of my life. If it's the same to you. I've been a wretched father to you all.'

'But Dad. The baby on the strand. 'S nothing to do with us.'

'So you say.'

'Don't you believe me, Dad?'

'Dunno. Dunno any more what's true.'

'Dad, it's true. I swear it. On Mam's ring.' She put her hand briefly down on it. 'See.'

He grunted. 'So you say.'

'Will you retract, Dad? For my sake, if not yours?'

He shrugged.

'Will you? Please?'

He picked up the ring and looked through it, straight at Shell. His pupils dilated. He put it back in his pocket with a strange smile. 'Maybe. If.'

'If?'

'If you tell me. Who the *real* father is.'

On the word 'real' he thumped the table. Shell jumped. The Detox Terrors were back. A fury was in his face.

'Dad! Does it matter?'

He thumped the table again. 'Of course it matters. I'll punch him to pulp. I'll thrash him to pigsmeat. I'll—' His fingers crackled. His eyes squeezed up hard. 'Tell – me – who – he – is,' he minced.

'Dad!'

'Tell me the name of that blackguard and I'll—'

'Dad. You can't thrash him. He's miles away. Gone.'

'I'll follow him. I'll shred him. The bastard.'

'You won't.'

'I'll have his hide.'

'I won't tell you, so.'

'You'd better.' He spat the words out like lava from a volcano. But a sly glint was in his eye.

She flopped back in her chair. His eyes narrowed. *Declan. Time's up. Toodlepip.* 'OK, Dad. I'll tell you,' she sighed. 'On one condition.'

'Jesus. Women. I'm the one driving this bargain. What condition?'

'You retract. And tell no one who the father is.'

He cursed again. 'That's two conditions. You'd drive a sane man to distraction.' He snorted. 'All right. I promise. I'll tell no one. But I'll have his hide, you'll see.'

'And you'll retract?'

He snarled, then nodded.

'It was Declan, Dad. Declan Ronan.' *Your secret's out now, Declan.* The words fell out like a suit of old clothes. Dad would tell nobody at first. But then, as soon as he'd a few pints down him, he'd tell Tom Stack, who'd tell Mr McGrath, who'd tell Mrs McGrath, who'd tell everybody in Coolbar. Mr and Mrs Ronan would be the last to know.

'Declan Ronan?' Dad gasped.

She nodded.

'The *altar* boy?'

She nodded again.

'The la-di-dah Ronans? Declan?'

'Yes.'

'So that's why he shot off to America. The monkey. I'll kill him.'

'No! He didn't know then. About me. About the – baby.'

'The baby?' His voice changed. 'Wasn't it twins then, like they said?'

'No, Dad. Course not.'

'A boy so. Like they said?'

'No, Dad. A girl. Like I said.'

'A girl?'

'A little girl. Tiny. With blue eyes, Dad. And she came out dead.'

'Dead?'

'Trix, Jimmy and me. We buried her in the field.'

His hands covered his eyes. His shoulders shook. *My God. The old fool's crying.* 'Ah, Shell. Forgive me. I *did* do this to you. I knew all along and I pretended not to know.'

'You'll retract now, Dad?'

He nodded. 'Anything, Shell. Anything you say.' His head went back down on the table. 'Your mam's own grandchild, Shell. A girl, you say? Was she like her, Shell? Was she?'

Shell got to her feet. 'She was, Dad. A little.' Her chair screeched across the floor. Dead with the blue eyes shining. Like suns, beaming. She grabbed the edge of the table, hard. The room was filming over. She didn't trust him. She'd better get him to retract fast while the going was good. She called out for the guard.

The guard came in and sent for Molloy. Molloy

was out. Sergeant Cochran arrived instead. She put on the tape and the ghost-hiss filled the room. He stumbled and floundered, then got out the words. *I, Joseph Mortimer Talent, of Coolbar Road* . . . In two more minutes, his confession was retracted.

Forty-seven

Shell thought that once he'd retracted the case would be closed. But a day passed and nothing happened. Then another and another. Dad was still detained.

Father Rose called one evening later that week. The boys and Trix were playing the card game Forty-five at the kitchen table.

'Hearts are up,' Liam called.

Shell, Mrs Duggan and Father Rose watched as the others played.

'You reneged,' Jimmy shouted at Trix.

'Did not.'

'You did. You should've put the ace down last time.'

''S my ace. I can put it down when I like. Isn't that right, Father Rose?'

'Don't ask me. I'm not familiar with the rules. We don't play Forty-five where I come from. What do you say, Shell?'

'If Liam led with a heart and you had one, Trix, you should have put it down.'

Trix pretended she didn't hear. Jimmy made a face

like a demented gorilla, then he rolled his eyes. Shell winked at him. The game went on.

Father Rose touched Mrs Duggan's arm, indicating the fireplace at the other end of the room. 'Can we three talk?' he said in a low voice. She nodded. They removed themselves out of earshot. Mrs Duggan fetched Father Rose a whiskey and ushered him and Shell onto two chairs.

'Any news? Will they let Joe out soon?' Mrs Duggan asked.

'No sign of it. I saw Molloy today. He insists the original confession stands.'

'That man. He's a dog with a bone.'

'He says he's waiting for the pathologists' report.'

'Is it due out soon?'

'Any day.' He dropped his voice. 'Don't tell anyone, but Sergeant Cochran slipped me something in advance.' He looked from one to the other. 'Apparently the babies have different blood groups.'

Shell's hand was on her throat. She could hardly breathe.

'One's an A. The other's an O,' Father Rose said.

'What – does that mean?' Shell faltered.

'I'm not sure. But maybe good news.'

'You'd think twins would be the same blood group,' Mrs Duggan mused. 'I'm an O. So are we all in this house. D'you know what you are, Shell?'

Shell shrugged. 'Dunno. Dunno what a blood group is.' She watched Father Rose as he took a sip of his whiskey. 'Did they find out why my baby died?' she whispered.

He shook his head. 'Sorry, Shell. Sergeant Cochran said that was all she knew.' He jerked his head towards the drawn curtains. 'It's a circus out there,' he said. 'There's press everywhere. Stack's pub is buzzing. And the gardaí are going round door-to-door. Father Carroll's announced a special Mass.'

'What for?'

'For the repose the two babies' souls.'

'Can I go?'

Father Rose raised an eyebrow. 'I'd sooner send you to the wolves.'

'But I *want* to go.'

Mrs Duggan's hand landed on her shoulder. 'We'll go together, Shell. All of us together. Like last Sunday. Will you be officiating, Father?'

'No. I've my Goat Island duties that day.'

'But surely—'

Father Rose shook his head. 'Father Carroll won't hear of it.'

Mrs Duggan raised a brow. Father Rose shook his head and raised up a palm. Mrs Duggan sighed. She went to quell an insurrection at the card game.

Father Rose settled himself in the chair. He took a long, slow sip of his whiskey. Shell kneaded a ball of fluff on her jumper. The fire crackled. *A and O. The two babies side by side on the slab.*

'It's been a terrible time for you, Shell.'

She shrugged.

'Mrs Duggan told me how you went in and got your father to retract.'

She nodded.

'How did you manage it?'

She looked up. Father Rose was not looking at her, but into his drink. *It's not the first sip, Shell, or the second. But the third.*

'I told him who the real father was,' she whispered.

Father Rose nodded. 'I see.' He got up from the chair and leaned against the mantelpiece, glass in hand, staring into the flames. 'On that subject, there's something I wanted to show you, Shell. If I may.'

She hunched her shoulders. 'What?'

Father Rose downed the whiskey. He put the glass up on the shelf and rummaged through an inner pocket. He pulled out an old envelope. 'Nora Canterville, our housekeeper, found this the other day. When she was sorting through the hymn books. She gave it to Father Carroll, who gave it to me.'

'What is it?'

'Take a look.' He passed it over. It was a shopping list in her writing. *Eggs. Back bacon. Pan-loaf. Oxtail soup. Stock cubes.* The list went on. Beneath was more of her scrawl, wilder, in a blunt pencil. *Sorry, Bridie. Honest to God. Didn't know you were going with him.* And on the other side, crammed in letters not her own: *He'd make a dog sick in those robes. You can have him Shell plus bra.*

She was at the Good Friday Stations again. Bridie's nostrils were flaring. She was showing her gums. Spite was in her eye. Simon of Cyrene had lifted up the back part of the cross. She remembered the note being written, how Dad had nearly caught them at it and her plunging it in the hymnal. The words swam before her. *Sorry. Dog. Sick. God.* Father Rose was waiting, saying nothing. *Please, let me die. Now.*

'The girl in the note, Bridie,' Father Rose said at last. 'She's the girl I saw you fighting with that day, isn't she? The day we drove over the coast road?'

Shell nodded, miserable. 'Bridie Quinn. We were friends. Until—'

'Until what?'

She couldn't answer.

'And who was it Bridie said would make a dog sick, Shell? Will you tell me that?'

Shell bit her lip. *Declan, your secret's out now.*

'Won't you?'

She swallowed. 'You know, Father, don't you?' *Face down in a cowpat.*

'I think I can guess. He's "not in Coolbar now", I think you said?'

She nodded.

'He's gone abroad? To America, maybe?'

She nodded again.

'And was he the father, Shell?'

'Yes.' Her voice was barely audible.

She looked at the note and longed to scrunch it up. The words *in those robes* were a torment. 'Is – is this note why Father Carroll won't let you say the Mass?' she stammered. *He thinks it's you, doesn't he? He thinks what Mrs McGrath thinks. What they all think.*

'He's his reasons, Shell. Good reasons, probably.' Father Rose reached for the whiskey he'd laid on the mantel, forgetting he'd already finished it. He looked into the diamond zigzags of the cut glass as if the shape of the rest of his life was etched there. Then he looked up. His tired lids lifted. A soft gleam found its way to her. He smiled.

'Father,' Shell said, 'tell Father Carroll. Tell him the truth.' She passed him the note. 'Please.'

He passed it back. It was like a daft card nobody wanted, the joker of the pack. 'No, Shell. You keep it. Father Carroll didn't pay it much attention, don't you worry. And doesn't a letter belong to its author, in the eyes of the law?'

'I wouldn't know.'

'It does. So the note's yours. And your friend Bridie's, I suppose.'

'She's not my friend. Not any more. She's not spoken to me since the summer. And then she went away.'

'But she's back now, isn't she?'

'Is she?' Shell looked up, confused.

'I saw her, I'm sure, recently.'

'Never. Where?'

'She was walking up the coast road, on her own. Thumbing a lift in the dark.'

Shell frowned. Mrs Quinn was before her, talking. *She's in Kilbran, with her Auntie May. Helping with the B & Bs.* 'When was that, Father?'

Father Rose considered. 'Let me see. I was on my way back from Goat Island after an evening Mass. Not this week, last. Just before Christmas so. I slowed right down to give her a spin, but when she saw who it was she shook her head and waved me on.' He grinned. 'She probably didn't fancy a ride with a priest. Not to mention the cut of my car.' He replaced the glass on the mantelpiece.

'You're *sure* it was her?'

'Certain. She's the kind of face you don't forget. You should call over and see if you can't make it up.'

Caterwauls and table-thumps rebounded across the room. 'Forty-five,' yelled Trix from the table. ''S my game.'

'Cheat!' hooted Jimmy. 'You reneged again.'

The cards at the other end of the room flew through the air like manna from heaven. Father Rose laughed and shook his head. His hand waved vaguely in the air. 'Isn't the world a mad fandango? Isn't it, Shell?'

Forty-eight

Not just Coolbar, but all Ireland waited for the doctors' verdict. Parliamentarians met in the Dáil in heated conclave. The airwaves crackled with lamentations. *Only look at the state of a country where such a thing could happen,* a woman TD bewailed. A tribunal of inquiry was called for on national news. Coolbar was in a state of siege.

But within the Duggans' house there was a hush at the centre of the storm. No one came near them. The radio, TV and telephone were unplugged.

The weekend came and went. On Monday, John, Liam, Jimmy and Trix went back to school for the new term. They didn't want to go, but Shell and Mrs Duggan made them. Dispatching them from her car into the chill January air, Mrs Duggan warned, 'If anyone alludes to you-know-what, just look blank.'

Inside Shell's head there was a chattering going on like birdsong. You heard it if you listened for it, not if you didn't. When the house went quiet on Monday morning, the chattering got so loud she thought her brains would burst.

He'd make a dog sick in those robes.

An A and an O.

Haggerty's Hellhole. It's where all the girls go to fornicate.

She was walking up the coast road, on her own. Just before Christmas.

When Jimmy came home from school, he'd a cut lip and bruised cheekbone.

'What happened?' asked Shell.

''S that Dan Foley and Rory Quinn. They jumped me in the break.'

'Jumped you?'

'Jumped me and pumped me. They wanted the facts.'

'The facts?' She thought of Molloy with his tidy shirt and needling eyes.

'The gory facts. About you and the baby.'

'What did you tell them?'

'I said you'd had triplets, one, two, three. And the third was hidden up Miss Donoghue's ass.'

'Jimmy! She's been nice to us of late.'

He shoved his swollen cheek out, tent-like. 'So.'

'Are you friends with Rory Quinn?' she asked.

'No. We're enemies. He's a filthy toerag.'

'Could you do me a favour? Tomorrow?'

'What?'

'Could you ask him where his sister is? Bridie? And when he last saw her?'

The next day he came home with a face like a whipped pup. 'Did what you asked, Shell, coming out of school. And this is what I got.' He held up a swollen finger. The nail was hanging off.

'What? Rory Quinn did *that*?' Shell was appalled.

Jimmy nodded. 'I asked him, about Bridie. And instead of answering he knocked me on the ground. He stamped on my finger with his big boot.'

'Just for asking?'

Jimmy nodded. 'He's a toerag.'

'He didn't tell you anything?'

'No. He just said wherever Bridie was was none of my business. I reckon he's not sure himself. Or he's ashamed.'

'Ashamed? Why?'

'That Bridie. She was always shoplifting. Me and Seamus Ronan saw her do it once in Meehans'.'

'So?'

'She's probably in jail. Not in Kilbran, like her mam says. But in jail. And they're too ashamed to say. So Rory flattens me when I ask. What d'you reckon?'

'Doubt it,' Shell said. 'They wouldn't send her to jail just for that. But it sounds like she's not at home and Rory, for one, doesn't really know where she is.' She took Jimmy by his good hand and went to clean him up. She'd to remove the fingernail, which was only hanging on by a thread. Jimmy winced, but didn't cry.

When she'd done she got the phone book out and found the number of Bridie's Auntie May in Kilbran. She dialled it when everyone was out doing the cows. It rang and rang, then a woman answered.

'Can I speak to Bridie?' Shell asked. She'd the phone line twisted round her fingers with fright. Her voice sounded like a squeak.

'To Bridie?'

'Bridie Quinn.'

'Bridie Quinn isn't here. Why would she be? She's at home in Coolbar.'

'Wasn't she there over Christmas? With the others?'

'No. She couldn't come. She was on a school trip, her mam said. Skiing in France.'

A school trip? In France? Since when had the pupils of the Presentation School ever got as far as Ringaskiddy? 'So she was just there for the summer, then? Helping out with the B & Bs?'

'We stopped the B & B racket a year ago. Who *is* this?'

'Just – just a friend.' She hung up before she got asked any more questions. She nearly tripped over the wire as she replaced the hook. Skiing in France?

That night the chattering came back loud and strong. She switched the light on in the small hours and got out the note. She hunched over it under the blankets as if it might contain an answer. *Bridie white and pale, miming a retch. Bridie in Kilbran, making breakfasts for the guests. Bridie in America, going from coast to coast, like in the song. Bridie in Coolbar, walking down the coast road, thumbing in the dark. Why don't you call over to her, Shell? See if you can't make it up? Mrs Quinn, her face livid, turning away. If I'd known the kind of things you two got up to. If I'd known earlier, I'd have—*

'What?' Shell whispered to herself. 'What would you have done, Mrs Quinn?' She switched out the light again. There was no answer but Trix and Jimmy's breathing so she tried an answer herself. 'Send us both off to England for an abortion, Mrs Quinn? Is that what you'd have done?'

Forty-nine

The next morning she woke up early. She pulled on her tights, then her pants over them. Over that she put on a warm shirt, with two jumpers on top. She crept downstairs and out before anybody was about. From the back barn she took Mrs Duggan's bike. She cycled down the drive, over the cattle grid and through the village. There was nobody to see her as she turned off onto the coast road towards Goat Island. She passed the Quinns' house on the left. A rusty bike was upended in the front yard. The curtains were drawn, dingy and yellow. Nobody was up. She'd half thought of calling there, but instead she cycled on.

It was slow going through the cutting wind of the morning. The sky was low and dim, but the birds were going strong. She reached the track that led down to the strand and the small patch of tarmacadam where Declan had parked his father's car. She left the bike by a paling and clambered down the shingle, onto the strand.

The tide was far out. The sands lay before her in long swaths of light and dark, pancake-flat. As the sun rose behind her, they began to gleam white and yellow. She walked across them, wishing she'd brought a scarf to keep her hair from flying about.

The sea has made the sand a mirror
Which my two feet destroy,
And in that mirror two eyes I see,
A sadness and a joy.

It was the ditty she and Mam had made up together in their walks on the strand. As she spoke the words, a lightness came over her. She hopped gaily as she walked, smiling for the first time in what seemed an age.

There were no craft out to sea or any sign of dog-walkers. She was on her own. She approached the rocky outcrop where the cave was. Her spirits fell again. The tattered remains of the gardaí's yellow cordon fluttered in the breeze. The sand was scuffed up all around. People had been in and out, it seemed, in their droves.

She went down on her hands and knees and went through the crack. *You're a ewe on heat, Shell. You're a bull with its horns stuck, Declan. In a thornbush.*

Inside the cave the smell of something stale and ancient prevailed. The cold and darkness of the place went through her like a knife. Her eyes could make out nothing much at first. Then the dark, encrusted walls appeared, then the scattering of pebbles. And there, just above where she and Declan had lain that time, was the rocky shelf. There was a bouquet on it. Not of flowers such as you might buy from the shop, but rather several sprigs from an unusual shrub, with milk-white berries clustered on them. They were tied together with a cream-coloured ribbon. She lifted the bunch up and smelled it. It was fresh and green. Somebody'd left them not long ago; yesterday maybe.

Anybody might have done it, she supposed. Anybody in all Ireland who listened to the news. Or any local from Coolbar. She put them back and crawled out, wondering.

It was a relief to be out of the place. Her mam had said it was a place of beauty, made by the wind and rain, but this morning it felt like a tomb, a tomb from which no dead could ever arise. She walked briskly back towards the car park, keeping to the lee of the cliff. Halfway along, the chattering was in her head again. She found a place to sit, out of the wind, where she could think.

The signs of Bridie being pregnant were there to see when you looked back on them. That last term at school, she'd often looked pale and tired. She'd turned her nose up at the school dinners, where before she'd been teased for gulping them down, however foul, like a human rubbish bin. By July she'd have started showing. She and her mam had probably had the fight to end all fights. They'd never got on: Bridie'd always said Mrs Quinn had a mighty temper. Perhaps Mrs Quinn had thrown her out. Or perhaps she'd walked out of her own accord. But she'd not been in Kilbran, as Mrs Quinn said, or in America, as Theresa Sheehy said. She'd probably thumbed a lift as far as Cork. She'd have had no money to speak of, no keys and no job. What would she have done?

Her father's voice came to her. *It's a desolation, Shell, down by the river harbour. The women there, all kinds, all ages. Some only your age, like that schoolfriend of yours, Bridie. As bold and brash as her.*

Is that what Bridie had become? A woman of the night? A woman of the streets? She'd always had a touch of the Mary Magdalenes about her, Declan had said. *Hickory, dickory, Bridie Quinn, ring the bell and let yourself in,* he'd quipped. Shell knew now what he meant. Only too well. The heel of her shoe ground into the shingle at the thought of him laughing away at every last one of them with his rhymes.

She looked out to sea. A lemon path from the rising sun cut through the calm water, vanishing towards the horizon. She closed her eyes and imagined how it must have been, the night not long before Christmas, when Father Rose had seen what he'd seen on the way back from Goat Island . . .

. . . There was Bridie, walking the coast road in the quiet December night. The moon was rising above her, the sea was flat and calm before her. She'd come back to Coolbar with a baby in tow. She was desperate for a bed, some kind words, someone to help with the infant. She was going to make it up with her mam. But when she'd got home, nobody was there. They'd gone to Kilbran for Christmas, just for a change. That's what Mrs Quinn had said and that part was true, she knew. But Bridie hadn't known. She'd thumbed a lift all the way from Cork only to find an empty house.

Shell *was* Bridie now, approaching Coolbar, unseen. She'd have glimpsed the Coolbar lights through the trees. She'd be gagging for a fag. An oily rag, as Declan used to call them. Night would be falling. She'd be like a ghost in the dark, a Christmas ghost, with nobody seeing her. She'd have been longing for someone to take the crying baby off her. Longing for her own bed, the familiar smell of the wash on the sheets, and the wind lashing the window, and the old dreams, the ones she'd had when she was small.

But the lights are out. The car's gone. Not a soul. She's on her own.

She doesn't know where to go. She keeps on up the coast road, why she can't tell. A car passes, swerves to avoid her. She jumps into the hedge. Hides the baby. *That was close.* She climbs the hill and cuts across the fields. Over the short grass, the gates, the hedges. Lugging the carrycot. The child's crying with the cold, a broken record. And the moon's up like a beach ball, bobbing on the sea. She reaches the path and goes down the cut, out onto the strand. It's bright like day out here. The wind's biting. She sits where Shell sits now, maybe. Her and the baby, both. And she thinks, *I'll walk into the sea as soon as the moon gets higher. Drown us both.* But she doesn't. She's chattering with the wind. The baby's screaming. She remembers the cave.

Haggerty's Hellhole.

The Abattoir.

The cave where Declan used take her. Where the

girls go to fornicate. Where the boys tied up the girls and left them. She creeps in there through the crack, pushing the carrycot ahead of her. The baby's crying still, only softer now, like a mewl from a stray cat. It's tired. Inside she strikes a match. And there's the shelf, the rock shelf, set into the wall. It's made for the cot. She lays him on it so he's high and dry. If the tide comes in, he won't be washed away. Perhaps he stops crying. He's happy out there, she thinks. He's still, the eyelids are down at last, and his cheeks are gone soft, like pouches. She tiptoes away, thinking, *He'll sleep sound now. I'll be back to fetch him. Later.*

Out in the air the waves are running in under the moon. It's misting rain and she's floating over the sands like a ghost. Must keep going to keep warm. The weight's gone. Somebody'll find it and take it away. Surely to God they will. It's nothing to do with her. She's light as a dream, and there's a strange waltzing in her head. Before she knows it, she's up the cut, out of the wind, and she's back on the road, walking. The baby's crying, only this time it's in her head, so she walks faster. A car's coming up behind her. She sticks out a thumb and it slows down. She turns to see who it is as it pulls up, but she sees it's the priest, the young fellow, in his daft, clapped-out car. She shakes her head, waves him on and he drives on. She's walking away from the strand further, away from the moon, towards the future. Until the next car comes, a dark saloon, warm and bright, a stranger in it. Anyone at all who'll whisk her from the hellhole that is all around her. He stops. He invites her inside with a fag lit, waiting for her. The headlamps are golden and he's off to the city. She's a ride all the way. The radio's blaring *Across the north and south, to Key Largo* and the rain's hammering it but the baby's still screaming in her head. So she steps inside, accepts a fag and shuts the door. And he's pulling away, away from the darkness into the darkness, away from Coolbar, for ever and away . . .

Shell took her fists from her eyes so the yellow streaks of pictures died away. The chattering quietened down. The sun had got stronger on the sand. She stood up.

A dog-walker passed by. A cracked eejit of a terrier was chasing the breakers.

That's how it was, she thought. *That's how the baby came to be in the cave.* There was no way of proving it. But she knew. Somewhere, in Ireland or beyond, Bridie was sitting listening to the news, saying nothing, keeping quiet. And somebody else, nearer to hand perhaps, was laying wreaths on the very spot where Bridie had left her child. Mrs Quinn, maybe? Who knew?

Molloy had been right. But it had been Bridie, not her, who'd been unable to stand the sound of the baby's cries. Could she still hear them now? In her dreams? Wherever she was?

Anger churned around in Shell like bad butter, anger at what Bridie had done, at Mrs Quinn, at Declan, at Molloy, at almost everyone in the village; even at Mrs Duggan with her baby boy with a hole in his heart that had been mended. She kicked up the sand. Then she remembered Father Rose, giving his first sermon. *Has it ever occurred to you that where there is no anger, there is also no love?* Tears from the wind slid over her cheek. She wiped them away, trying to drown his voice. But it was no good. Father Rose was still talking in her head as she retrieved the bike and pedalled away from the place. She remembered the lucky sheep that had leaped from the bonnet of the car in the nick of time and been saved. *There but for the grace of God go I, Shell. Or you, Shell. Or any of us, Shell.*

The tarmac fizzed under her as she cycled back to Coolbar. At the Quinns' house there was still nobody up. But in the hedgerow opposite was a white shrub in bloom that Shell recognized.

The tender bouquet, the rock shelf, the frozen child: a heartbreak on the world.

Fifty

News of the doctors' final report on the bodies of the babies appeared the next day in the county paper:

TWIN TRAVESTY

A team of Dublin pathologists has proved conclusively that the two dead babies, a boy and a girl, found near Castlerock are not twins. Fraternal twins can sometimes have different blood groups, as these did, but it has now been further established that the babies had different gestational ages. Although born at the roughly same time, they were conceived at least five weeks apart, the team concludes. The baby found on the beach was thought to be born at around 40 weeks (at full-term), whereas the one born to the unnamed girl at the heart of the case was born premature, at about 35 weeks.

Evidence also indicates that the latter baby, a girl, was stillborn. The doctors' report suggests that the umbilical cord became tangled around the baby's neck during labour. Tragically, the report concludes that had she been born with a qualified midwife in attendance and with the appropriate hospital care afterwards, she would probably have lived.

The Gardaí Síochána are now expected to drop all charges against the father, held in custody since Christmas. His erroneous confession has prompted serious concern in the Dáil about the handling of this case, with some TDs calling for an independent inquiry into how the gardaí conducted themselves. Superintendent Garda Dermot Molloy is currently unavailable for comment.

The news broke across the village. Everyone kept saying they'd known it all along. Mrs McGrath was heard to say that the baby in the cave was probably a 'tinker child'. She said she'd seen Travellers camping up the bog road a few weeks back and what more could you expect from the likes of them?

Shell read the words over and over but at first they meant nothing. *Gestational. Erroneous. Prematurely. Tragically.* Then she remembered the grey worm-like cord looped around Rosie's neck. She remembered her minuscule limbs. She thought of the baby in the cave and the baby she'd held in her arms, of Bridie disappearing, and of Declan, passing from one to the other of them either side of Easter, like a horse moving over to graze a different patch.

A girl and a boy.

A and O.

Full-term, premature.

It all made sense.

She sat at the casement window in the Duggans' house looking out on the winter copse. The dead babies weren't twins, but half-brother and half-sister, born into the self-same vale of tears.

She prayed for the repose of both their souls.

Fifty-one

With the charges against Dad now dropped, he was
due home that very afternoon. She went to the house
to prepare for his return. The cold had settled into
the walls. A litter of post was on the mat. She flung it
on the table. The three beds in her room were a
jumble of unmade covers. She stripped them down.
She opened the piano and took the bottle of whiskey
out. It was half full. She tipped the amber fluid down
the sink, but not before taking three sips. She waited
for the warmth to come on the third, like Dad had
said it did, but all she felt was an angry scalding in
her throat and the start of a sneeze in her nose. She
retrieved the pink dress from its hiding place under
her bed and, brushing off the dust, hung it back in
Dad's wardrobe. A malaise was in his room. His bed
was a wreck, the curtains undrawn. The air was close
with the smell of bad dreams. She opened a window
and the wind rushed in. She stripped his bed down.

Tired, she sat on the chair, listening. At first she
could hear nothing, not even the wind. Then the stir-
rings started. The little creaks, a sigh, the last shred

of a long-drawn-out piano chord trembling somewhere near.

She flicked through the letters. Bills. Two late Christmas cards from nobody she remembered, far-flung friends of Mam's youth who didn't seem to know that she was dead. Then a white envelope she'd nearly missed popped out. There were blue airmail stickers, strange stamps, an address of lazy scrawl. It was to her. Her eyes went wide. *To her?* She'd never before had a letter from abroad. She opened it.

A card inside depicted a robin perched on a snowy branch. It held an envelope in its mouth. Its wings were spread and one eye winked. Within, lines of writing slanted upward, chasing from one edge to the other:

Dear Shell. America is mad. New York is madder. I drive a big truck up and down the island. The sky's like candyfloss, I'm sure it's fake. We're building and drinking and gallivanting and there's no stopping us, me, Gerry and the lads. I'd my Christmas bonus pinched from me or I'd have sent you a new bra. Digs are in a place called Hell's Kitchen on Eleventh Avenue and you'll say it's where I belong. We're down the Irish bar most nights. The Shamrock, I ask you, worse than Dad's fecking leprechauns. But the stout's good. A man walked in just now with a ferret on a lead and it's not the drink talking. The girls are cracked. They drink Singapore Slings with ten shots in them and still want more. I went up the Empire State Building yesterday and nearly fell off. The yellow cabs bobbed down on the other side of the clouds like tiny abacus beads. They made me dizzy. But not as dizzy as you made me, Shell. I still remember. Love from u-know-who.

She saw him, crouched over the dark pint. The dollars flying out of his pocket. The muggers lying in wait. The clutter of glasses. The girls batting their eyelids at the world. The fag-ends. The man whistling at the ferret to jump through a hoop. The buildings lurching forward, toppling back. The cabs winking. And the cut of him, with the building dust in his hair and the Coolbar line to his face. And him writing the card, not looking at the girl opposite with the stars-and-stripes eyes, but moving the biro from west to east, like bread rising or a plane going home. *Shell smells of flea balls on the dirt floor.* And the trail of devastation he'd left behind him.

She switched on the electric-bar fire and held the card to the filament. The paper wilted then latched into flame. She put it on the tiles and watched the robin, the cabs, the Singapore Slings burn. Declan Ronan, the man for the main chance. Would she ever in this mortal life set eyes on him again? *Toodletits, Shell. Tarala, Declan.* Did it even matter?

She threw the remains in the bin and dusted down the piano and the sills. Then she made the beds up clean with brand-new sheets.

Fifty-two

The bedrooms aired and the place dusted, she fetched Jimmy and Trix home from school.

'Why can't he stay in jail?' Jimmy moaned when they got in.

'I want to stay at Duggans',' Trix grumbled. 'And watch TV.'

'Whisht, the two of you,' Shell said. 'I'll buy you sweets if you'd only stop.'

She sent them out to play in the back field.

She cleaned the grubby windows.

She made a batch of scones.

A car drew up outside, ahead of time. She froze. Mr Duggan was driving Dad home from Castlerock under strict instructions to elude the lure of the bar. *Will his hands still shake? Will he open the piano and hit me when he finds the whiskey gone? Will he shout if I break the egg yolk for the fry?* She looked out of the window with floured hands and pinched face. But it wasn't Dad. A familiar purple drew up: Father Rose and Jezebel.

He came in the door with a soft '*Hulloo, are you within?*' and that same smile of his. She offered him the chair and washed off her hands. 'Can I get you something, Father?'

'I can't stop,' he said. He perched on the piano stool, his back to the keys. His jacket flapped open to reveal a sweater with a polo neck obscuring the dog-collar. He looked different without the little square of white: a man of small concerns, walking the same crust of earth as anyone. She made conversation, but the words meandered down blind alleys. Father Rose sat there staring into the middle distance, a little like Dad used to do.

'I'm leaving, Shell,' he said at last. 'I've come to say goodbye.'

'Goodbye?'

'I'm called away.'

'What do you mean?'

'I'm called away by the Church.'

'Are they sending you to another parish? Already?'

He shook his head, smiling.

'Where then? Abroad?' She imagined him in the heart of Africa, walking among the poor, lifting up sick children to the mercy of the Lord.

'County Offaly.'

'County Offaly?'

'Yes, Shell. There's a house up there for priests with sick vocations. For those of us whose callings have gone sour.'

She stared in bewilderment.

'It's a retreat for doubting priests.'

'Is that what you are – a doubting priest?'

'I'm in spiritual crisis, Shell.'

She remembered him in the dark church, the day the pains started. *Have you come to shelter, Shell? A church at least has that use.* 'I don't understand,' she said, frowning. 'What is it you doubt about?'

'Do you really want me to tell you?'

'Yes, Father,' she whispered. 'If you will.'

He leaned against the piano and ran his hand soundlessly over the keys, newly dusted. 'When I used walk into a church, Shell – any church – I'd feel a presence. The smell of the divine, something more than just the bricks. Always I'd feel it and always I'd be glad. But this past year, in Coolbar, Shell, the feeling's dwindled.'

'Dwindled?' *My own stupid state of grace.* 'How d'you mean?'

'I've sat in that church for hours. I've hunted in my mind, into the alcoves, around the statues, across the pews and up by the tabernacle. I've stared into the light perpetua. But all I've heard is the wind. All I've smelled is the wood polish. All I've felt is myself, alone in a universe of loneliness. And in the faces of the parishioners I've not seen the image of God like I'm supposed to. I've seen something brittler. Something more impermanent.'

'Father – Father Rose . . .' she faltered.

He raised a friendly brow.

'I used feel that. Me too. The wood and the wind in the church, and the nothingness. Then you came, and it was different. You made it different. You made me believe again. In Jesus. In heaven. And then Mam came back. From the spirits.'

'Did she, Shell?'

She nodded. 'She still comes odd times. She sits at the piano, where you are now. When Jimmy's here, she's inside him, guiding his fingers over the keys. I know it.'

He smiled at her.

'*You* did it, Father. You made her come back. It was after hearing you talk I began to feel her round the place.'

He shook his head. 'If she came back, it was yourself brought her,' he said. 'Not me.' He took from his pocket a folded slip. 'There's an address for you, Shell. My mother's house. A letter there will always reach me, wherever I am.'

He handed the paper over and stood to go.

'Father' – she searched for a question, any question to delay him – 'how long will they keep you in Offaly?'

'Days, weeks. Months maybe. Until the way becomes clear. We've to agree, me and them. We've to arrive at the one mind.' As he spoke, he made for the door. Shell followed him out to the yard and watched him get in the car. She saw the passenger seat, littered with familiar clutter. The fags. A map. The licence. He wound the window down.

'Father . . .' she stumbled as he started the engine.

'What, Shell?'

'D'you ever feel, Father . . .' she blurted. 'D'you ever feel Michael like I feel Mam?'

The engine spluttered, died. 'Michael?'

'Your brother.'

302

He rested his hands on the steering wheel and stared at the smooth back field, rising. The remnants of the yellow tape marking where the baby had been exhumed fluttered in the breeze. Trix and Jimmy's figures were huddled among the top trees. 'It's funny your asking that. I used to, once. Just after he died. Michael always longed to be a priest, not me. I was the daft, harem-scarem one. It was as if he was telling me to take up the call where he'd left off. But somewhere in my teens he went quiet.'

'Did he?'

'Yes. Perhaps he'd nothing more to say. I'd done what he wanted: gone for Holy Orders.'

'Perhaps now – perhaps – he'll come back again.'

Father Rose smiled. 'Maybe so, Shell. I could certainly use the help.'

'When you're in Offaly, Father, you could pray to him instead of God. Perhaps he'd be closer. Perhaps he'd tell you what to do.'

He considered it. 'I could try.' But he didn't look convinced. He turned the ignition on and the one time when she wished it could have broken down, the engine started fine. He gave a final smile, breaking up the shaving shadow across this face. 'We'll surely meet again, Shell,' he said. His palms drifted briefly above the steering wheel, the wheels slid forward. 'Somewhere in this benighted isle.'

The car edged off the verge onto the road. 'Goodbye, Shell. God bless.' The words were muddled somewhere in the engine noise.

'Goodbye, Father Rose,' she whispered back. As

the car took a bend in the road, she shut her eyes. She could see the field, the grave, the remnant of yellow tape, but in the middle, surrounded by streaks of light, was the man, or rather the yawning absence of him. And then a crucifix with nobody on it, groaning in the wind. She opened her eyes. She stared at the place where the purple car had vanished around the bend, hardly believing he'd really left. In its place, another car appeared, a sleek estate: Mr Duggan, with Dad beside him.

'That eejit of a curate,' Dad said as he got out. 'We nearly collided.' He closed the car door and smiled.

Shell sucked her lips between her teeth and bit into the gums. She nodded at him. 'Hi, Dad.'

'Shell,' he said, approaching her and extending his arms. 'My own girl. It's good to be home again.'

Fifty-three

Dad wasn't a different man, only quieter. He was mad for the playing cards now, not the drink. He was down in the village playing Forty-five most nights. He still read like a demented prophet from the pulpit every Sunday. After tea, he rattled round the rosary mysteries like a train hurtling through the night. He stopped the collections and went back to his farm-labouring. He'd groan about the state of his bones, pouring the distalgesics down his throat. She'd a job to manage him. But she persuaded him to replace the ancient broken twin-tub Mam had used with a newer automatic model. Before spring came, she sowed the back field with grass and put up a brand-new washing line, one that folded down like an umbrella and twirled around in the wind. She left the cairn of stones where it was. It was like a beacon, collecting weeds and lichen.

Shortly after Father Rose left, Father Carroll said a funeral Mass for Baby Paul, as he was named, and her baby. When they asked her what she'd called the little girl, she lied. She didn't want any more gossip. So she said the name was Mary Grace, not Rose. The babies were buried in the churchyard in two small coffins in the far corner reserved for unbaptized souls. They'd a long wait in Limbo until the end of time. 'I'm sorry for your trouble,' Mrs McGrath said afterwards, her hat lurching off to the side. 'I'm sorry for your trouble,' said Mrs Fallon, her hands folded over her bag of wrinkled crocodile. 'Come round for a slice of coffee cake sometime,' said Nora Canterville. Shell shook their hands and nodded, her cheeks sucked in and her eyes staring down at the thick tan tights around their lumpy ankles. *Suffering Saviour. Spare me from legs like theirs.*

Mrs Quinn came to the Mass too, but on her own. She sat up in the gallery and said nothing to nobody. She watched the interment from the church porch and left the moment the prayers over the grave were finished. Shell saw her walking up the hill, hunched over on herself. Only she and herself knew it was her grandson being buried that day.

The following Sunday, Father Carroll announced that a new curate would be with them by Easter, a widower who'd retired from business and taken to the Church late in life. People in Coolbar never mentioned Father Rose, but in Shell's mind the memory of the man did not fade, but grew. His words, his smile, his gestures wove in and out of her days. *We'll surely meet again, somewhere in this benighted isle, Shell.* She thought of him in County Offaly, kneeling before the light perpetua, and she prayed for his path to be made clear. She kept the address of his mother safe in her powder-blue mass bag.

Her old primary schoolteacher, Miss Donoghue, called round one evening and pleaded with her to go back to school. 'You're not stupid,' she said. 'You never were.' Shell refused. She'd done with the place, she said. But in the end she agreed to Miss Donoghue's offer of an evening grind. Miss Donoghue insisted on not being paid and Shell could not say no. She began to go over every Tuesday, Dad's night off from the cards.

One fine week at the end of winter, the funfair came to town. The year before, Jimmy and Trix had been devastated at there being no money to go. This year, Shell made Dad give her some money for a few rides. The three set off together into town on a Saturday afternoon.

The whole of the park by the pier flashed and blared as they approached, bursting with mad machines. Stalls glittered. The air pulsed with heavy rock. They plunged into the crush.

'Can I've some?' Trix shouted, pointing to the candyfloss stall. Shell bought three fat spools and they licked them clean. They rode the dodgems and the ghost train. Soon she'd little money left. They wandered around the rides, trying to choose their last go.

A woman walked past them, brushing Shell's sleeve. Shell turned to look at her, but all she could see was her retreating back. Her hair was tied up with a chiffon scarf, like the olive-green one Mam had used for strolls on the beach. Hands in her pockets, she was heading towards the pier, a familiar lilt in her stride. Her head was off to the side as if she was thinking of faraway times and places, just as Mam did when she strolled along the strand or played the quiet piano pieces. The people on either side bobbed around her, but she never paused, picking her way forward. As she stepped away, the sound of her singing began in Shell's head. But this time she recognized the song:

> She stepped away from me
> With one star awake
> As the swan in the evening
> Flies over the lake . . .

Then the tune faded. *Mam. Don't go.* Shell grabbed Trix by the hand and rushed after the figure, but she'd already vanished into the crowds. No. There was her head again, her elbow. She'd the smooth leather coat on, the black one, her best.

'Shell,' grumbled Jimmy. 'Where are you going?'

She'd landed them by the Big Wheel. There was no sight of the woman anywhere. 'Dunno. Here. I s'pose.' Her eyes roved the crowds.

'The Big Wheel,' Trix said, her eyes alight. 'I'm not too small for it, am I?'

I've lost her. Maybe I was imagining things.

'Am I?' Trix's voice, almost a wail.

'No, Trix. Hush. Not if we all go up together.'

She bought the tickets with the last of the money. The man fitted them into the same carriage. He locked the bar down across their legs and the wheel spun round, inching them backward as more got on. When everyone had boarded, the wheel picked up its pace. Faster and faster, it spun up and back, knocking out their breath. Trix gripped her on one side, Jimmy on the other, their six hands and ankles muddled. Back and up, *whoosh*, with the wind flying through them.

'Holy Mary,' Shell gasped. Her stomach somersaulted.

'Look, Shell. Look.'

They were at the top of the arc with the white of the sun bursting and the sea glittering. Then down and forward, and the fair running smack up to them again. And there, on the far pier, walking away like the librarian had done, was the woman in black and green, a living poem. Strolling down and away, her scarf unwinding. Shell blinked, squeezing her eyes, wishing she could see better. *Whoosh*. The wheel scooped her insides out like ice cream. The figure was further away. She craned her neck just as the woman turned. Her hand was in the air, her scarf afloat. She was flickering, a flame, growing thinner and drifting out over the soft seascape, her chiffon billowing like a wave until she was a slender match, hardly more. *Mam*. She called out with her soul in her mouth. A last farewell. But she was going, going for good this time, back to the place from which she'd come.

The last slither vanished and there was the sea. Nothing but the sea. The whole mass of it, large and shining, restless, eating up the sky. Chasing the day to another continent. The wheel spun and there was the coast and the land and the dark hills faraway. The people, the houses, the sounds. The living and the dead. The dreams and laughs and tears. The here-and-nows and the here-afters. Bridie, white-cheeked, shaking the rain off her see-through umbrella as she walked away up the hill. Father Rose in Offaly, crouched in his evening shadow, waiting for God like a lighthouse beam. And Declan, up in a bulldozer with his rhyming slang, digging up the great city. *Mam.* Mam in the place of spirits, Mam in her memory, Mam in her blood. Jimmy yodelled as if from Alpen heights, his arms flung over her and Trix. They peaked and swooped the blue. Trix's hair and hers streamed together like tangled kite tails. Trix, Jimmy and she, a silent row going up the back field, picking up the stones. Together always. Free. And Mam's perpetual light shining on them. And their lives ahead of them, around them, spilling from them as they screamed *Whoooooooooo* like three demented owls. What joy it was to be, what joy.

Acknowledgements

I could not have written this story without the generous support of fellow-writers and friends Tony Bradman, Fiona Dunbar and Lee Weatherly. Warmest thanks also go to Tony Emerson, Helen Graves, Síle Larkin, Rosarii O'Brien, Carol Peaker and Ben Yudkin. My agent Hilary Delamere has guided me throughout with the clearest of vision, and my editorial team has been a joy – David Fickling and Bella Pearson at David Fickling Books, and Kelly Cauldwell, Annie Eaton and Sophie Nelson at Random House. And thank you to my darling mother, who has in her time picked up many a stone, and to Geoff, my wise and kindest critic.

This is a work of fiction. Neither the characters nor the events depicted are based on real life and the author and publisher disclaim, as far as the law allows, any similarity between the book, the fictional characters and/or events depicted and any individual and/or real life event.